Sand Cove 2:
Cold Summer

Sand Cove 2:
Cold Summer

Niyah Moore

www.urbanbooks.net

Urban Books, LLC
300 Farmingdale Road, NY-Route 109
Farmingdale, NY 11735

Sand Cove 2: Cold Summer
Copyright © 2021 Niyah Moore

ISBN 13: 978-1-64556-310-5
ISBN 10: 1-64556-310-3

First Mass Market Printing January 2022
First Trade Paperback Printing March 2021
Printed in the United States of America

10 9 8 7 6 5 4 3 2 1

Distributed by Kensington Publishing Corp.
Submit Orders to:
Customer Service
400 Hahn Road
Westminster, MD 21157-4627
Phone: 1-800-733-3000
Fax: 1-800-659-2436

Prologue

Stephanie

The stench of dry blood filled my nostrils and nearly choked me as soon as I stepped foot into the victim's house. Blood was smeared on the wall to the right of me and on the carpet. As I walked carefully, I thought to myself that I should've been used to this by now, but gory murder scenes like this one always pulled me in and hit me like a wave as if it were my first time experiencing it.

In the kitchen lay the victim. She was a white female with black hair and light brown eyes as she stared off into space. The assailant cut her open from the stomach and left her insides hanging out.

"I need to step outside," I said to my partner, Stanton, as I tried to gulp fresh air.

There was no fresh air in the house, so it wasn't working.

"Sure thing. You okay, Agent Tyler?" he asked, giving me a concerned look.

"I'll be fine."

I walked to the front door quickly before I threw up. As soon as the fresh air hit my lungs, I started feeling a little bit better . . . until I looked straight ahead. The road leading to Sand Cove was staring me in the face, and I couldn't believe I didn't notice it on my way there.

This was my first time being that close to Sand Cove in months. We didn't solve Luca Moretti's murder, so the case grew cold and closed. The lead I thought I had in Luca's assistant wound up being a dead end just like the others. I was more than disappointed; I felt defeated and salty. I really wanted to solve it because I had a hunch that the killer was a resident of Sand Cove, and I hated that I couldn't prove it.

Taking another deep breath, I glanced down at my vibrating phone to see that it was my daughter, Chloe. She had the most perfect timing.

I answered, "Hello?"

"Hi, Mom," Chloe said.

"Hey, Chloe Bear. How are ya?"

"Good. I'm picking up things from my dorm and getting ready to head home for the summer."

"Oh? Are you not staying with your dad for the first week of summer vacation?"

"No, I decided to stay with him the week before school starts again. Is that okay with you?"

"Of course it is. It's always good to have you home."

"Awesome. Dad is helping put my stuff in his garage. He's thinking about letting me get an apartment for next school year, so I won't have to stay in the dorm."

"An apartment? Wow. Sounds expensive."

"Dad said he'd handle it."

"That's good, Chloe Bear," I replied, trying not to sound too worried about her living alone in New York City.

"Mom, I'll be fine," she said, sensing the nervousness in my voice.

"I know. It's just that you're growing up so fast on me."

"It's called life, Mom. Anyway, I gotta run. I love you. See you soon."

"I love you too. See you when you get here."

If Danny promised he would take care of an apartment for her, then I was all for it. I wasn't sure how he could afford it, but it wasn't my business. I was going to have to see it and make sure she would be in a safe neighborhood. Though I was convinced by now that she could handle her own in the big city and had plenty of friends, the protector in me had to make sure with my own eyes.

Stanton stepped on the porch and stood next to me. "You sure you're okay?"

"Yeah, you know how I get with bloody scenes."

"I know. That's why I had to come out and check on you."

"Thanks. What's the story here?"

"She appears to be the sixth victim of a serial killer. The same type of wound to the stomach with insides spilled out. No forced entry, so it's safe to assume she knew the attacker just like the others. The murder weapon was not found in the house. These guys are searching the back yard currently and dusting for fingerprints. There seem to be shoe prints in the blood, though."

"Any ID on the body?"

"Not yet. There's no ID, driver's license, or purse in the home. The attacker might've taken her car if she had one. There aren't any keys in the house."

"Hmmm, all right. Let's see if a family member will call in after the news runs," I said.

"Okay. You plan on taking another look inside?" he asked.

"Nah, I can't handle it today. You got this one, right?"

"Yup. I'll loop you in when I need you."

"Sounds good." I put on my sunglasses and headed for my car.

The residents of Sand Cove thought they were so perfect because they had the perfect scenery, perfect houses on a secluded beach, perfect jobs that created wealth, and perfect weather. They were far from perfect, however. But there wasn't anything I could do without hard evidence. I took another look at the road to Sand Cove, and I shuddered. Then I made a U-turn and headed toward the highway.

Chapter 1

Tahira

Dressed in a sheer white wedding gown, I ran down the long hallway of a cathedral with my hands holding up my dress in bunches with my heart racing. The hall seemed endless with each stride, and it felt like I was never going to make it. I was late to my own wedding, and I wondered if Alohnzo was stressing. I was sure he thought I had changed my mind. I would never change my mind about being his wife, but I had cold feet.

My mum told me to focus on my love for him and not what others would think about me getting married so quickly after my husband was murdered. I was starting to sweat, and I was afraid that the hours of makeup would be ruined if I didn't slow down. Beautiful organ music played as a choir sang in the far distance, and I felt excited. This was my day, and I had nothing to be afraid of.

I was going to marry Alohnzo, the man of my dreams. He showed me that his love was perfect, and the way that he loved me wasn't some dreamy fairy tale. Alohnzo was everything I never imagined. He was an alpha male who always knew what he wanted and when he wanted it. Alohnzo was all about his love and protection for me, and I felt safe. I felt secure. These were things I had never felt with my deceased husband, Luca. Alohnzo was confident and poised in the most inconvenient situations. And I was going to be his wife.

Out of breath, I finally came to the pair of oversized wooden double doors. I hesitated for a few seconds, trying to regain my composure as I wiped my face and touched my hair that was pulled into an updo. I closed my eyes before hurling the heavy double doors open. I slowly opened my eyes to see 200 sitting guests turning my way. I instantly stopped breathing, and my knees started to tremble. As if I could hear Alohnzo's voice telling me to focus on him, I looked past the guests to meet his worried expression. He suddenly looked relieved that I didn't stand him up at the altar. He nervously smiled my way. His brother, Alistair, patted him on the back with an identical grin.

I stepped inside of the cathedral, feeling my stomach swirl, but I refused to take my eyes off Alohnzo. His deep brown eyes, his golden skin, that handsome grin, and shadow beard made my heart skip a few beats. The butterflies in my stomach moved, and although I felt like I was going to faint from all my emotions, I took in another deep breath through my nose and exhaled.

As soon as I took two steps down the aisle, the door slammed shut behind me. Startled, I jumped, looking behind me to see who would slam the door that way, but no one was there. The room suddenly spun around, and all the guests disappeared into thin air. Speechless, I looked at Alohnzo. He didn't seem to notice our guests were no longer in the cathedral. He reached out his hand for me to join him at the altar.

I marched down the aisle. With each step, the floor beneath me felt weak, as if I were walking on some thin ice covering a lake. I took another step, and then I heard a snap. I halted and looked down. Without warning, I started falling straight to the bottom of pitch blackness, screaming. I dropped to the bottom but somehow landed on my feet, and a single light appeared above my head.

Where am I?

"Alohnzo!" I shouted up with fear and panic filling me.

I couldn't hear anything, not a single sound.

I turned around to see if I could make out my surroundings, but I couldn't. With a snap of a finger, I was standing in my living room. It didn't look the same, though. Where was my furniture? Where were my paintings? The room had been stripped bare. I heard footsteps coming toward me down the hall. I turned to the hallway.

"Alohnzo?" I called, feeling my voice shake.

I waited for his response, but I still couldn't hear anything. No one was there.

I turned toward the living room, squinting through the dim lights, and saw someone sitting in an orange armchair wrapped in a thin gray blanket.

"Alohnzo?" I walked toward the person.

The closer I got, I realized it wasn't my sweet Alohnzo. It was my deceased husband—alive—but he didn't look the same.

"Luca?"

As if activated by my voice, he rose silently from the chair, staring at me with heavy-lidded eyes and a hanging mouth. His cheekbones accentuated his skeletal face, looking like Michael Jackson in "Thriller." I swallowed the hardness that was trying to form in the back of my throat. Instead of running away or screaming, I stood still, staring him in his face.

"Tahira," he whispered as his wrinkled hand reached for my face.

I froze as he gently traced my chin with his wrinkled fingers. I tried to move, but my feet felt like they were glued to the ground. He grabbed my throat and squeezed with unbelievable strength. The more he pressed, the stronger he became.

"Why?" he asked. "I loved you."

I struggled to move his hands, but he was too strong. I fought with all my might to break free, but I tripped over my own feet. Crawling on my stomach like an army soldier in the mud, I did my best to get to the front door. I looked behind me, and he was right there. I tried to go faster, but it was no use. He grabbed my foot, and in one swooping motion, he pulled me into the darkness.

"Aaaah!" I screamed in the highest pitch.

I opened my eyes as I inhaled deeply and realized that I was no longer in Luca's grasp. Frantically, I looked around the room because the bad dream felt too real. I wasn't in a wedding dress, and it wasn't my wedding day. I was in a hotel suite in London, and the sun was trying to peek through the curtains. I was in a cold sweat, and my chest was heaving up and down.

I didn't expect to spend eight months away from Alohnzo. In those eight months, it didn't matter if I was at my mum's or in a hotel . . . my bed was cold and lonely. I missed Alohnzo's muscular arms and how he would wrap them around me. I missed the smell of his Cool Water shower gel. No other man had been the object of my affection and desire the way he had. I was in love with Alohnzo.

I wanted to be back in Sand Cove because I missed everyone, but the house I shared with Luca was another story. When I thought about returning to the house, I felt nervous and afraid that Luca's ghost would haunt me while there. The nightmares I was already having brought on this anxiety, and that was the main reason why I hadn't rushed to get back.

I looked at the time. It was a little after 5:00 a.m., so I got out of bed and inhaled and exhaled deeply to catch my breath. Those dreams about Luca were feeling more real with each one. I turned on the lights, went into the bathroom, and splashed water from the faucet on my face. I had to get myself together because I was catching a flight back home in a few hours. I walked to the closet and pulled out my luggage. Placing it on the bed, I unzipped it. After taking the clothes out of the drawers, I put them neatly in the suitcase. Then I walked around the hotel room, making sure I didn't leave anything. Everything was packed and ready to go.

I went into the bathroom and started the water for a shower. While it ran to get hot, I brushed my teeth. After taking a shower, I dried off, put on lotion, and dressed. Then I called room service to eat my last breakfast in London.

Chapter 2

Alohnzo

It was midnight, and I couldn't stop thinking about Tahira. She was always on my mind, all day and all night. I stared out of my bedroom window as thunder rumbled, and a bolt of lightning split the night's sky in half. The moonlight highlighted the palm trees as they swayed as if they were waltz dancing with the wind.

As the storm was building, I became worried. It was getting harder to eat, sleep, or think straight without Tahira. When I was in London with her for two months, we had so much fun together. We went sightseeing to Big Ben, the Tower of London, and Tower Bridge. We ate Tahira's favorite foods, fish and chips with onion rings dipped in tartar sauce, and spicy crab croquettes at the Lobster Bar. I didn't want to leave, but I had to return home for work. Since Alistair abandoned the company, the bulk of his clients were left to me, and my workload was heavy.

I didn't think Tahira would like to stay away from me in London for so long. She promised she was coming back but would change her mind. This time, she had given a date and a time, and I couldn't wait to hold her in my arms.

I checked my phone, hoping she called to let me know she was going to really come home this time, but she hadn't. I got into bed, lying on top of the covers, and closed my eyes.

I hated my alarm for waking me up at 6:00 a.m. because it felt as if I hadn't slept at all. Yawning every couple of minutes, I managed to get out of bed, take a shower, and get dressed on time. As soon as I was in my car, I called Tahira again, but she didn't answer. I left another voice message.

"Tahira. I'm not sure if you've received my messages, but I hope you're already on the plane. I wanted to pick you up from the airport, but you didn't let me know what time your flight would be landing. Anyway, call me."

Ending the call, I started the car, pushed the button to open the garage, and backed out. Once down the driveway, I hit the button to close the garage. Before passing Alistair's house, I saw that the "For Sale" sign was gone and wondered who bought it. I hoped whoever Alistair might've sold the house to would be a good fit into our community. I wished he would've let me help him make that decision. He hadn't lived here long enough to determine who would get along with everyone. If he hadn't disappeared and changed his phone number, I would've been able to talk it over with him. While Alistair had been away, I had my landscaper take care of his front lawn and areas surrounding his home because it was starting to get out of control. I didn't want Tru or Noble to complain about it, so I took care of it.

I headed down the street.

My phone rang, and I quickly grabbed it. I was disappointed as soon as I saw that it was my mother. I hesitated before I picked up because I wasn't in the mood to hear any negativity, but I was also curious to see what she wanted. "Good morning, Mother."

"You were supposed to call me back last night," she complained.

"I'm sorry, I got caught up with some unfinished work," I said, making something up.

"I see. Did that widow move in with you yet?"

"No, and please don't call her that. Her name is Tahira, and she does have her own home."

"Good. Have you heard from your brother lately?"

"I have his email address, but I haven't reached out. The sale sign isn't up this morning, so I guess he finally sold the house."

"To whom?"

"Mother, I don't know, but I'll try to find out soon."

"I'm worried," she said. "I don't know why he would disappear and stay away from us like this. It's been too long, and it's not like him. Your father is supposed to be retired by now. He doesn't want to do anything unless Alistair is here."

"I think it's time to talk about me stepping into Pop's role without Alistair. We don't know if or when he's coming back. I have what it takes to lead this company. I think it's time for Pop to make a decision, don't you?"

"I didn't know you wanted to fill your father's shoes without Alistair. It's your father's dream for both of his sons to run the company together. He's waiting for Alistair to return, but don't worry, I'll talk to him."

"Thank you, Mom. I appreciate that. Alistair ran off and didn't say a word. How is that fair to us?"

"I hear you, son. My only concern is that Alistair isn't okay, but in the meantime, I think you will be perfect in the role, and you are more than capable of handling things on your own. Why don't you come by for dinner this Friday, and we'll talk about it together? How does that sound?"

"Sounds great. I'll be there."

"See you then. I love you, son."

"I love you too. See you soon."

I waited for her to end the call first in case she had anything else to say. The last thing I wanted was for her to call me back and accuse me of hanging up on her purposely.

I hoped going to my parents' home wouldn't be a waste of my time. If my father was bent on waiting for Alistair, I was prepared to resign to start my own business. I didn't have a clue about what that business would be, but I was open to whatever would be a significant investment. I had never discussed leaving the company, but I wanted them to understand where I was coming from. I was successful and good at being a financial advisor. I was the best Pop had. Though I was paid well, I didn't want to settle in that position. I wanted to *be* the boss.

My phone rang again. This time, it was Tahira, and my heart skipped a few beats.

"Hello?" I answered so fast as if she would hang up if I didn't.

"Hey, Alohnzo," she said, sounding cheerful.

"Tahira, hey, is everything all right?"

"Yeah, everything is fine. I meant to call you on my way to the airport, but it was too early in the morning your time, and I didn't want to wake you up. I have a layover in Newark, New Jersey, for about an hour, and then I'll be arriving around three in the afternoon. I can't wait to see you."

"I can't wait to see you, either. I was worried about you."

"I figured you would be. I was trying to get things together to leave. After breakfast, I took a nap but then overslept. I was running late to the airport and almost missed my flight."

"Oh no. Sounds like a rough start."

"Yeah. I need to tell you about what else that has been going on with me."

"Okay."

"I . . . I have also been having nightmares, but it's fine. I think I'm experiencing some posttraumatic stress or something."

"You sure?"

"Yeah, but I'll be fine. I'm glad I'm almost home. I can't wait to lie with you, kiss you, hold you, and make love to you."

"I've been dreaming of those things for months now. I'll be there to pick you up from the airport, so don't you worry about a ride home."

"You'll be working, and I can take an Uber. I'll let you know when I'm home."

"No, Tahira. I'm coming to pick you up. I'll be there at three, and that's that."

"Okay. I won't argue with you, my love. Thank you so much."

"It's no problem. Nothing and no one will ever be a priority over you, not even work."

"I love you so much," she said.

"I love you more. See you when you arrive."

"Okay. See you." She hung up.

I exhaled, feeling relieved. Butterflies swirled in my stomach, and I perked up. I couldn't wait to wrap my arms around Tahira and plant the juiciest kiss on those beautiful lips. I drove to work, feeling excited because my baby was finally coming home.

Chapter 3

Noble

"We have to do something about Constantine Enterprises before we end up broke and filing for bankruptcy," Tru said, putting lotion on her thick and gorgeous legs while wearing a bathrobe.

"I need you to be positive," I answered, feeling as if my wife were overly dramatic. "I admit things aren't going as planned, but why don't you have faith that we can turn things around?"

"Because the company cannot survive, especially with sagging sales. We might have to consider shutting down the business permanently."

"Hell no! That's not an option."

Our cosmetics were no longer being sold in the larger retailers because those retailers were shutting their stores for good, but we could overcome this obstacle. It was going to take work, but I was willing to roll up my sleeves and figure this out.

"You do understand that the rise of e-commerce companies such as Amazon is making it harder to attract the customers to buy our products," she said.

"Fuck Amazon. We just need to change our sales strategies. I'm ready to give it one last try. Tru, baby, listen to me. We can do this."

"I don't see how you think we can," she answered while rubbing the excess lotion through her hands. "We already let most of our employees go, and we don't have enough money to come up with a strategy to start all over again. Revamping is not an option right now. Enough is enough, Noble. We have our home and our lives on the line, and you want to risk it all? For what?"

"Baby, I get it. You're frustrated, and so am I, but I need you to have faith in your man. I'll come up with another alternative. Just watch. We'll be back on top."

"No, Noble, we don't need any alternatives. It takes more money to make money, and we don't have money because *someone* wanted to gamble everything we had in the first place. It's okay to let go and realize when things just aren't going to work, but this doesn't mean you're a failure."

Just like Tru to throw my gambling in my face. I hadn't gambled ever since the FBI agents exposed my secret. I was done with it.

"You act like your money and Luca's didn't save us," I said.

"It did, but it hasn't been a year, and we're right back in the hole, and this time, there's no one to borrow from and no savings to back up our asses. Anyway, I don't want to argue about it. I've made up my mind, and I'm going back to law school."

"Law school? Are you serious? You don't think we have enough money to relaunch our business, but we have enough to send you back to law school?"

"Hey, I still have the money that my dad gave me to get my law degree. Baby, I supported you and your dream of Constantine all these years. After graduation from college, you were set on this business, and I lived that dream with you. The mistake we made was thinking this company would last forever with all the technology changes and the evolution of social media without being prepared for it. Nothing lasts forever."

"Johnson & Johnson has lasted over 133 years, Tru. We barely reached ten years. You know how many challenges they have faced as a company? How many decades they survived? We got this."

"Baby, Johnson & Johnson has over 200 subsidiary companies with products sold in over 175 countries. We can't compare ourselves to a multinational giant like that." She stood up and placed the lotion on the dresser.

"Why can't we? I have a dream, Tru, and I still feel like Constantine can be saved. With the right investor, we can do it. One of my childhood memories of my grandmother was watching her sit at her vanity, and she had all these pretty products . . . perfumes, powder puffs, and creams all encased in gorgeous jars. All iconic beauty brands. I wanted to honor my grandmother's memory with our company."

"I get it, Noble. I've heard your beautiful story millions of times. Baby, sometimes, we must live in reality. There were things we could've done differently years ago. . . . Your gambling debt cost us big time. Face it; it's time to let Constantine go." Tru kissed me on the cheek and went into the walk-in closet. "I gotta make the kids breakfast, get them dressed, and get them ready for school since Ximena is gone. It's their last week of school before the summer break."

"What you mean she's gone?"

"She left for Mexico last night. Her family vacation, remember? She'll be gone for two weeks."

I nodded. "Oh yeah, that's right. I'm going to call Alohnzo to see if he can help us."

She came out of the closet dressed in a thin-strapped summer dress and flashed me a sharp look. "Don't you dare ask him for money, Noble."

"I'm not going to ask him for money. He's a financial advisor, and I'm a customer. I should've asked for his financial advice and guidance a long time ago."

"You don't think it's too late for that?"

"Never too late."

She sighed and shrugged. "Okay, but I'm still enrolling in law school." Then she walked out of the bedroom.

Feeling my head pulsate, I rubbed my temples as I picked up my cell phone and dialed Alohnzo.

After a few rings, he picked up. "What's up, Noble?"

"Hey, you got time to see me for an appointment today? I need a financial advisor."

"I have an appointment in about fifteen minutes. After that, I don't have one for a couple of hours. I do have to be at the airport to pick up Tahira by three, so if we don't run into that time, we're good. What you need?"

"I need advice and help with my business. What kind of services do you offer?"

"Well, I help organize finances as well as project results. I help with building savings and investments, trust funds, estate planning, and I also help people to see how well prepared they will be for retirement. I can help with reaching financial goals and offer investment research for business ventures."

"I need help with Constantine, bro. I need business advice and a plan to get things back on track."

"Okay. Bring your income and expenses reports, and we'll see what I can do."

"Sounds good. What time?"

"Ten a.m. is free. Will that work?"

"Yeah, that's perfect. That gives me about an hour and a half."

"Good. Will Tru be coming with you?"

"No, she has to be with the kids. Our nanny is on vacation."

"No problem. Instead of meeting at the office, let's talk over breakfast."

"That works for me. Where you want to meet?" I asked.

"How about Bellaire Boulangerie on Cross Creek Road off Pacific Coast Highway?"

"Sounds good. By the time I get dressed and everything, you should be done with your first meeting."

"Okay. See you then."

"See ya. Thanks, Alohnzo."

"No problem, Noble."

Taking a deep breath, I thought about my grandmother and her legacy. I was going to have to fight and do everything in my power to keep my dream alive. By the time I got in the shower, dressed, and downstairs, Tru was making the twins' plates of pancakes, eggs, and sausages.

"Good morning, Daddy's babies. Daddy gotta go make some things happen today." I kissed each of them on their foreheads.

"Good morning, Daddy," they replied in unison.

Tru poured a splash of orange juice into her champagne as she said, "Let me know how it goes with Alohnzo. I wish I could be there."

"I'll let you know everything—no need to worry, baby. Your man got this. You trust me?" I asked as I wrapped my arms around her waist.

She nodded, "I trust you, babe."

"Good. You guys have a wonderful day."

"You too. Wait, you don't want coffee or breakfast?"

"No, I'm meeting Alohnzo for breakfast."

"Okay," she replied. "Let me know how it goes."

"I will."

I walked into the boulangerie, and my eyes immediately went to the mouth-watering displays for the customers to gaze at. The aroma of fresh-baked bread, coffee, various tarts, and Danish pastries in the air was more delicious than any scent I had ever smelled. It was the kind of place I could sit in for hours, just staring out of the window. The place was classy and upscale, precisely what I would imagine for Alohnzo's taste.

Alohnzo walked in behind me.

"Hey," I said, giving him dap with my right fist. "This place is a nice gem. You come here often?"

"When I can. It's one of my favorites. The coffee is the best," Alohnzo replied.

"I definitely need some coffee, and I didn't eat breakfast yet."

I noticed there wasn't anyone to seat us. Alohnzo walked to the counter to place his order with an older woman wearing a pleasant smile. I took a good look at the menu to see what I wanted to order.

"Hey, Grace. May I please have a ham and cheese Croque Monsieur, a chai tea latte with almond milk, and whatever my friend is having here?"

"Oh, you treating?" I asked.

"I got you today. Trust me, everything on this menu is too good to pass up. I've had everything. You ever had a coconut mocha before?" Alohnzo asked.

"No, but it sounds good."

"I recommend it."

"All right, um, let's see. So many things to choose from, but let me get the quiche Lorraine, coconut mocha, and chocolate hazelnut croissant."

"You'll love the coconut mocha," Grace said. "It's the people's choice. Will you gentlemen be eating in or taking out?"

"We'll have it here," Alohnzo replied. "We'll be sitting at my usual table in the corner by the window." He handed her the card before she could read the total and placed a twenty-dollar bill in her tip jar.

I followed him over to the table in the corner right next to the large open window.

We sat, and I handed him a folder out of my briefcase. "Here are the financial reports from this year and the previous year. I also have tax returns from the past three years."

Alohnzo opened the folder and looked at my paperwork page by page in silence.

"How's Tahira?" I asked.

"She's good. She's on her way home."

"Oh, good. Tru has been a little crazy without her." I tapped my fingers on the table nervously.

"Yeah. Me too." Alohnzo frowned a little as he continued to read over my paperwork. "You guys are really struggling with sales. Why do you think customers aren't shopping with you anymore?"

"I think it's because we don't have a social media presence, and our website isn't being maintained. We've been relying on our brick and mortars, but unfortunately, a lot of our stores have closed."

"I see. You'll need to build a social media presence and have a user-friendly website where customers can shop if you want to find new customers. You ever think about selling your products on Amazon?"

"I refuse to share any profits with Amazon. I really want to rebrand, get a fresh look, and start all over. Some new products need to be developed, but as you can see, we don't have enough money for that."

"I hear you. Are you guys open to outside investors or new partners?"

"Alohnzo, I'm open to almost anything. Tru, however, is going back to law school, so she won't be a part of the business much anymore. I need to continue my grandmother's legacy . . . give my kids something to inherit."

"Well, I might know a few investors who have invested in other companies like yours. I'm also looking for potential business ventures for myself since I may not be working for my pop much longer."

"He fire you?"

"No, nothing like that. It's just time for baby boy to leave the nest."

"You think you would want to partner with us?" I asked.

Alohnzo had never talked about owning his own business. He seemed happy working for his father's company, getting rich off managing rich people's finances. He was like a Black Jeffrey Epstein minus the sex offender stuff.

"Possibly. I still may step into my pop's shoes and take over as CEO if he ever retires. If he doesn't retire soon, I'm ready to do something else. I've been thinking about investing money elsewhere for a while now."

"You ever think about starting your own firm and continuing financial advising?"

"No, though, that is a promising idea." Alohnzo paused before he continued, "You mind if I'm honest here, Noble?"

"I want you to be honest. That's why I called you."

"Your financials on paper are scary, and you've accrued a ton of debt. I think your best bet would be to close or sell."

That wasn't what I wanted to hear.

"You only looked at my paperwork for two minutes, and that's what you come up with? I can't—and I won't sell my company. Come on, financial advisor, I know you can come up with something better than that."

Alohnzo looked up at me and replied, "Listen, I've seen businesses nose-dive like this before, and the only thing that could help them was to close the doors for good or sell if someone were interested. The tricky thing with selling is finding someone who can pay off your debt and start over."

"I know that, but it's not impossible."

"Let me have twenty-four to forty-eight hours with your financials, and I'll get back to you with some options. I can't guarantee anything, but I'll do my best."

"I appreciate that. Listen, I put my blood, sweat, and tears into this company, so whatever you can recommend other than closing or selling, I'll take it."

"I hear you, but give me a few days to work this out and see what I can do. What about loans? How's your credit?"

"You don't even want to know. I have too many loans that I'm behind on."

Alohnzo nodded and closed the file. "Well, you might want to prepare yourself for any outcome, including selling or closing. I don't want you to be unrealistic in your expectations and set yourself up for disappointment. Noble, I want to set you up to win."

Swallowing the hard lump in my throat, I stared out of the window. Shutting down or selling was one of my biggest fears. Call it stubborn or out of my mind, but I believed in my business, even if no one else did. There had to be another way to keep my doors open.

"The only way you can set me up to win is to find someone willing to partner."

Alohnzo's phone rang, and he looked to see who was calling. "Excuse me while I take this call."

"No problem."

"Hello? Mother, slow down. What? He had a stroke? Where is he? Okay, I'm on my way. Okay, I'll try my best to find Alistair." He ended the call with worry lines forming in his forehead. "Sorry about that. My pops just had a stroke, and I gotta get to the hospital. I'll look more into your file and get back to you as soon as I can."

"No problem, man. Family comes first."

Alohnzo picked up my file and walked to the counter. "Hey, Grace, can you wrap up my food to go?"

"I'll take mine to go as well," I said, standing behind him. "I hope your pops is good."

"Yeah, me too. Now, I gotta find my brother."

"Do you know where he is?"

"No, but I have his email address. I'm sure he'll answer if I tell him what's going on."

We grabbed our food, coffee, and walked out of the restaurant into the parking lot.

"Hey," I said to Alohnzo before he could get into his car, which was parked next to mine.

"Yeah?"

"No rush on my stuff. I know you must take care of family business first. Constantine isn't going anywhere."

"I appreciate that, but I still plan to get back to you in twenty-four to forty-eight hours. Cool?"

"Works for me. See ya later."

"See ya." Alohnzo nodded his head as he got into his car.

I got into mine and sat for a few seconds. My food and coffee were piping hot, so I decided to drive to Zuma Beach, which was about fifteen minutes away. I parked, got out, sat on the hood, and enjoyed my quiche, croissant, and coffee while staring out at the water. Alohnzo and Grace were right. The coconut mocha was damn good. Taking a deep breath between bites, I prayed Alohnzo could help me save my company. After I ate, I sat for about ten minutes before I got back into my car and headed to work.

As soon as I got into the building, my morale dropped. Our office used to be filled with employees before we had to let them go. We no longer had a secretary and personal assistant, but I was going to keep coming, no matter what. I couldn't imagine what I would do if I couldn't be here. This company had always been my dream, so being on the verge of losing it was a big deal to me—huge even. Since I was a little boy, I knew that I would be somebody's boss. I loved this company so much because it was the thing I promised my grandmother before she died. This was my connection to her.

I picked up the mail from the box and walked to my office, then sat at my desk and sorted through the small pile. There was one from the leasing manager, which made me pause. I opened it and closed my eyes after I read that we had three days to pay or we would be evicted for defaulting on the lease agreement. We were two months behind but thought that we would've had the money to get caught up.

I flopped down in the chair, loosened my tie, and blew out frustrated air. Things were progressing much faster than I wanted them to. Would I have to close the doors or sell? I shook it off and felt hopeful.

"Grandma, I know I took some wrong turns, but I promise, I'm fighting for you," I said as my stomach twisted in knots.

Chapter 4

Kinsley

As the sun rose, the sky was in hues of pinks, oranges, and yellows, and it reminded me of sherbet. I was lying in a hammock on the deck of our beach house, gently swinging. I looked up at the tree branches and leaves as they swayed in the warm breeze. I drew in deep breaths of fresh air as I listened to the sounds of the red-legged thrushes, golden swallows, and ocean waves. Flowers surrounded our deck, donning their best verdant hues like a shattered rainbow. This place was my piece of heaven.

Alistair and I repaired plumbing, painted the interior walls white and exterior yellow. We added a sunroom and den. I would've never known that he was so good with a hammer and nails. We enjoyed this new life we made for ourselves. He made me feel loved and wanted, something I had never experienced, so I gave him all of me.

While at peace with nature, I ran my hand across my growing belly. I was thirty-two weeks pregnant, which meant I was pregnant before coming to the island. It was really a beautiful surprise that we both were thrilled about. I didn't want to know the sex of the baby because I wanted to focus on having a healthy baby. Alistair wanted to know, but he was comfortable with waiting until delivery because it was something I wanted.

Finding a doctor was a little hard when I first found out about the pregnancy because of the language barrier, but we found one who spoke English well. The medical appointments were expensive because I didn't have health insurance, but we had more than enough money, and I was able to get everything I needed to have a healthy pregnancy.

I was going to have a baby Kelly. I never imagined myself as being the mother type, but my life with Alistair had been more than perfect. Though he wasn't the Kelly I pictured I'd spend the rest of my life with, Alistair had shown me that he was the one meant for me.

Alistair came out of the screen door with a handmade ceramic mug of coffee in his hand and said, "Good morning, Mrs. Kelly."

"Good morning, Mr. Kelly."

I loved the way Mrs. Kelly sounded as it came out of his mouth. We eloped on Isla Colón, which was the main island, only a month ago. The main island was a central hub with restaurants, shops, and nightlife. I enjoyed Starfish Beach there because of the numerous sea stars that were on the ocean floor. We naturally picked up a little Spanish to interact. I was officially his wife. I snickered to myself every time I pictured his mother hearing the news for the first time. I could see her walking in a circle with her fists balled up and lips tightly pursed together like the clasp of a coin pouch. Obscene curse words would fly out of her mouth. I was so happy to be away from the nasty woman.

Staring lovingly at him, I asked Alistair, "What's on your mind, handsome?"

"Alohnzo sent an email."

I hadn't heard his name in a while. "Really? About?"

"Pop had a stroke. It's not looking good, and I need to be by his side in case he dies. Not to mention, I couldn't find anyone to buy my home in Sand Cove. Thankfully, I had already pulled it off the market last night before bed. We gotta get back to the United States."

As soon as he said that Amos had a stroke, I didn't feel anything. Was I supposed to? It was unfortunate, but the way Amos treated me left me feeling nothing for him.

"I noticed you said *we* gotta get back. . . . You expect me to return when I'm close to my due date? Nah-uh, I'm not going back. I refuse to have anything to do with your parents."

"Sorry, honey, but you don't really have a choice. I'm not leaving you here alone. Don't worry about my parents. You'll be safe in my house."

I sat up in the hammock and stared deeply into his eyes. "Wait. What? So, you want to go back to Sand Cove for good?"

"Yeah. I mean, why not?"

"There's a couple of reasons . . . Amos, Mabel, Alohnzo."

"Listen, I understand how complicated things were between you and them, but that's all over with now. You must understand that I'm the oldest, and I have an obligation to my father. I gotta run the company with Alohnzo."

The air between us became thick, and the tension I never thought we would have started mounting out of nowhere. I never wanted to return to California—ever again—let alone Sand Cove.

"Before Alohnzo emailed, you already decided not to sell the house, so this was something that's been on your mind for some time?"

"Yes, and I'll explain. I enjoy this piece of paradise with you, I really do, but we can't raise a family on a secluded island. What are we going to do when it's time to get the baby to school? You saw how hard it was to find a doctor. Plus, this house is too small. We need a nursery. My house in Sand Cove is perfect for a family, and I need to get back to tend to my horses at the ranch."

"I'm quite sure your parents' stable keepers and groundskeepers have been taking rather diligent care of your horses while you've been away. We can add another room for a nursery, or we can find another house on the mainland, so those are not factual issues, Alistair. They're excuses."

"My mind is made up, Kinsley. This is not up for debate or discussion. We're going back, and as my wife, I expect you to be by my side. I'm going to look at flights now." With that, Alistair walked into the house.

I hopped out of the hammock as if I weren't as big as a house. The thought of returning to Sand Cove and seeing Alohnzo nauseated me. What would he think about me now that I was his sister-in-law? I sighed, feeling like I wanted to throw up. To stop the sick feeling, I drew deep breaths and exhaled slowly.

Once inside the house, I said, "What about my furniture and the house?"

"Sell the house. I'll buy new furniture." He shrugged as if that were all to it.

Putting my hands on my hips, I stared at him while he sat at the table and made calls. I could not believe that I had no other choice. I held my tongue to stop myself from saying something that would cause us to be at odds.

Chapter 5

Tahira

The flight from Newark to Los Angeles took about five hours. I slept most of the time, and it felt good to get some rest without waking up drenched in sweat. As I headed down the escalator with my luggage, Alohnzo was waiting for me as he promised. Instantly, excitement filled me. Alohnzo was as handsome as the day I first laid eyes on him. I smiled widely, but I noticed something was different about him. Though he smiled, his eyes were sad. As soon as my feet left the escalator and touched even ground, he swept me up in his arms and swung me around. He kissed my cheek and then my lips. His body was trembling, though he was strong enough to hold me.

"Hi, beautiful," he said as a single tear slid down his cheek.

"Hi, handsome. Are you okay, or are you just that happy to see me?" I asked.

He put me on my feet and took my luggage in his right hand. "I'm ecstatic to see you . . . but Pop had a stroke earlier. I just left the hospital. He's in ICU, and I feel helpless. I don't know what to do."

"Oh no. What are the doctors saying?"

"He's in a medically induced coma, on life support, and he has some bleeding on his brain. All we can do is pray right now."

"Aw, man, this is tough news. I'm so sorry, Alohnzo. Do you need me to go to the hospital with you? I can be there for support."

He reached for my hand with his left hand, and we walked out of the airport. "No, it's okay. You just got home, and I don't want you to have to sit in the hospital for hours."

"I don't mind, but I still feel some jet lag. Have you been able to contact your brother?" I asked.

"Yeah. He responded to my email. He'll be here late tonight or tomorrow morning," he replied, sounding unenthusiastic about it.

"That's good, isn't it?"

"It is, I guess. You already know how complicated my relationship is with Alistair. I'm pissed at how he left and didn't say anything. Regardless, he's on his way now, and I hope Pop pulls out of this."

I took my cell out of my purse to text my mum.

Me: Mum, I landed safely. I love you.

Mum: Glad to hear it. I love you too. I enjoyed our time together.

After I returned my phone to my purse, I stared at Alohnzo. His hair and five o'clock shadow of a beard were always lined and well-groomed. Butterflies were flapping around in my stomach like crazy. For the last few months, I craved to see him, feel him, smell him, and I thought Luca's death was going to be the release valve I needed to be genuinely happy, but I was still learning how to love myself and how to live without Luca.

We crossed at the crosswalk toward Alohnzo's car in the parking lot.

"It feels good to be home," I said.

"I'm happy to see you. You know Tru missed you just as much as I did. She kept asking me when you were coming back."

"I haven't talked to Tru in a few days, and I feel kind of bad about it, but I just needed some time to myself, you know?"

He popped his trunk with his remote and placed my suitcase inside. "I understand. Noble told me that Tru hasn't really been the same since you left."

"Yeah, she told me that too. I'll go to her house while you're at the hospital."

"That'll be nice. Tru's going to be happy to see you. Does she know you're here?"

"Nope. It will be a delightful surprise."

After closing the trunk, he opened the passenger door for me to get in. He quickly picked up a folder from the passenger seat.

"That's a pretty thick folder you got there," I said, sitting in the car.

"Yeah." He closed the door. Once in the driver's seat, he continued, "Noble asked me to look over his business financials to see if the business could be saved." He put the folder in the backseat before putting on his seat belt and starting up the car.

"What do you mean? I thought everything was fine with Constantine."

"No, things aren't too good. I don't think I can help, but I promised I would look into it a little deeper to give him options."

"Tru didn't say anything about their business. I figured they were able to rectify the damage, especially since Noble didn't have to pay that money back."

Alohnzo headed toward the exit. "I thought so too."

"Yeah . . ." I paused, thinking about the fun we all used to have together. "I know it's the start of summer, but have you been thinking about the bonfire? It's your turn to host, you know."

"I haven't given the bonfire too much thought. I may need your help since I'm no good at planning parties."

"That won't be a problem. I love planning parties."

"You and Tru just have a natural knack for stuff like that." He picked up my hand and kissed the back of it.

I smiled. I was feeling better about being back home already. Oh, how good it felt to be in my love's presence again.

Chapter 6

Tru

To my surprise, my morning ran smoothly. For kinder-garteners, Noelle and Noble Jr. were advanced in every subject, and they usually argued over everything, but that morning, they made it easy for me to get them ready and off to school. While the twins were at school, I did house-work. Wearing a purple scarf to cover my hair, a tank top, and shorts, I cleaned the dishes, swept and mopped the floor, started laundry, and dusted the shelves. No one could truly clean my house the way I could, although I liked the way Ximena cleaned. I was worn out before I could clean upstairs, but I was enjoying my alone time. It felt good not to have to stress and deal with meetings and employees all day.

I didn't understand why Noble couldn't see that in a little while, there would be no more Constantine. I had al-ready enrolled in Pepperdine Caruso School of Law and was accepted to start in the fall. It was time to focus on me, for once, and do what I wanted to do. Noble was so set on his company and wasn't giving up even when all the signs of failing were there, and I felt terrible for him, but he needed to take accountability. He wouldn't be in this situation if he didn't have that gambling problem.

Taking my thick, curly hair out of the scarf and constraining bun, I put my feet up on the glass coffee table, lay my head back on the couch, and looked up at the white ceiling. I was exhausted, and I was trying to prepare myself mentally to clean upstairs.

A car honked, and I went to the window. I instantly smiled to see Tahira getting out of Alohnzo's car. I didn't know she was coming home, and I panicked because I had just taken my hair out of the bun. I quickly ran over to the hall mirror and finger-combed through the curls into a high ponytail before going out the front door.

"Tahira?" I sang, feeling shocked. I wasn't expecting to see her anytime soon.

"Hey, Tru. I'm back."

I speed-walked down the walkway and met her at Alohnzo's car. We hugged.

"Welcome home. Hi, Alohnzo." I waved at him through the car.

"Hey, Tru. I gotta run to the hospital. My dad is in ICU after a stroke. I'll see you later."

I held my heart. "Oh no. I'm sorry to hear that. Let's try to get together soon."

"Yes," he said. "I'll see you later, baby."

"See you," Tahira replied with a smile as she took her luggage out of the trunk.

Alohnzo drove away, and Tahira walked with me to the front door.

"Have you been home yet?" I asked, looking at her luggage.

"No, I came to you straight from the airport. I haven't been in the house for so long . . ." She paused. "I can't go inside yet."

I frowned a little as I closed the door behind us. "You were in the house simply fine before you left. Is Luca's death fucking with you?"

"Kind of. It's so weird. I've been having nightmares about him, and I'm just a little creeped out. Though most of his things are out of the house, I need to make it my own."

"Ooooh, what about remodeling?"

"Hmmm . . . I haven't thought about remodeling. I could make some changes. Maybe that will help shake the Luca vibes in there."

"I can help you," I said, sitting on the couch. "I love interior decorating."

Tahira placed her luggage on the side of the couch, sat next to me, and sighed. "It feels so good to be back. How's everything been around here?"

"Life goes on, but it has been quiet. Alohnzo has been buried in work to stop himself from missing you so much, so we haven't had our dinners like we usually have. Noble has been worrying himself sick over Constantine, and I almost thought you weren't coming back."

"I almost thought I wasn't either. I love London, but there's no place like Sand Cove."

"Truth, but I'm glad you got to get away. Sand Cove hasn't felt like Sand Cove ever since . . ." I stopped myself from talking anymore about Luca and changed the subject. "You still loving Alohnzo, I see."

"How can I not? He's still perfect. Where are the kids? School?"

"Yeah, the munchkins are at school. I gotta pick them up in a few hours."

"Oh, okay. Where's Ximena?"

"She's in Mexico visiting family, so I'm managing the kids and their schedules while she's gone. As you can see, I'm dressed this way because I was just cleaning the house myself."

"You don't work at Constantine anymore?"

I shook my head. "No, the company isn't really operating at its full capacity. Noble talked with Alohnzo this morning to see if he can help us, but I don't see the point. We're too deep in the hole to climb out. If Alohnzo can find a way to save us, it'll be a miracle."

"I'm sorry to hear that, Tru."

"It's fine. Noble can't let go because that company is his baby."

"So, what is he going to do if Alohnzo doesn't figure out a way to help?"

"I have no idea, but I'm going back to law school. I've already enrolled."

"What? Congratulations, Tru. That's great."

"Yeah, I'm looking forward to it," I said. "What you plan on doing now that you're back?"

"I don't know yet. I want to get back into acting, so I'm going to call my agency and see if I can land a few auditions."

"Now, that makes me happy. I know you're going to kill it and be that big star you always wanted to be."

"Thanks. You've always been so supportive, Tru. I really appreciate you."

"Of course. You're my bestie."

Tahira replied, "And you're mine."

My phone rang from the coffee table. I leaned over and grabbed it. "Hello?"

"Hello, is this Trudee Mason?"

"Yes. May I ask who's calling?"

"This is Isabelle Sanchez. I'm Ximena's immigration attorney. Does Ximena Flores work for you?"

"Yes," I replied with a frown, looking at Tahira. "Did you say immigration attorney?" I put the call on speakerphone.

"Yes, I did. Do you mind if I ask you a few questions?"

"No, I don't mind. How can I help you?"'

"How long has Ximena been working as your nanny and housekeeper?"

"She's been a live-in nanny for about a year and a half."

"Will her job last for at least another year?"

"Yes, and maybe two or more years."

"Did you know that her visa expired six months ago?"

"No, um, she didn't mention it. I saw her check her passport before her flight last night. Is everything all right?"

"Well, I want you to know that Ximena was detained by Customs and Border Protection at the airport."

"Oh no," I gasped. "Is she okay? Do I need to come to get her?"

"She's fine. You don't need to come. After the CBP officers completed their questioning, she was sent on her flight to Mexico, but she cannot return to the United States yet. However, I may be able to apply for a waiver of admissibility to get her visa renewed or a green card since the job will be longer than two years. The good thing is that she has a clean record, and I do not see any inconsistencies in her story to render her inadmissible into the United States again."

"Okay," I said, feeling myself panic a little. "How long will this take? We were expecting her to return in a few weeks after her time with her family in Mexico."

"I'm not sure. Once someone has been deported, federal immigration laws make it exceedingly difficult for that person to return. She would like for me to apologize to you and your family that she will not be returning as soon as she hoped."

"Okay. Thanks for the information. Is there a number to contact her?"

"No, not at this time. Thanks for taking the time to speak with me, Mrs. Mason. Have a good day."

"You have a good day as well."

I was speechless. Ximena had been deported. What was I supposed to do now?

"Are you okay?" Tahira asked, observing me.

Tears were building, and a lump was forming in my throat, but I refused to cry. We couldn't afford to hire another nanny. "I wasn't expecting to hear that. I can't imagine what she's going through right now."

"I didn't know she wasn't a citizen," Tahira said.

"During our interview with her, she mentioned that she had a valid visa to work. We never spoke about it again. Damn it. I was prepared to take the kids to school for another week, but now, it looks like I'll be doing it every day, which, I mean, there's nothing wrong with that. It's just that I wanted to be able to focus on law school."

"You still have some time before school starts, though, right?"

"Yeah. It doesn't start until the fall. I gotta let Noble know. This is going to add more stress."

"I'll help you out with the kids. Just let me know when you need me, and I'll be here."

"Thank you so much. Ximena did more than just take care of the kids. . . ." I stopped myself from blurting out the affair I had. Ximena and I hadn't been together sexually once Noble told me to stop. We never crossed that line again.

While Tahira was away, Ximena filled that void. What was I going to do without her? I continued to fight the urge I felt to cry. I needed to get out of the house.

"Hey," I said, "why don't we go pick up some sage to burn in your house? I know this little specialty spiritual shop along the coast. You might even want to get some crystals."

"Oh yes, I heard nothing but good things about crystals. I've never had to burn sage before, but I am all for trying anything to get rid of that haunted feeling. Let's go," she said.

"Cool. Let me run upstairs to freshen up, and then we can go."

Chapter 7

Alohnzo

It was 10:10 p.m., and I was ready to leave the hospital. I was exhausted, and I wanted to spend time with my girlfriend. I waited for Tahira too long to be away from her any longer. Mama didn't want me to leave her side while we sat in my father's room, watching as the ventilator breathed for him. All my life, I feared death, and at that moment, I didn't want to deal with the fact that my father may have already been dead. My eyes remained on my father lying in that hospital bed with tubes everywhere, and my heart felt like it wasn't going to throb any longer if that machine made the long beep sound. Numb, I couldn't feel anything around me.

I needed to get out of there, so I stood up.

"Please, don't leave, Alohnzo," my mother pleaded as tears cascaded down her face.

"I'll be right back," I said gently.

I stepped into the hall and called Tahira to see if she was okay since it had been a few hours since we talked.

"Hey. You okay?" I asked.

"Yeah. Tru and I went to a little shop and got some sage. We burned some in the house. I took a bath, and I was thinking about going for a swim, but strange weather right now. How's Pop?"

"The ventilator is breathing for him. . . . We may have to decide to pull the plug if he doesn't wake up soon."

Tahira's British accent was filled with sadness as she replied, "Oh no."

"My mother hopes Alistair will show up before she makes the decision."

"Do you think he's going to show up?"

"He said he would."

As soon as I said the words, I saw Alistair walking from the other end of the hallway. He looked a little darker, as if he had been in the sun for too long, and he grew a goatee.

"Speaking of," I said. "Alistair is here now. I was going to leave here in a bit, but it may be longer now."

"There's no rush, baby. I'm not going anywhere. Look after Pop, and I'll see you soon."

"Okay. Talk to you later."

I ended the call and waited for my brother to reach me.

"Hey, big little brother," he said.

"Hey, little big brother," I replied.

We hugged briefly. Though I was mad at him for disappearing, this wasn't the time to fight about it. Our father was dying, and as brothers, we needed to be there for each other.

"How's Pop?" he asked, looking nervous.

"He's on life support. If he doesn't wake up soon, we may have to pull the plug."

Tears instantly filled his eyes. Sounding exasperated, he said, "Damn. Is this really happening right now?"

"It's really happening. Mom's waiting for you in there."

Taking a deep breath, he replied, "You coming in with me?"

"If you need me to."

"I need you, bro."

This was a rare moment between us. Alistair had always been that big brother who never let me see his vulnerable, afraid, or sad side. He toughed out everything growing up. He was a natural show-off, competitive as hell, but at that moment, none of that mattered.

I opened the door, but he hesitated to walk in. One look at Pop lying there and Alistair couldn't handle it. Though he walked in, it looked like he was going to faint, but he didn't. As soon as he reached the bed, he broke down as he lay his head on Pop's lap.

As if the last breath had been pulled from his lungs, he said, "Pop."

Mama looked on as she cried silently. She let Alistair have his moment. I put my arm around our mother and held her as I had been doing most of the day.

Once Alistair was finished weeping, he wiped his tears and said, "Mama, I'm sorry for leaving without saying anything."

"Where were you?" she questioned.

He should've known she was going to ask. Although it shouldn't have mattered where he was, I was curious as well.

Alistair didn't hesitate to respond, "Bocas del Toro, Panama. I just needed to get away for a little while to clear my mind."

"You had to sell your house and go out of the country for eight months to clear your mind?" Mama fussed. "You know how much stress you caused your father?"

"Mama," I said, stopping her from saying anything that would suggest Alistair was the cause of Pop's stroke, "he's here now, and that's all that should matter."

She shook her head but didn't combat me with sharp words, though she wanted to.

"I didn't sell the house. I'm back now, and I'm not leaving." He sat in the chair next to Pop's bed and held his hand.

"I'm going to get out of here and get some sleep. Mama, you should get some sleep as well. I'll be back in the morning, and if Pop doesn't wake up by then, I support any decision you make."

She nodded and said, "I'll be leaving in a little bit. You get some rest."

I put my arm around her and placed a kiss on top of her head.

"Alistair, I'll see you later," I said.

"Okay, bro. You out of here?"

"Yeah. Try to get some sleep if you can," I said.

He placed his head on Pop's chest, and I walked out of the hospital room.

I pulled into my driveway and waited for the garage door to lift. A woman was walking down Alistair's walkway with a small bag of trash. Alistair hadn't mentioned that he had someone with him. As she got closer to the garbage can, I realized it was Kinsley. She saw me and paused before throwing the trash away. At that moment, I didn't know what to do or say, but Alistair's sudden departure made sense to me now. She left, and he went after her.

She lifted the top of the trash container. After she tossed the bag inside, she closed the lid.

I rolled down the window and asked, "What are you doing here?"

She scowled as she stared at me as if she hated me. "That's no way to greet your sister-in-law." She stood in front of the garbage can so I could clearly see her as she rubbed her round stomach and flashed her wedding band.

I rolled up my window, drove into my garage, and pressed the button to close it. What had Alistair done? Mama was going to lose her mind, but I wasn't going to be the one to tell her. He was going to have to let her know on his own.

I turned on the light, sat on the couch, and called Tahira.

She answered, "Hello?"

"Hey, I just made it home."

"I'm glad you're home. I can't sleep. I'm coming over."

"All right." I ended the call and sighed.

My father was dying, and I felt helpless. I couldn't care less if Alistair married Kinsley. My only issue was that she would be living next door. As I rubbed my temples, Tahira walked in.

She came to me and sat on my lap. I cradled her in my arms and leaned back on the couch. It was her first night home, and I hadn't been able to spend time with her like I wanted to. Cupping my face with her hands, she kissed my lips. Her kiss felt like a magical relief pill that made my headache instantly go away.

"You okay?" she asked.

"I will be. Are you okay? You said you couldn't sleep."

"It's been hard to sleep lately. Tru thinks I should remodel the house and make it feel like mine, but I don't think that will help."

"Maybe you should sell it."

"I thought about that, but where would I move? I love Sand Cove too much to leave."

"Move in with me."

She studied my eyes to see if I was sincere before she replied, "I love the idea of living together, but what if it doesn't work out? Then I'll be homeless."

"You think that we wouldn't work out?" I asked, feeling confused.

"Things happen in relationships. I don't want to risk anything right now."

I wasn't sure why she was saying that. I loved her, and I thought she loved me. I wanted to propose and marry her one day, but would she reject me if I asked her to spend the rest of her life with me?

Easing her off my lap, I stared into space. I wasn't sure if it was my father's condition or how long she had been away, but I felt disconnected.

"Alohnzo, I don't want you to take what I'm saying the wrong way. I think it would be smart not to move in together."

I walked to the kitchen without responding, turned on the light, and went over to the wine cabinet. Pulling a bottle of rosé, I also picked up a wineglass.

Tahira slowly entered the kitchen. "Alohnzo?"

I popped the cork and poured, refusing to look at her. I couldn't respond when I didn't know how to process her words.

"So, you're not going to say anything?"

I finished the glass in one gulp before I replied, "You don't want to live together, and you don't like your house because of the memories tied to Luca, so . . . What are you going to do?"

"I don't know yet."

I poured more wine. "Tahira, I love you, and I was going crazy with you all the way in London. I think selling the house and moving in with me would be perfect, but I guess we are looking at relationships differently."

"I love you, Alohnzo, and you should know that by now."

"Do I? You spent eight months away from me, and to me, it didn't seem like you wanted to return. If I didn't nearly beg you, you would've stayed away."

Tahira sighed, "I'm not sure why you're so upset. I—"

"Because it's clear you want to be tortured living in a house you can't stand. I thought what we had was special, but—"

"There is no but. What we have *is* still incredibly special, Alohnzo."

"You sure? I can't tell. You're here, but it's like you're *not* here." I gulped more wine.

"You're in pain right now, and I get that, but don't take it out on me. If you need time to deal with what's going on with your father, I'll give you that. I still need some time to deal with my issues as well."

"You need more than eight months?" I snapped.

She crossed her arms over her chest as she shook her head. "Wow, Alohnzo. Are you *serious* right now? I lost my husband."

I narrowed my eyes at her. Hearing her call Luca her husband pinched a nerve. "I don't get you. Luca made your life hell, and although he died while still being your husband, you hated him. Why are you having nightmares about him? I thought you were so relieved he was gone. Do you miss him? Do you wish he never died?"

A flick of lightning flashed, and thunder roared. Suddenly, the rain started to pour. The fire in her eyes could've burnt me to ash.

Without another word, she headed out into the rain. I went to the front of the house and looked out of the window. I watched her jog with her sweater as a shield over her head until she reached her home.

My heart sank, and the pit of my stomach formed a series of knots. The fear of losing Tahira and my nervousness after saying too much were all mixed up together. I went back to the kitchen and continued to drink until the bottle was empty. I felt a pull in my pounding heart, yelling for me to fix this mess, but I was too filled with resentment and grief. I had been holding in my anger at her for staying away so long. I thought she would never want to leave my side ever again.

I was wrong.

Chapter 8

Kinsley

Coming face-to-face with Alohnzo nearly took my breath away. Seeing him reminded me of why I fell in love with him, but his disgusted expression told me why he didn't feel the same about me. I was never going to see his incredibly charming smile ever again, so I kept that piece of memory of him tucked away in the back of my mind. I wondered what our history would have looked like if I hadn't played games with him and was honest from the beginning. Would we be in love and living in bliss? I shook those thoughts out of my head. What happened between us was supposed to happen that way.

While with Alistair on the island, I got to know him without any distractions, but it didn't make me forget about Alohnzo. When I thought about him, I didn't say it aloud.

Everything about Sand Cove reminded me of Alohnzo, and that was why I didn't want to be there. I didn't expect him to welcome me with open arms, but I wanted him to look at me as if I meant something to him once. Perhaps I didn't mean anything to him, but did he have to dismiss me with his eyes? My past was my past, and I didn't need him throwing my stupid mistakes in my face.

Alistair purchased brand contemporary furniture to furnish the house, and it was going to arrive in the morning. He said that I could arrange the furniture any way that I wanted. It was going on midnight, and all the stores were closed. I was so hungry. Thankfully, I had half of a turkey and swiss sandwich I didn't finish earlier and a bottle of water from the airport. I stood at the kitchen island and ate.

I expected Alistair to stay at the hospital for a long time because of how upset and sad he was before he went to the hospital. I wanted to go there with him, but he didn't think it would be a good idea. I mean, I guess I understood why, but at the same time, his family was going to have to get over the fact that I was his wife and we were having a baby. No time was going to be the right time.

After I finished the sandwich, I went upstairs, took a shower, and made a pallet on the floor with the blankets I packed in my luggage. Before I could close my eyes, I heard the garage open. Within a few minutes, Alistair entered the bedroom. He had a bag of food and a carrier with two sodas.

"Hey, I didn't think you'd be asleep, so I grabbed some chalupas."

I got up and turned on the light. "Thank you. I had half of a turkey sandwich, but I'm still hungry. How'd it go?"

He sat on the pallet and placed the food and drinks between us. "He's on life support. Mama and I decided that if he doesn't wake up in the morning that we'll pull the plug. If he doesn't breathe on his own . . ." He paused and cried.

I moved the food and wrapped my arms around him. I rubbed his back. I couldn't find the words to say, but

I was happy I could be there for him. Although Amos wasn't one of my favorite people, it hurt me to see my husband in pain.

"I'm going back to the hospital in the morning. I need to take a shower." He got up.

"Okay. Did you see your brother up there?"

"I did."

"You guys talk?"

"A little bit." He took a good look at my worried expression before he walked into the bathroom. "You saw him or something? Why you look like that?"

I nodded. "I saw Alohnzo for a quick second when I took out some trash. He was pulling into his garage, probably coming from the hospital."

"What he say?"

"He asked me what I was doing here."

"What you say?"

"I told him the reason why is because I'm your wife, and we're having a baby."

Alistair looked irritated as he rubbed the top of his head. "You couldn't wait, could you? You wanted to throw that in his face so bad."

"What? No. I wasn't about to let him treat me as if I don't belong here."

"But you already know that you do, so there was no need to say anything to him." Without saying anything else, he went into the bathroom and slammed the door.

I jumped as tears threatened to form. I knew coming here would be a mistake. We were happy in our own little piece of paradise. If this was going to be the way things would be while here, there was no way I would be staying, and I wasn't going to sell my house. I had a feeling that I was going to need it. I took out a chalupa, but I instantly lost my appetite. I put it to the side of the pallet and sipped my soda before I lay down to get some sleep.

Chapter 9

Noble

While sitting in the office for a few hours, I was trying to figure out how I was going to pay the lease in case Alohnzo didn't have a resolution for me. My mind was too busy to go home afterward, so I went to the cigar lounge to have a smoke and a few drinks. By the time I was ready to head home, it was after 11:00 p.m.

Tru was sitting on the couch in the living room. She wore a worried expression as she reached over to turn on the lamp.

"Tru, you didn't have to wait up for me," I mumbled.

"Why not? I was worried about you. You didn't call me to tell me about how things went with Alohnzo. Tahira came by, and Alohnzo dropped her off. He went to the hospital to see his dad. I take it that you two didn't get to come up with a solution for the company, and you were trying to think of a backup plan."

"Yeah," I said, flopping down on the couch next to her. I buried my head in her lap like a little boy. "He's going to get back to me in twenty-four to forty-eight hours."

"You've been at the lounge?"

"Look, Tru, please don't say anything about the way I smell. I'll take a shower in a little bit. I just need you to hold me."

She caressed my head and replied, "Okay."

"We got a three-day pay-or-quit eviction notice at the office."

"Yeah? Well, I knew it was coming."

"I didn't think they would slap us with one after all the years we paid on time. We've been in that same building since we started. I don't know what to do. Alohnzo suggested selling or closing after only one minute of looking at our income and expense reports. He's going to look over it some more to check other options, but I guess I should tell him now that we're getting evicted."

Her hands felt good as they rubbed over my short waves. I held on to her legs.

"I know you're in a shitty mood, but I need to tell you what happened with Ximena."

"Isn't she with family in Mexico? Wait, don't tell me she got kidnapped by the cartel and—"

"Noble, no. She was arrested at the airport. Her visa expired six months ago. An immigration lawyer called and said she's trying to get her something more permanent to stay since she has a job. So, for now, she will remain in Mexico."

"Well, I mean, we really can't afford her anyway, so this could benefit us."

"Benefit us how? Who's going to take care of the house and the twins?"

"You can, or your mother will help," I replied simply.

What was wrong with doing things the way we did them before we had a nanny? Tru's mother was an immense help to us. I was sure she wouldn't mind helping.

"I won't have time for all that because I'll be starting law school in the fall. My mother is carefree, living her retired life in San Diego. I don't want to ask her to come up here to help us."

"You already got accepted?" I lifted my head from her lap and stared at her.

"Yes. I'm going to Pepperdine."

"Why didn't you just say that this morning?"

"I didn't want to ruin your mood before you met with Alohnzo."

"So, I guess that's it, huh? Close Constantine for good, so you can go to law school. What am I supposed to do?"

"Take care of the house and the twins for a little while," she said. "Take a break."

"How will we pay all these bills? Our mortgage ain't cheap, you know."

"Our mortgage and bills will be paid with what's left in our account for at least six months. The business is draining us, so if we don't give up the business now, we won't be able to pay our bills anymore. Listen, if you sell Constantine, that will at least give us enough money, hopefully, to be cool for another year or so."

"Seems like you have everything figured out," I huffed as I got up from the couch and headed upstairs to take my shower.

"Noble," Tru called after me, "don't act like that."

I didn't respond. Even Tru had given up on me. What was a man supposed to do when his own wife no longer believed in him?

Chapter 10

Tahira

Another nightmare jerked me out of my sleep. In this one, Luca kept jumping out of places like the closet and the shower. There was no way I could go to sleep after that, so I went downstairs for a drink of water, making sure to turn on all the lights as I went.

Thoughts about selling the house came to mind. Remodeling it wasn't going to stop the memories I shared with Luca, and it didn't seem like the nightmares were going to go away anytime soon. I took my cold cup of water upstairs and thought about swimming, but it was raining outside, and it was fifty-five degrees. I would catch a cold swimming out there if I did.

Reluctantly, I dialed Alohnzo. I needed to see if he was awake so I could go to his house to sleep. This tension between us wasn't something I wanted. I needed him.

"Hello?" he answered, sounding just as wide awake as I was.

"I can't sleep," I said.

"Neither can I . . ." He paused before he said, "I'm sorry about earlier. I'm a little uptight. I don't really know how to deal with what's going on with Pop. I didn't mean to take it out on you."

"I know. I'm in a weird space too. You're right. I need to sell the house, so I'm going to. I don't want to spend another minute inside of it. Is it still okay for me to move in?"

"Of course, it is. You should come over right now."

I was hoping he would say that. "All right," I replied, throwing on my jacket, slippers, and grabbing my keys. "Open the door." I ended the call and walked down the stairs. I locked the house and jogged next door.

The rain wasn't pouring, but it was drizzling.

When I got to his door, he unlocked and opened it.

He took my jacket and hung it up on his coatrack after I took it off. Gently placing his hand in mine, he took me to his bedroom. Once there, he wrapped his arms around me, and I rested my head upon his chest. All my fears stopped as if my heart took over from being in his arms that way. He squeezed me as if he needed to check to see if I was really standing with him.

At that moment, somehow, my insecurity came back as I asked, "Do you really want me to move in with you? What will your mother think?"

He stared down at me with a serious look. "As long as you're with me, Tahira, the rest of the world can go fuck themselves. Seriously. I mean that."

I put my arms around his neck and thanked him with a deep, passionate kiss. Electricity flowed through me. I missed him so much. I would never leave him for that long ever again. His hands covered the small of my back as his soft lips continued to kiss me. In his arms, I felt loved, safe, and so much passion. He was bringing me back to life, reviving what I thought I lost and restoring what had shattered. As we lay on his bed, we made out and cuddled. We lay in each other's arms, not saying anything, just enjoying the sound of the light rain and how good it felt to be back in each other's arms. We fell asleep intertwined as if we were too afraid to let go.

Chapter 11

Alohnzo

Tahira and I slept well together. If it weren't for my phone ringing, we would've stayed asleep comfortably in each other's arms. When I saw that it was my mother, my heart started beating hard as I feared she had pulled the plug on Pop.

"Hello?" I answered.

"Alohnzo, your father is awake," Mama said.

"He is?" I asked, sitting up. "Is he functioning okay? Is he brain dead or anything like the doctors were saying?"

"No, no. He's speaking, not clearly, but he's alert. It's a miracle. It truly is. He has some nerve damage, but he's smiling. He's especially happy to see Alistair."

"That's good. What time did Alistair get there?"

"About an hour ago. What time will you get here?"

"I have to shower, but I'll be there shortly."

"Okay, see you then."

I ended the call and looked over to see Tahira staring at me with tears in her eyes.

"I heard the news," she said. "Your mother's voice came through the phone."

"Yeah. I'm going to head to the hospital, but I'm taking the rest of the day off. Think about where you want to go for lunch and let me know."

"Okay."

I gave her a quick peck on the lips before getting out of bed. "What you going to do while I'm gone?"

"I'm going to find a realtor to put my house on the market."

"I know a few realtors."

"Of course, you do," she said with a bright smile. "I was trying to figure out who Luca and I used, but I can't remember or find the information. Can you give me the best referral you have?"

"No problem. I got you. I have the perfect guy. He's the same realtor the Masons and I used. Since he's familiar with Sand Cove, he'll know exactly the type of people to sell to, people who would fit into our community." I winked at her and went into the bathroom to shower.

I was happy Pop was alive, but I started thinking about my plans for my future. Did I really want to run the company with Alistair? We didn't get along longer than five minutes most times, which was why our offices were on two different floors. I needed to have my own dream, so doing anything with Alistair made me change my mind about taking over Amos Kelly Advisors once Pop stepped down.

After the shower, I got dressed. The smell of something good cooking made my stomach growl. Before heading downstairs, I grabbed my cell off the dresser and called my good friend, Jake, to see about helping Tahira sell her house.

After the phone call, I went downstairs. Tahira was moving her hips, off rhythm, of course, to some salsa music. I smiled at how cute she looked even when off-beat. I didn't care if she had rhythm or not. She was everything. When she spun in a circle, she noticed I was standing there, watching.

She smiled, but not bashfully. "Hey, I made you some breakfast before you get started on your day." She looked out of the window. "The pool guy is here. I can't wait for the sun to start shining. It's been so foggy lately. That sky needs to be as blue as that ocean. I'll get in the pool for the time, but I need to be one with the ocean. I miss that feeling."

"I can't wait to see you out there." I stared at the thick-sliced bacon, eggs over medium, wheat toast with butter, and a jar of my favorite peach jam on the counter. "This looks yummy. I just got off the phone with Jake. He said he would love to meet you and talk with you. You need to get the house appraised."

"Wow, you work really fast. You mean business, Mr. Kelly. Thank you for that. Will Jake help me with finding someone to appraise it?"

"I'm sure he can. After I leave the hospital, I gotta call Noble so that we can discuss what I think about his business."

"I think he'll appreciate that. Tru told me about the eviction notice from the building they were leasing. They gotta be out of the building in two days now."

"Ouch. Damn. That's good to know because when I talk to potential partners, I won't leave that part out." I opened the refrigerator and pulled out the grapefruit juice. I got a glass out of the cabinet and poured it. "What do you think about me becoming Noble's partner and helping him put his business back on track?"

"Do you really want to be business partners with your friend and neighbor? You'll be with each other constantly . . . at work, at home. I don't want to put a damper on any plans with Noble. However, Luca always said that Noble was someone he would never go into business with. When things are good, he goes back to gambling. I know Luca was one of the most negative people in the world, but he was good with his money. He made smart investments. I would think about it some more."

I gulped the juice and nodded. Tahira was right because Noble hadn't proven himself to be a good businessman. His own wife had abandoned the business.

Tahira made a plate for both of us and garnished the dishes with sliced strawberries and parsley. I sat at the table, and she joined me.

"I should buy Constantine from him," I said. "That way, he can get some money out of it instead of losing the business and going broke."

"You think it can be saved?"

"Yeah, it has a lot of potential, just not in Noble's hands, unfortunately. I would completely rebrand because the foundation is there; it just needs a boost. Did I tell you that I'm leaving my father's business?"

Tahira chewed a piece of bacon with wide eyes. "Why? I thought you loved working there."

"I used to, but that was before I started having my own visions. I want to advance, but Pop controls everything. I'm a businessman, and I should be allowed to make decisions without him criticizing me. Pop hasn't officially retired, but when he does, he wants Alistair and me to run it together. Not to mention, Alistair is back here for good, and he married Kinsley—"

"What? He married Kinsley, so does that mean she's living next door?"

"Yeah, and she's pregnant." I stuck my fork in the egg and shook my head. "I mean, I don't really care that he married her, but why does he want to stay here again suddenly? He can put his house back on the market and sell it like he was going to do when he left. Now the woman I used to sleep with is my sister-in-law. Not to mention, she was our father's prostitute. Can't leave that part out."

"I remember you telling me that. What will our annual bonfires look like now? We saw what happened last year. She hates us."

"Our annual bonfires don't have to include them. They can do like they did before and disappear."

She laughed and shook her head, reminiscing about that night. "You and I can do so much more this year because we aren't hiding our feelings."

I finished my breakfast and kissed Tahira. "I love you. I'll try to be back as soon as I can, so we can enjoy some alone time."

"I like that. I love you more. Have a good day."

When I arrived at my father's hospital room, I walked into the middle of Pop talking.

"I won't retire yet. I feel like this is a sign from God," Pop said out of his twisted lips.

"Amos, you're in no condition to work. You said you were going to retire, so you need to go on and retire," Mama fussed.

"Mabel, mind your own business. Amos Kelly Financial Advisors needs me."

Mama looked up at me as I approached the bed.

Pop attempted to smile, but his deformed mouth would only allow a crooked one. Seeing him that way hurt my heart. I was happy that my father was still breathing, but this wasn't something I expected ever to see.

"Hey, Pop," I said, leaning down to hug him.

"There's my boy," he replied.

I kissed his forehead. "Now, what you in here talking about? Work? Nah, that's out. Doctors should be ordering you to stay home and rest."

"They're ordering him to stay home and rest. The bastard is too damned stubborn to follow the doctor's orders," Mama quickly said.

I hugged and kissed her while Pop huffed and puffed like he was having a tough time breathing. Mama grabbed the oxygen mask and put it over his mouth and nose.

"See, Pop," Alistair said, "you can't get your blood pressure up. Alohnzo and I will handle the business while you rest."

"No," Pop replied, removing the mask. "You will stay in the position you're in. The only way I'll retire is when I'm in a grave."

Shaking my head, I replied, "I see things won't change, and I feel stagnant as one of your advisors, Pop. I'm sorry, but I'm putting in my resignation today. I won't return to Amos Kelly Financial Advisors because you don't get it. I don't want to upset you while you're recovering, but this . . . I can't handle it anymore."

I walked toward the door and started to leave, but my mother was on my heels, saying, "How could you say that? And at a moment like this?"

"It's the perfect moment." I walked out, and she continued to follow me. I turned to her and continued, "He just told Alistair and me that we're not good enough to run his company. He would rather die before handing it over."

"Now, you're putting words into your father's mouth. He didn't say that."

"That's exactly what he said. Look, Mama, I love you. I love Pop, but when it comes to business, he only wants things one way, and that's his way."

"Please, just let him rest, and he'll reconsider. I'll talk to him."

"No, thank you. I'm fine, Mama."

"Okay, well, it seems like you know what you want to do. Just the other day before all this happened, you made it seem like you couldn't wait to run the business. Are you saying this because Alistair is back?"

"No, I'm saying it because I need to let you know how I feel. I don't want to be in Pop's shadow any longer. Alistair can do whatever he wants."

"All right. You sure? I just want you to be happy. I love you, my son."

"I love you too, Mama."

I hugged her and walked down the hall to the elevator.

Pop wasn't going to reconsider anything. I knew that look in his eye, and my outburst could cost me the relationship I had with him. That man was going to work himself to death. As much as I loved my father, it was time for me to move on and stand on my own.

Tahira wanted to rest and didn't feel up to going out for lunch, which was fine with me because the hospital visit had me emotionally drained. Once she took a nap, I made some calls to five clients to let them know I had quit my father's company, and I wouldn't be advising them anymore. They were bummed, but I assured them that any of the top advisors would be more than capable of handling their accounts.

I also mentioned the opportunity for them to invest in Noble's company. I gave each client the financial rundown and didn't leave anything out. Unfortunately, it was hard to get them to partner with him, and it was even harder to sell them on the idea to buy him out. They didn't want to inherit debt for an African American-based company because they didn't think it could survive in the market. They all felt it would be a bad investment, but they also didn't have experience in retail companies. Constantine had enormous potential, and if in the right hands, it would make money back, plus some.

Just when I was going to call it quits, I thought of one last person. Marcus Travers was a long-time client. He was African American, so when I presented the opportunity, he had an instant interest in Constantine.

"I do have experience with working with distressed Black businesses specializing in retail," he said.

"That's perfect," I replied.

"Okay. I'll partner with you. It would be Mr. Mason's best bet to sell the company to us. You and I can turn the company around. Speak with him and let me know."

"I sure will. Thank you, Marcus."

"No problem. Thank you for thinking of me."

"I'll get back to you as soon as possible."

"Perfect."

I ended the call and sent Noble a text message.

Me: Hey, I looked everything over. Let's talk.

Noble: Come by the house. I'm at home.

I walked over to the Masons' with the folder and took a deep breath before ringing the doorbell.

Tru answered the door in baggy gray sweats, a black mug in her hand, and her midnight tresses were all over her head. I had never seen her look this way since I had known her.

"Good afternoon, Tru. How are you?"

"Afternoon," she replied. "I'm having a rough morning. He's on the balcony."

"Sorry to hear about your morning." I stepped inside. "I hope the day gets better."

She closed the door with a smile. "Thanks."

I walked across the living room and through the kitchen to the sliding door. Noble was standing facing the beach with one hand holding a glass of brown liquor. The other was tucked in his slacks with a gold Rolex wrapped around his wrist. I slid the door open and stepped onto the deck.

He didn't turn to look at me as he kept his eyes fixed on the ocean waves. "Can I get you a drink?"

"No, thank you. Is everything all right with you and Tru?"

Noble struggled to keep up the façade of peace and contentment he usually wore as a mask, but he could no longer hide behind it. "No, we're kind of beefing right now about the business, so I hope you came to tell me some good news."

I rubbed the back of my neck deeply with one hand, hoping he would accept what I had to offer. "You asked me to find options, so I made some calls."

"Don't beat around the bush." His eyes moved to his glass as he swirled the liquor around.

"I'm not. I couldn't find any partners from my client list because they don't have experience in a retail business, and they feel your debt is too high. I did, however, find someone willing to partner with me to buy Constantine from you. He specializes in distressed businesses. We're willing to offer one point five million to you and Tru for the business, and we'll use two million to pay off your debt."

Noble took a deep swallow before he rested the glass against his thigh. He gave me a stern look. "You expect for me to give my company, one that I put everything I had in it, to you and some stranger?"

"You wouldn't be *giving* it to us. You would be *selling* it to us."

"I thought you would consider being my partner. You changed your mind?"

"I did consider it. Look, Noble, you don't have a working capital anymore. I would essentially be bailing you out in exchange for 50 percent, and that isn't something I can do."

"Who said I would give you 50 percent? I was thinking more like 30?"

"So, let me get this straight. You want me to take care of the debt and put the business on track for 30 percent?"

"Yup."

"That's interesting. You've put the company at significant risk and—"

"You think I would do it again? So, you're basically calling me a shitty partner."

"Look, all I have is the paperwork you gave me." I held up the folder. "The company made close to $15 million last year, yet somehow, the company is at the point of bankruptcy. Luca's loan helped a little, but your taxes wiped out whatever profit you made. Noble, you have a great business, and it has the potential to sustain, but it has to have a new owner to do so."

Noble chuckled and shook his head. He snatched the folder from me and replied, "I thought we were friends. I came to you for help. I see what's going on here. You see an opportunity to make yourself rich at my expense, and you think a funky one million is all it's worth?"

"My partner and I would have to clear the debt, have working capital, invest in rebranding, and build a social media platform for more advertising, so that's way more than one million out of our pocket. If we didn't have to invest in any of those things, we wouldn't have to have this conversation."

He nodded with water rimming his eyelids. He sucked a gulp of air as he faced the beach and replied, "Get the fuck out of my house."

I thought Noble would be frustrated but not mad. I was trying to help him the best I could, but I wasn't going to risk losing a shitload of money simply because he was my friend.

"Damn, like that?"

"Straight like that, and while you're at it, you can go straight to hell!"

I walked to the sliding door and made my way out of the house. I was hurt, and I felt my stomach burning. I didn't appreciate Noble's tone because I hadn't disrespected him in any way.

Tru's voice stopped me before I could leave. "Alohnzo?"

"Yeah?"

She got up from the couch and stood in front of me with a look of concern. "My husband is so extremely passionate about Constantine that he can't reason. He was optimistic that you could save him, but I knew the chances were slim. He'll calm down, and I'll make sure that he apologizes."

"If he loved Constantine so much as he claims, he would've never risked his beloved business on bets, but it's his business. After today, the offer will be withdrawn as I would like to move to other potential investments."

She nodded. "I understand. Thank you for looking into it for him. That was truly kind of you to do in the first place."

"No problem. Have a good night."

"You too. Tell Tahira that I'll call her later."

"Okay." I opened the door and walked out.

Tru closed the door behind me.

I trotted down the walkway and walked toward my house while calling Marcus.

He picked up on the first ring. "Alohnzo, good news from Mr. Mason?"

"No. He's stubborn. He doesn't want to sell. He would prefer to partner with just me."

"Hmmm . . . Well, what do you think about that?"

"Noble poorly handled the business and the finances, risking not only his business but his personal assets as well. Why should I bail him out to be in the same boat in a year?"

"You don't think he would learn from you and change?"

"He could, but if he's not open-minded, how far would we get? Would he let me bring my offers to the table, or is he only looking for someone to bail him out? Plus, he's talking about giving me only 30 percent. That's an insult."

"I understand where you're coming from. Listen, I have a fantastic opportunity on the table. Two brothers have spent three decades as winegrowers, and they own a five-acre estate, including a vineyard between Zuma and Carbon Beaches. They're older, don't have any children or family to leave their business with, so they want to sell. Their biggest revenue is their online store and wine club, where customers receive wine regularly. Collectively with the online store, tours, and wine tastings, they bring in about $985,000 a quarter. I know you don't know much about running a vineyard or the retail side of things, but you know business, and we would inherit their estate keepers and winemakers. I would love to partner with you on this because I think we can come up with ways to double their revenue within the first year."

He had my full attention. "What's their asking price?"

"Everything is negotiable. I'll arrange a meeting, and let's see what we can negotiate. Sound good?"

"Sounds great. Thanks, Marcus."

"No problem. I'm glad you called me earlier. You have helped me as my financial advisor for years, and my finances quadrupled. I'm happy that I can return the favor. I'll call you as soon as I have the meeting date and time."

"Okay, I'll talk to you soon. Thanks again." I ended the call and smiled.

Noble couldn't separate his feelings from what needed to be done for his business. In business, you had to make wise decisions. He was demonstrating why it would be a bad idea to go into business together. I was going to find the perfect company where I could build an empire. I hoped Noble would come to his senses, but I was okay if he didn't.

Alistair was pulling his Range Rover into his driveway as I was walking up to my house. He got out of the car and said, "Alohnzo."

"What?"

"You know you broke Pop's heart today, right?"

"Well, he broke mine. He'll never leave us in charge, Alistair. He wants to control everything even after he almost lost his life. You know what that means to me? It means he doesn't trust us. He trained and groomed us for this business all our lives, but for what?"

"You know how Pop is, though. That's why I don't take anything he says personally. He's a workaholic, and he's passionate. That's all. As much as I would love to run the business right now, I'm going to play my position and support him while he's still here on this earth."

"Good for you . . ." I paused because Kinsley walked out of his house. She was standing on the porch, watching us. I leaned closer to Alistair and said in a faint voice, "What you think Pop is going to say when he finds out about you and Kinsley?"

"He shouldn't have anything to say. I made an honest woman of her, something he could never do. You sure Pop would be the only one feeling some type of way?"

I narrowed my eyes at him. I never had feelings for Kinsley, so what was he talking about? He could miss me by assuming I cared for her. "You know me better than that, bro. I don't catch feelings easily."

"Could've fooled me. You didn't waste any time making a move on your neighbor's wife."

Unbothered by his statement, I said, "Anyway, I may have found a new gig to keep me busy, so I won't need Pop's direction anymore. I'm good."

"Already? Damn, you work fast. What you got up your sleeve?"

"You think I would tell you when you try to compete with me all the fucking time?"

Alistair chuckled as he rubbed his chin. "It's all good. I love you too, but on a better note, Pop will be home in a couple of days. He wants you at the house so that you can sign some papers."

"What papers?"

"Your resignation."

I sighed at how dramatic Pop was being, but responded, "Yeah, okay." I turned from him and walked to my door.

"You have a good night, little big brother," Alistair called.

I really wished he would crawl back under whatever rock he came from.

Chapter 12

Alistair

If Alohnzo had been patient with Pop, he wouldn't have missed out on what Pop had in store for us. As soon as Alohnzo left the hospital, Pop changed his mind and decided to retire. Since Alohnzo didn't want any part of the company, he was going to leave Amos Kelly Financial Advisors solely to me. I was cool with that. Although I would be Pop's right-hand man while he was still functioning as head of the company as he transitioned out, I was one step closer to inheriting it all. I was the oldest, and that was the way it should've been anyway.

I didn't get Alohnzo. How could he quit the family business while our father was lying in the hospital after surviving a stroke? His actions seemed very selfish to me. I was living out of the country and came back to be there for Pop. We might've been brothers, but we weren't built the same.

I walked toward Kinsley, feeling bad about how I reacted the night before when she brought up Alohnzo. There was no need for me to be insecure. She wasn't in love with him anymore, and Alohnzo never wanted her in the way I loved her.

She rushed down the stairs and quickly threw her arms around my neck. "I'm sorry about last night," she apologized.

I kissed her lips. "You shouldn't be apologizing. I'm the one who needs to say sorry to you. I overreacted. You also need to be careful and stop moving so damn fast."

She smiled while shaking her head. "I can still move normally. I'm pregnant, not handicapped."

I looked at my wife, and she was looking too damn good. I lifted her off her feet and carried her into the house.

She shrilled in delight, "Put me down, Alistair."

I whispered in her ear, "You love me, baby?"

"I do, always and forever."

I placed her on her feet once inside. With my fingertips, I lifted her chin and gave her a passion-filled kiss. Then I looked around and saw the furniture placed nicely.

"It looks good in here."

"You picked out some nice stuff. I wouldn't have picked a white couch, but it brightens up the room. How much longer are you planning on keeping me a secret from your parents?" she asked, biting her lower lip.

"Honestly, sweetheart, I wish that I didn't have to keep you a secret." I held both of her hands in mine. "Don't mistake that as being ashamed of you because I'm not. I wouldn't have married you if I were ashamed. Once Pop recovers and is at home, I'll tell them. I don't care what they got to say about it. I love you and our baby."

She pulled on my shirt to follow her to the bedroom. She was so sexy to me. Kinsley had my heart. I looked down and saw the pink rose petal trail going up the stairs.

"I want tonight to be all about you and me," she said.

Our mouths and tongues touched as she moaned passionately. Pushing her against the wall, my hands groped generously at her plump ass. I lifted her and carried her to the bed. She wrapped her legs around my waist, pulling my hips to anchor against her. My hands pulled at the hair tie that held her beautiful red curls together in a ponytail, allowing her thick tresses to spill over into my hands. I loved her hair and the color of it. I loved running my fingers through her hair, gripping her soft coils tightly as I deepened my kiss. She whimpered softly against my lips.

I undressed her, and she undressed me. I caressed her body as she lay on her side. Finding the right position without having thoughts of squishing my baby was a challenge most times, but Kinsley took hold of me and slid me into her wet center. While lying on our sides, I thrust in and out of her. She felt so soft, warm, and ready for me. I held on to her breasts and didn't stop until we came together.

Pop was released from the hospital three afternoons later. I pulled up to the estate called Sugarcreek and parked at the end of their driveway. To my surprise, Alohnzo was pulling up next to me wearing shades. I didn't expect him to come after the way he had been acting.

I got out of my car, and he got out of his. "Good afternoon," I said.

"Good afternoon," he replied as if he didn't want to. "I just want to sign these papers and get out of here."

"Wow . . . Okay. So, you're going to keep up with this attitude?"

Alohnzo refused to answer as he rang the doorbell.

I pushed past him, opened the door, and walked into the warm house. Why was he ringing the doorbell like some stranger? We grew up in this house.

"Why are you acting like a fucking weirdo?"

"Shut up," Alohnzo replied.

We walked through the foyer and down the hall to the family room in silence. Mama's kitten heels sounded against the polished hardwood floors as she walked toward us.

She greeted us with hugs. "My sons, my babies."

"Hello, Mama," Alohnzo and I said in unison, sounding like identical twins.

"Have them sit at the table, Mabel," Pop said, as he walked to the table with his cane. He didn't talk with a slur this time, and his mouth wasn't twisted as bad as it was when he first came out of his coma.

"Y'all heard your father. Go ahead and sit," Mama said.

I pulled out a chair. The kitchen table held a vase with white orchids in the center and was large enough to fit six, but Pop and I sat close to each other.

Alohnzo didn't move as he replied, "I'm not staying long. Alistair said you wanted me to sign some paper."

"Sit down first," Pop demanded.

Alohnzo sat across from me but refused to take off his shades.

I shook my head in disbelief.

"After talking with your mother and Alistair, I have to think about my health. I'm officially retiring. This will be my last week. I'm leaving the company for both of you. Alohnzo, it's up to you if you want to accept." Pop's words came out slowly, but they were clear.

Though I thought Pop made up his mind on letting me run the company alone, I waited to see Alohnzo's response.

"Thanks, Pop. I'm glad you're putting your health first. That makes me most happy, but I met with a few people this morning, and I just closed a business deal with a partner. I'm going to focus on that business, so I will not be returning to your company."

"Really?" Pop's eyes were wide with fascination. "I would love to hear more. I already know you think like me, so whatever it is must be lucrative. Let me say that I'm proud that you have your own mind to want to build a legacy of your own. I wish you nothing but the best. You don't need to sign anything, and I accept your verbal resignation. Alistair, are you ready to take on the business without your brother?"

I nodded with a wide grin. "Of course. As we discussed yesterday, I won't disappoint you. I'll make you proud too, Pop."

"That I know for sure. You both are destined for success. Now, I need to know something because legacy is everything to me. What's going on with your love lives?" Pop eyed me.

I looked at Alohnzo to see if he ratted me out, but I couldn't see his eyes to see if he knew what Pop was hinting at.

"Well, I'm involved with someone," I said, reluctant to share.

"How involved?" Mama asked as she folded her arms across her chest.

"While I was away, I got married, and now, we're having a baby."

"What?" Mama's eyes almost popped out of her head as she glared at me. "To whom? When? Why?"

I thought before I responded. I loved Kinsley, but I knew the stain she left on my family's name. To be honest, she and I were supposed to live our lives as if my family didn't exist, but I wasn't going to be happily secluded. I wanted to yell out that I was in love with Kinsley, but it wouldn't come out.

"Kinsley," Pop said knowingly.

"Kinsley?" Mama scoffed, moving her cold stare to him.

"It wasn't hard to figure it out, Mabel. The man disappeared the same time she did. If he found her, of course, I did as well. Their marriage is legal, so that makes her our daughter-in-law. You guys are having our first grandchild. Is it a boy or a girl?"

"We don't know yet. Kinsley would prefer not to know until birth."

"Lord, Lord, Lord. Where did I go wrong? I can't get rid of this bitch for nothing, and now you're telling me she's having a baby? How far is she?"

"Thirty-two weeks."

"So, she's almost nine months? Okay, I get it. You chased her and married her because she told you she was pregnant."

"No. We had no idea she was pregnant before she left. She didn't find out until a month after we were already settled there."

Mama made a sucking sound as she held her tongue against her teeth. "I won't accept this. Never!"

Before I could reply, Pop questioned, "Did she travel back with you?"

"Yes, she's at the house. Mama, I don't want you going over there and starting trouble."

Mama rolled her eyes at me. "I cannot believe you." She shook her hands in the air before she stared at Alohnzo. "And what about you? Let me guess. You're crazy about that widow, aren't you?"

Alohnzo finally removed his sunglasses to stare our mother in the eye as he replied, "Her name is Tahira, for the last time. Yes, I love her, and I plan to propose sooner than later. It would be nice to have my family's support, but if not, it's cool. It's not her fault that her husband was murdered."

Mama put her head down as she shook it slowly. She took a deep breath and said, "You all disappoint me greatly, but I'll tell you what. Bring Tahira by to meet us. That will allow me to get to know her. What do you think, Amos?"

"I like that idea. We'll have a nice dinner here. Is Tahira still pursuing being an actress?"

"Yes. She just returned from London a few days ago, but she plans to find some acting opportunities soon."

"All right. Look at your schedule and let us know what night works best for you," Pop said.

"Wait, so it's okay to sit down with his deceased neighbor's wife, but you won't offer to sit down with Kinsley?" I questioned, not feeling their favoritism.

"First of all, no one told you to go off and chase your father's whore," Mama said.

"Out of respect for my wife, please don't call her that."

"You want me to respect that piece of trash after what she put your family through? How *could* you, Alistair? She trapped you in her web, and you're stuck now. Did you even have her sign a prenuptial agreement? Hell, do you even *know* that baby is yours? She was fucking your daddy and your brother in the same month. With the way it's looking, that baby could be any of yours."

"I used a condom every time," Alohnzo said quickly.

I ignored my mother's ill words and replied, "She's not what you think. I know the *real* her, and so what if she made some mistakes? She's human. I see something in her and gave her a real chance at love because everyone needs love."

"Oh, is that so? You have no idea, Alistair. She's *exactly* what I know she is. She's a manipulator, con artist, and a prostitute. You don't know the half." Mama laughed, shaking her head. "Go ahead, Amos, and get to the point of why you're asking about their love lives so that I can be done with this stupid conversation."

"I asked that question because who you marry becomes a part of this legacy. Your children and their children will never have to work. I wouldn't want a woman to come through here like a tornado and try to take a piece of what we've worked so hard for. Do you understand where I'm coming from?"

Alohnzo nodded before I did.

"Good," Pop said. "Alistair, you and I will talk about your transition to the head of the company. Alohnzo, I wish you nothing but the best with your endeavors. I know you will set up quite an empire of your own. I can't wait to see it all."

"Thanks, Pop," Alohnzo replied. "I appreciate that. When I have a launch party, you'll be on the list."

I gritted my teeth as I watched Alohnzo soak up Pop's praise.

Mama added, "I guess at some point I need to stop being so overprotective and dictating when it comes to your love lives. I'll be fine if you all agree to stop hiding things from me from now on. I think I can handle you and Tahira, Alohnzo."

There was a gleam in her eye that only shined when she was thinking about Alohnzo and Tahira.

I shook off the bit of jealousy I felt because I was now going to oversee Amos Kelly Financial Advisors without Alohnzo, and I was going to prove to them why I was the best choice. In time, Kinsley and I were going to prove them all wrong as well. She wasn't some cheap whore like Mama was trying to imply. She was a beautiful woman who wanted to be loved. I still couldn't believe how these fools mistreated her. But none of that mattered because *I* was the man to love her.

Alohnzo hugged and kissed my parents before he walked out of their house.

I walked over to the bar area and poured myself some French Cognac. I grabbed a crystal snifter, downed it quickly, and felt the fire burning my throat and chest. Then I poured another.

Mama left the dining room after giving me the side-eye.

Before taking another drink, I turned and stared at my father. He was the older version of me with salt-and-pepper hair neatly combed and cut low. His graying beard accentuated his strong jaw and sharp nose.

"Let's talk on the patio," he said. "I need some air. Grab the bottle and get me a glass."

I picked up the bottle of Cognac, our glasses, and carried them out with us to the patio. Pop sat at the patio table with the red umbrella in the middle. I sat next to him as he placed his cane against the table. As I stared out at the stable, I thought about seeing the horses. We had twenty thoroughbreds, which consisted of five broodmares, nine mares, and six yearlings. I took them to many expos. We were going to sell the yearlings. We usually only kept them when the older horses were close to passing away.

I looked down as I poured Dad a drink. "Pop, you sure you should be drinking?"

"I'm sure. Tell me more about you and Kinsley."

I handed it to him.

He took a sip and exhaled. "Come on with it. Why are you hesitating?"

I couldn't help but think about my father being with Kinsley. That was the first time I pictured him with her. Things were different now because she was my wife. I had always been close to my parents, and I loved them with all my heart. I respected Pop, and I didn't want ever to disrespect him, but talking about Kinsley made me feel uncomfortable. Pop was still waiting for my reply. I ran my hand over my deep waves in my short-faded hair.

"Come on now," he said with a slight grin.

"Pop, what makes you think I have anything to share with you about *my* wife?"

Pop nodded, savoring the taste of the Cognac. "Alistair, you're one of the best businessmen that I know, but I never taught you to be stupid. Don't be fooled by those hazel eyes, red hair that smells like fresh strawberries, and her beautiful, light brown skin."

Downing my drink, I poured some more Cognac. I needed the liquid courage to have this conversation with my father. He wasn't just my father. He was Kinsley's past lover, a jealous ex who couldn't stand to see me win her heart. I could see it in his eyes.

"Well . . . Pop, as I said before, Kinsley is my wife, and she's carrying my baby, your grandchild. The things that happened between the two of you are in the past, and we're moving forward."

Pop moved the Cognac around in his sifter as he replied, "That's the thing about life and emotions. You have no idea when and what will affect those two things." He raised his glass to toast with me.

"Touché," I answered.

He had a smug grin on his face, and at that moment, I felt a little tension between us. I watched him as he stared off into the distance. He hadn't let Kinsley go. He was still holding on but didn't want to seem like he was, especially since I married her.

"Well, Pop, I gotta get home so I can prepare for my return to work tomorrow."

"Yes, get some rest. You've been gone for a while, and there are some changes you need to catch up on. Have a good night."

I stood up and patted him on the shoulder. "You have a good night as well, sir."

I walked into the house toward the front door.

Mama was getting ready to head upstairs, but she stopped at the bottom of the staircase when she saw me.

"If I were you, I'd get a DNA test, son."

I sighed heavily. "Really, Mama?"

"'Really, Mama,' nothing."

"I'm sure Kinsley would've said something."

"Humph, you think so? She would take that to her grave if that meant losing you. That whore doesn't know a damn thing about being an honest woman."

"Mama, I really don't like that you always have something negative to say about my wife. We can't change the past, but I want you to let it go. You don't know anything about her and how she's changed her life since being with me."

She shook her head slowly as if she felt sorry for me and went up the stairs.

I brushed off what my mother said because she couldn't stand Kinsley and would do anything to ruin my happiness with her if that meant getting rid of her. I walked to my car, and I didn't realize that my fists were balled up until I saw my reflection on my shiny car door. I took a deep breath, shook out my hands, and left.

Chapter 13

Tahira

Alohnzo's suggested realtor, Jake, was professional, fast, knew the market, and Sand Cove. We picked an ideal listing date, assessed the condition of the house, and fixed the minor repairs like the leaky faucet in the kitchen. Tru and Alohnzo helped me to declutter and donate things I no longer wanted. We hired a cleaning crew to deep clean and a few painters to make the walls look fresh. For a week, Jake only needed to show the house to a very few select buyers. He had a list of people who had been waiting for the chance to live in Sand Cove. Celebrity Judge Sidra Embry was at the top of the list. She didn't mind my asking cost and felt it was worth every penny because it was a private community with its own beach. We accepted her offer, and I was able to close the deal at thirty days.

"Welcome to Sand Cove, Miss Embry," I said as I handed her the keys.

"Please, call me Sidra. Thank you so much," she replied happily. "I'm so excited."

Sidra was no taller than five feet, and she wore her hair in a short cut. Her Southern accent was adorable.

"You'll get to meet the rest of the neighbors soon. Alohnzo's brother, Alistair, lives in the first house, and the Masons live in the last one."

"I can't wait to meet everyone. Thank you again for your warm welcome."

"No problem. Thank you for buying the house."

I walked away from her, and into the house I was now sharing with Alohnzo.

Living with Alohnzo felt like a dream. I had been afraid that he would change and be this horrible person like Luca, but that wasn't the case. Alohnzo was busy because he successfully purchased Pinnacle Vineyard with his business partner.

He called and said, "Get dressed. I have a surprise for you."

I loved his surprises, so I didn't hesitate to get into the shower and dress.

Sitting at the vanity in the bedroom, I applied light makeup, sleek, smoky eyeshadow, and slowly removed the pins from my hair. My hair had grown about an inch while in London. I used my fingers to fluff the curls gently to cascade past my shoulders.

I had just finished putting on my Rhianna red lipstick when Alohnzo walked into the house. "Tahira?"

I grabbed my heels, clutch, and spritzed perfume on my neck and wrists. Then I met him at the bottom of the stairs.

Alohnzo was standing in a blue button-up and dark blue jeans. "You're stunning," he said.

I hugged him. "Aaaaw. Thank you. So, what's the major surprise, handsome?"

He took my hand, and we walked out of the front door to the car. He didn't respond until we had our seat belts on. "If I tell you what it is, it wouldn't be a surprise anymore." He squeezed my inner thigh right where my dress stopped.

I smiled as he backed out of the driveway and closed the garage.

We drove, listening to songs by Erykah Badu, Jill Scott, and Dwele. I liked his music selection for the night. Soon, he pulled up to Pinnacle Vineyard. Even at night, I could make out the rolling landscapes, trees, and grapevines. I smiled.

Alohnzo came around and opened the door for me. He held my hand as we walked toward a table that was covered in white linen. I admired the candlelit centerpiece.

"This is bloody wicked."

"Thank you." Alohnzo beamed with pride at me. He loved it when I used my British slang. He pulled the chair from the table so I could sit, then helped me to scoot it closer.

"This place should definitely have a bed and breakfast to go with the wine tasting and fine dining," I suggested.

"That sounds amazing and something to consider." He sat across from me with the brightest smile.

"I remember how all this looks from the pictures you showed me."

"You'll be back in the daytime soon to see it."

A waiter poured us two glasses of sauvignon blanc. After he left, Alohnzo reached across the table to take my hands into his.

"Tahira, I have to ask you something." He squeezed my hands nervously.

He got down on bended knee, and my heart started racing. Was he proposing? My thoughts were flying around my head, and he had this gleam in his eye that hinted that he was ready to make me his wife. As soon as he had the black square box in front of me, I placed both hands over my mouth. I had dreamed of marrying him, but I had no idea that he really wanted to, especially after I spent most of the year in London without him.

"I wanted to share this moment with your mom, Tru, and Noble. I'm sorry Noble is still pissed at me, and Tru didn't want to leave him out. I did call your mom and asked for her blessing on a Skype video call. She was more than happy that I want to make you mine for a lifetime. I can't imagine living my life without you, and I've never felt this way about anyone. Tahira, will you marry me?"

He opened the box and took out the gorgeous diamond-encrusted band with a solitaire diamond in the center.

"Yes, yes, yes. I love you." I accepted his ring as he slid it onto my finger. With tears in my eyes, I hugged him as soon as he stood up.

There was no way the grin was going to be wiped off either of our faces. I thought of calling my mum, but it was 2:15 a.m. her time. I admired my ring throughout the rest of the dinner. As we waited for dessert, Alohnzo asked, "What kind of wedding do you want to have?"

"With Luca, we did the whole big wedding, so I kind of want to do something smaller and more intimate. What about your parents?"

Alohnzo nodded slowly. "I talked to them about wanting to marry you. They want to meet you. With my new business venture, I haven't had the time to take you over there for dinner. I think when they see how awesome you are, they'll love you. My mother can be a bit much at times, but you're amazing, and if she doesn't see it, then don't worry about her. Just know that I'll never allow her to disrespect you in any way. I'll always have your back."

I smiled warmly at him. Alohnzo had a way with words that made me melt.

As soon as we were in our bedroom, he whispered against the back of my neck, "I'm so happy you want to be my wife." He grabbed my hips from behind and pressed his hard body into the back of me.

Spinning me in his arms, he held me while gazing into my eyes. His smooth lips attached to mine as he kissed me passionately and deeply. With his teeth, he tugged on my bottom lip, and I moaned against his mouth. He lay me on the bed, his hands went up to my dress, and he spread my thighs as he gripped them. Our kisses were passionate as we hungrily devoured each other. My fingers unbuttoned his shirt eagerly. He let me go momentarily to take his clothes off. Then his hands quickly resumed their place on my upper thigh. His mouth moved from my lips to taste the skin of my neck.

"Alohnzo . . ." I moaned as his lips made my skin feel so good.

His hands were traveling higher up my dress. His fingers played with the hem of my panties before he slipped them off and dropped them to the floor. He played with my short-trimmed hair that neatly covered me before his fingers made their way into my wet folds.

"You're always so wet for me."

I giggled as his fingers caressed me. I gripped his wrist so he wouldn't move from that spot. His eyes fixated on the way I was riding his hand. My body started trembling with need as his thumb shifted to brush over my swollen clit. I closed my eyes and panted.

His left hand moved up from my waist to the top of my dress. I helped him push the dress down to my torso. Alohnzo unhooked my black strapless bra. My breasts tumbled forward, and he immediately latched eagerly on to my dark nipples. He alternated between each breast as if he couldn't get enough. I eased out of his clutches and removed my clothes. Then I spread out on the bed naked, and his body covered mine.

Light from the morning sun came into the bare windows and gently caressed our skin. I had woken up a few minutes before him, and I couldn't help but admire my fiancé's handsome face as he slept on his back. I envied his long, dark lashes. Why did men always have to have the most beautiful eyelashes? The way the sun danced all over his body had me feeling tingly inside. I was so in love with him. I stared at my ring as it shined in the sun. This was a dream come true.

"Such a beautiful face," he said, staring at me.

I leaned over him and placed a kiss on his lips. "Good morning, my love."

"Good morning."

"You want to meet my parents tonight?" he asked.

"Sure," I said, feeling a little nervous.

"We'll have dinner with them, if that's okay."

"That's fine."

"Good. Let's shower, get some food, and then go to my hangar and jump in one of the planes. I'll let you pick which one we take."

"Ooooh, I can't wait."

My cell phone rang, so I picked it up from the nightstand. It was my agent.

"Good morning, Rachel."

"Good morning, Tahira. Is now an appropriate time to talk?"

"Yes. How are you?"

"I'm good. Listen, so I was trying to get some auditions for you, but we have a huge problem."

"What's the matter?" I asked, feeling my heart beat a little harder.

"Luca blacklisted you. He called every casting director in Los Angeles. Since he's not alive to take back what he has said about your professionalism, they want to respect him and do not wish to see you in an audition. I'm terribly sorry."

Tears came to my eyes as I replied, "There's no way to undo it? I mean, he's dead, for Christ's sake."

"I'm sorry. It's impossible to remove names once listed. For that reason, I'm going to have to drop you from the agency. I would encourage you to go to auditions that do not require an agent. Sorry, sweetheart."

I sniffled as tears cascaded down my cheeks. "Thanks, Rachel."

I ended the call and cried.

"Why are you crying?" Alohnzo asked, putting his hand on my back.

"The agency just dropped me because Luca blacklisted me. I don't know what I'm going to do. I won't get a decent audition without an agent."

He hugged me. "With me, you'll never have to worry about working."

I cried into his shoulder. "I know you'll take care of me, but I want to make my own way. I have my own dreams and goals, Alohnzo."

"I understand. Well, don't give up. Something will happen."

He kissed me, and I nodded. Though his words were trying to comfort me, I couldn't help but feel as if my dream of becoming a big star would never come true. Luca made sure of that. What was I supposed to do now?

Alohnzo's parents' home stood out with the manicured lawn. From the iron gates to the ranch-style stables behind it, I was at a loss for words. I had never seen a Black family own so much. As soon as we entered the elaborate home, I felt trembly inside. I kept pushing my hair behind my ear nervously and wringing my hands. I tried my best to shake my mood about the news my agent gave me, but it didn't work very well. I was in a bad mood, but I did my best to mask it for Alohnzo.

His parents were standing in the foyer where the walls were the color of French vanilla. His mother was average in height. Her deep brown curly wig looked natural and made her look young, as if she drank from the fountain of youth. Her eyes weren't soft or warm as she sized me up from head to toe, looking for my imperfections.

I shifted my eyes from hers to her husband's. He was tall, handsome, and regal. Alohnzo and Alistair looked so much like him that it was uncanny. His smile was incredible and charming.

"Hey, my son," his mother said as Alohnzo hugged her.

After Alohnzo hugged his dad next, he stepped back and introduced us.

"Mama, Pop, this is Tahira, my fiancée. Tahira, these are my parents, Mabel and Amos Kelly."

"You proposed already? When?" Mabel scowled as if someone had passed gas, and she could smell it.

"Mabel," Amos's calm voice said as he reached for my hand. "Let them come in good before you start." He gave me an apologetic grin as I placed my hand in his. He kissed the top of it. "It's a pleasure to meet you, Tahira. Goodness, you're pretty."

"Thank you," I replied.

"Amos," Mabel griped. "Stop with your flirting. Come in, come in. Let's go to the dining room. I prepared this food."

She led us through the hallway, where family photographs in silver frames hung nicely along the walls. I smiled at Alohnzo and Alistair as children with big smiles. They looked like the happiest kids. Amos trailed her while Alohnzo held my hand and squeezed it lightly. We entered the dining room, and I couldn't stop admiring everything about the place. The table had the most delicious-looking food: lamb chops with rosemary, corn bread dressing, creamy mashed potatoes, and a green leafy salad.

"Mama, you cooked all of this by yourself?" Alohnzo asked, eyeing the table.

"I know I usually only cook for holidays, but this is a special occasion. I didn't know you had already proposed, but let me go get some champagne from the cellar."

"I proposed last night."

"Congratulations," she said before walking down the hall toward their wine cellar.

"Thank you," Alohnzo replied.

"Please sit," Amos said.

Alohnzo held the chair for me as he always did before he sat next to me. Amos sat at the head of the table.

Mabel returned with two chilled bottles of champagne. "This should do." She sat to the left of Amos, across from Alohnzo.

Amos said, "Let's bow our heads and close our eyes to bless the food. God, bless this food my wife so amazingly prepared. May you also bless Alohnzo and his beautiful soon-to-be wife, Tahira. Thank you, Lord, for the life you've given us to continue to live. In Jesus' name, we pray, Amen."

"Amen," we said together.

Alohnzo smiled at me, and I smiled back.

Mabel started with the lamb chops and passed the dish around. She did the same with each dish until our plates were the way we wanted them. Amos popped the cork of one bottle of champagne and poured each of us a glass.

Mabel said, "Tahira, I hear you're from London. Which part?"

"I grew up in Greenwich."

"Greenwich. Nice. What was it like?"

"I had so much fun as a kid, but I didn't have many friends. My mum always took me to parks and playgrounds to visit. My teenage years were a bit tough because I grew up in a pretty rough part. It's been amazing watching London change over the years, though, from crummy and run-down to gentrification." As I talked of home, my accent grew thicker.

Amos said, "I like your British accent. We've been to London a few times. I like it there."

"There's truly no place like home, but Los Angeles has been my home for quite some time now," I replied.

"What are your intentions with my son?" Mabel asked. She took a few sips of champagne before she continued. "I heard you got most of Luca Moretti's estate, so it can't be money, can it?"

"Really, Mother?" Alohnzo looked embarrassed.

"It's fine, Alohnzo," I said, keeping a smile on my face. "That's a fair question. I know things seem sudden with Alohnzo and me, but before and after my husband was murdered, Alohnzo was there for me. I care for him very much. I always have, and I always will."

Mabel stared through me as she said, "How do I know you didn't kill your husband for the money?"

My smile immediately faded as I stammered, "Ex-c-c-use me?"

Alohnzo interrupted before Mabel could get in another cruel word. "With all respect, Mama, do not insult my fiancée."

"I have not insulted her. I'm simply asking an important question."

"Do you know that Luca was a verbally abusive asshole to her? Do you know how his affairs made her feel? You should. Instead of judging her when you know nothing about her, try relating to her."

Mabel clutched her pearls around her neck as Alohnzo let out her secret in front of me. "Well . . . I know what it's like for a man to betray your trust." Mabel's eyes grew watery, but she held back her tears as she continued. "Though I don't know what it's like to love another man other than my husband, I can relate in some ways." She cleared her throat. "I'm sorry for my harsh interrogation."

"That's a start," Alohnzo said. "I want to be clear. I love this woman, and she deserves a fair chance to be a part of this family. She's a good person with a good heart. She's one of the sweetest, kindest women in the world. If you would've seen the way Luca treated her . . ." Alohnzo paused as he got emotional. He tried to regain his composure quickly to avoid becoming unraveled.

Mabel dabbed the corners of her eyes with a cloth napkin. "You have a kind and gentle heart, Alohnzo. You always have. If she is all that you say, then she deserves you, and you deserve her. Treat her well."

"Of course, I will," Alohnzo replied.

Mabel's eyes were a little softer when she looked at me as if she understood the pain of being cheated on.

Amos said, "No amount of money could ever buy the kind of love that I see when you look at each other. What you two have is real. It reminds me of when I first met Mabel. You remember, sweetheart?"

Mabel nodded at the memory. "Yes, I do . . . As much as I want to tear you to pieces, Tahira, I won't. Forgive me as it's hard for me to trust people. My son adores you. The way he looks at you, I know it's true love."

"That's all I ask," Alohnzo said. "I hope that you guys continue to get to know her because she's not going anywhere."

"Tell us more about your business venture," Amos said. "You haven't told us what you managed to get your hands on. The suspense is killing me."

"Well, Marcus Travers and I purchased Pinnacle Vineyard."

"The Schmitz brothers' winery and vineyard?" Amos asked with excitement in his voice.

"Yeah, that's the one."

"We went to a wedding there once, didn't we?" Mabel questioned.

"Yeah, we did. That's a beautiful place, right along the water. Good ol' Marcus Travers. He's been a client of ours for some time, right?"

"Yes."

"See what taking good care of clients has done for your networking?"

Alohnzo nodded. "Absolutely. Pop, I'm more than grateful for what you have instilled into me as a business-man. The plan is to dive more into the wine business and launch our own line of wines and champagnes. Tahira is going to be the face of the first brand."

"I like that." Amos raised his champagne flute and said, "Here's to our son and our future daughter-in-law."

We raised our glasses. Before I could sip, out the corner of my eye, I saw Mabel glaring at me. When I made eye contact, she gave me a half smile. I didn't have her trust just yet, but I was going to be myself. Even if she never liked me, it wouldn't matter. Alohnzo was the best thing that could've ever happened to me, and I was glad he wanted me to be a part of his world.

Chapter 14

Sidra

I was a Los Angeles district court judge who filmed a syndicated reality courtroom show adjudicating small claims disputes. My show ran for fifteen seasons, and I made five million per year before it was canceled. Once the show was over, I decided to retire from law altogether. Retiring was something I had looked forward to. Purchasing the home in Sand Cove made me feel complete.

Before moving to Sand Cove, I had only heard about the existence of it on the news after Luca Moretti was murdered. I had no idea that Sand Cove had become a tiny Black community, and once I found that out, I wanted more than anything to become a part of it. Who wouldn't want to live in Sand Cove? When I saw that the breathtaking beach house had gone on the market, I jumped at the opportunity. Regardless of what my family and friends thought about me buying the late Luca Moretti's beach house, I made an offer, and Luca's widow accepted.

I was originally from New Orleans but moved to Los Angeles in the late '80s to further my career in law. My life hadn't always been this sweet. I grew up poor, so I cherished everything I earned in my success. I might've evolved into a phenomenally successful woman who loved the city of L.A. and the beaches, but I held on to my deep Southern roots and my Southern accent.

"I can't wait for all this to be over with," I said underneath my breath as I watched my 23-year-old daughter, Tori, instruct the moving men where to move her things. Three cameramen followed behind her every move.

Victoria, aka Tori, was my last child. She looked cute in her feed-in cornrows going down her back, and her diamond studs were shining in the three holes in each of her ears. She wore ripped jean shorts and a white sports bra with a loose-fitting crop top over it. She loved her life, and she loved being a reality star even more. I think my time on reality TV inspired her to want a show of her own. This was the first season, and I had agreed to let her film our moving process, but as I watched her, I prayed I wouldn't regret it.

My other two daughters were in their thirties, living their own lives. Nina was a family doctor, and Rena was a family court lawyer. Both were married but didn't have children just yet. I was patiently waiting for the day, but my daughters were too busy even to see me half the time. Now that I had this beautiful house in Sand Cove, I couldn't wait to watch my daughters and grandbabies play on the beach.

My boyfriend, Grant, in all his six-foot chocolate glory, walked out of the house with a bowl of gumbo. He was the most stunning man. He was slim but toned. Although I was 57 and he was 45, he was my dream man, and I was lucky to call him mine.

"This is a beautiful house, honey," he said. "You going to have peace with all these cameras documenting Tori's life in your home? I thought you would've had her get an apartment and film there."

"Ugh," I groaned. "I was just thinking to myself that I hope I won't regret this."

"Mmmm, this gumbo sho' is good, baby. You put your foot all up and through this," he said, taking a spoonful of rice into his mouth.

"I'm glad you like it. I haven't had a chance to eat because the moving men arrived earlier than expected."

He slurped the juice from a crab leg. "I better go inside with this."

I looked at the juice that had dripped on his white polo shirt. "Yeah. It's getting all over the place."

"You mind if I take some for Jarrell? He'll probably want some."

Jarrell was his 14-year-old son, and he was raising him alone as a single father. Jarrell's mother was incarcerated and had been since he was only 3 years old.

"You know I don't mind. Let's get inside, and I'll look to see if I can find the Tupperware."

We walked behind the cameramen as they followed Tori up the stairs to her bedroom. We headed in the opposite direction of the kitchen, and I opened a few boxes.

"The view is amazing here. Too bad it's foggy today. I would say let's take a walk on the beach, but it's a little windy for summertime. I still can't believe the beach is private, and you only have three other neighbors."

"That's what sold me. No one comes down this road, and I get to stay under the radar."

"You meet your neighbors yet?"

"I've only met Luca's wife and her boyfriend, Alohnzo. They live to the right of me. I look forward to meeting them all."

"Does it creep you out that the old director was killed in here?" He looked around as if he would magically see a ghost appear.

I waved my hand at him. "No, I don't think about it . . . found them." I took the stack of Tupperware bowls and tops over to the kitchen island where Grant was tearing that gumbo up. "You still undecided on moving in?"

"Now that these cameras are here, I don't think that'll be a good idea. Let's see what happens after the show airs."

I sighed a little. I was hoping that Grant would finally want to live together. I had been an extremely independent woman since the divorce from my first husband. Truthfully, I had been that way since I was a kid because I had a mother who had three jobs to take care of us, but it would've been nice to have a man around the house again.

Grant slurped down the rest of the gumbo, wiped his hands with a napkin, and took a good look at the way I was making the to-go bowl for his son. "Sid, you know I love you more than anything in the world. We've been together ten years now, and our relationship is special. You really sure you want me and Jarrell to move in?"

"Yeah, I want to share this with both of you. I want to share every part of my life with you."

"Okay, but you turned down my marriage proposal twice."

"You already know how I feel about marriage. We don't need to be married to spend the rest of our lives together, do we?"

"No, but I've never been married, and I don't believe in shacking up."

"There you go with your religious beliefs. If two people love each other, why do they need a piece of paper to validate them?" I sealed the bowl and threw my arms around his neck. "Just consider it, boo. You can wake up every day to me, and I can be naked and make you breakfast."

"You know I love your stuffed French toast with strawberries on the side. You sure know how to make a man feel like a king, but know that as your man, it's my job to keep you happy." Grant kissed me passionately. "I'll be back later tonight. You still making that peach cobbler?"

"It's already done. It'll be waiting for ya when you come back." I handed him the to-go bowl of gumbo. "Tell Jarrell that he can come by anytime and bring his friends to hang out on the beach."

"I will." He walked out of the kitchen.

Grant was the kind of man who enjoyed all the same activities I did, like watching basketball, singing karaoke, drinking games, and bowling tournaments. He could make friends with his coworkers and speak to everyone while out. He was full of confidence and loved meeting new people. I couldn't wait to meet all the neighbors and introduce him. Tahira and Alohnzo were sweet, and if the other couples were anything like them, we were going to have a fun time.

Tori came into the kitchen with a blanket in her hand. Her best friend, PJ, was right at her side. The cameramen were documenting everything.

"Seriously, though, I can't believe how big this house is," PJ said to her. "You know I'm definitely going to be coming over often to enjoy that beach."

"All that's missing is a spa on the deck. Mommy, can we get a hot tub on this deck?" Tori asked with her eyes sparkling.

"Of course, we can. That would be perfect, wouldn't it? Order one and put it on my card."

Tori nodded and turned to PJ. "I got a blanket so we can sit on the sand."

"Yes, honey," he said, snapping his fingers. "I'm down for that. Plus, I'm waiting for you to tell me when you're going to sit on you know whose dick."

"PJ! Lawd," I said, but I wasn't entirely shocked at her best friend's boldness. I was just hoping the network would bleep it out.

"What?" he asked with a laugh.

The cameras were on me and filming, but I continued saying, "For crying out loud, wait until you're out there to talk like that, you hear?"

"My bad, Mama Embry," he replied before covering his mouth.

They walked out through the sliding door and headed down to the beach.

I sighed and prayed her little reality show would only last one season because I didn't know how much more of this I was going to be able to take.

Chapter 15

Tori

I didn't have to dream about being rich because we were. All my life, Mommy had luxurious cars, big houses, and enough money to do whatever we wanted. I never had to want for anything. Mommy was the queen of dinner parties and gatherings while I was growing up. She couldn't go to the mall, grocery shopping, or anywhere without someone recognizing her. She would always smile graciously and sign autographs. Mommy had many friends and distant relatives from Texas who would always call her for a favor or for some charitable cause. I wanted to be just like her with my own shine. She had hopes that I would follow her and become a lawyer. I dropped out of college because it was too hard. I didn't like studying or trying to be like my sisters, Nina and Rena.

I didn't want to be known as the TV judge's daughter, so I became a socialite in Los Angeles, hanging out and rubbing elbows with the most popular crowds. I had one point one million followers on Instagram. An opportunity came for me to have my own reality show, so I jumped at the chance. This was my time to create my own path.

PJ and I sat on a blanket in the sand while the crew filmed us.

"Like I was saying in the house, when you going to sit on Makani's dick? I know it gotta be big."

I laughed, shaking my head. "You are so nosy. I've been so busy lately."

"So, when we throwing our first beach party?" PJ asked. "This is the perfect place to throw an invitation-only bash."

"I'm working on a plan. We'll have this beach so lit. We would have to invite everybody we know."

"And everybody would show up and show the fuck out. What are the men looking like around here?"

"There are only four houses, and from what Mommy says, the men are off the market and a little older. So far, I only met one who lives right there." I nodded my head toward Alohnzo's house. "He's fine as hell but taken. His chick used to own the house my mama bought. I haven't met the other neighbors yet, but I hear they're married."

"Damn. That sucks. It would be nice to have a love interest in this beautiful private paradise."

"Don't act like I can't bring a few love interests to play over here with me."

"You ain't said nothin' but a word, girlfriend," PJ laughed. "You got plenty to work with. Just let me know when and the time of the party, and I'll bring some fun too."

"I got you, boo. Soooo, I have slimmed my little fan club down to just Sevante and Makani. These days, I can't choose between them. I mean, why should I have to? Men do it all the time. They have all the cake they want."

"I'm jelly, bitch. Sev got that silky milk chocolate thing happening, and Makani, well, he's a little rough and thuggish but sexy as ever."

"Right. I don't want to be locked down to anyone, but if I had to choose, who should I pick?" I played with one of my braids.

"Don't pick. Just have fun. Enjoy the ride while it lasts, honey."

"What about you, PJ? Who you feeling these days?"

"Nobody. I'm single and free as a bird. I don't have time for the hounding and asking where I'm at."

"That part."

We laughed together.

"You think Mama Embry is going to let you throw a party?"

"Hell yeah. You already know Mommy will let me do whatever I want. Ooooh, before I forget, let me get online right now and see about ordering this spa. I'm going to need to do express delivery." I took my cell out of my pocket and tapped Google Chrome.

"Tori?" I heard a male voice call.

I turned toward the house and squinted my eyes because I didn't have my contacts on to see Sevante walking down the steps.

"I should've known he was going to pull up on you," PJ said, shaking his head. "Did he tell you he was coming?"

"No," I said, smiling as Sevante got closer.

Sevante's Hershey's chocolate bar complexion was shining under the sun's rays. The short-sleeved shirt he was wearing fit his muscles right. The way he walked upright and straight toward us as if he were a model had me biting my lower lip.

I checked my incoming calls and texts because I didn't remember seeing a text or a call from him.

"You called me?" I asked, staring up at him.

"Nope," he replied. "I was supposed to?"

I nodded. "Yeah, would've been nice. You know I'm filming a show."

He shrugged. "I'm not worried about these cameras. Damn, it's nice out here. I've never been over this way. Is this beach private?"

"Very much so," I replied.

"Have you been in the water yet?"

"No. It's not really hot enough."

"Any sunshine in Cali is an excuse to hit the water. I should've brought my board to hit the waves."

"You're a surfer?" PJ asked, with his lips puckered up as if he ate something sour.

"Absolutely. It's a terrific way to exercise. I'm surprised Tori hasn't told you. That's how we met."

I quickly reminisced on the day we met at Santa Monica Beach.

I was hanging with Yanni, a girl I met a few years back at a house party. We hadn't hung out in a while, and we were catching up. We were playing in the water, taking pictures, and posting them to our social media accounts.

"That's the one right there," Yanni said as she glanced over my shoulder while I posted.

"Yeah, I like this one."

I turned my head to see this dark-skinned god wearing a wet suit with his board in his hand, entering the water. He was focused on scoping the waves.

"Damn, baby is fine as fuck," she said, seeing what I was seeing.

He heard us and stared in our direction.

"Shit, did he hear me?" she asked, quickly putting her hand over her mouth.

"I did," he replied. "Thank you for the compliment. How are you beautiful ladies doing this afternoon?"

"We're fine," she replied.

I didn't respond as I stared at how handsome he was.

He paddled into the water and through the small waves. I continued to watch until he caught a wave he wanted to surf. He was good. Yanni and I were so captivated that we couldn't stop staring. I even snuck a few photos of him riding the waves on my phone.

"Girl, I'm getting ready to head home. I got a few things to take care of," she said. "It was fun catching up, though."

"Aw, you leaving? I had so much fun."

"Yeah. Call me so we can hang again."

"For sure. See you later," I said.

I thought about leaving or going to the pier to get something to eat. Just when I was walking out of the water, I heard him ask, "Leaving?"

I turned around to see him coming up the shore with his board in his hands.

"I'm not sure. I may hit the pier before I go home. I want some cotton candy."

"Sounds good. My name is Sev, well, Sevante, but people call me Sev. What's yours?"

"Victoria, but everyone calls me Tori. I prefer Tori."

"Nice to meet you, Tori. Listen, I don't want to come off like I do this all the time, but can I join you at the pier and get your number?"

"What you gonna do with my number?" I asked, eyeing his chin, his lips, his nose, and his eyes.

"What else is there to do with a phone number? Can I call you?"

"Sure," I replied. "You swim with your phone on you?"

He laughed shyly but realized he didn't have his phone on him. "It's actually in my car. Can you walk with me?"

"I don't know you like that to follow you to your car, so give me your number, and put on some clothes so we can go to the pier."

"It's good that you're safe. You're right. You don't know me, but I can assure you I'm not that kind of guy. If I give you my number, are you going to call me?"

A sly grin swept across my lips. "You give me your number, and you'll see."

"Okay. Stay right here. I'm going to run to my car and change out of this wet suit. Don't leave."

"I won't," I replied, smiling.

The memory faded as I stared into his eyes.

Sevante motioned for me to stand up. I knew what that meant. He wanted a hug and a kiss.

I stood up with a big smile on my face. He towered over me as I stood on my white polished toes. I was in his arms for a hug, and the smell of his heavenly cologne made me weak in the knees. He squeezed me with both strong arms as he lifted me off my feet.

"What's up, shorty? I feel like I haven't seen you in forever," he said.

"Hey, Sev. It's been a minute."

He placed a sweet quick peck on my lips before placing my feet on the blanket. "What y'all getting into tonight?"

"We're going to the Precinct," PJ said quickly. "You ever been?"

I hadn't agreed to go clubbing with PJ, but he liked to make my plans for me. He could do that because he was my best friend in the entire world. The Precinct was a sizeable gay bar with many festive events. I couldn't imagine Sevante ever going there, but I watched his reaction to see if he would be shady.

"Nah. Never heard of it. Sounds fun, though. Mind if I roll?"

I smiled. "Sure, if you don't mind being around PJ and his peeps."

Sevante picked up on my hint and nodded. "I don't mind. I'll be there with you, so it's all good." He gave me his sexy-ass smile.

I giggled as I played with my braids.

He gently took the same braid from me and rubbed it between his thumb and pointer finger. "Your braids look nice."

"Thanks. I got it braided early this morning."

"Ugh. If y'all going to be gazing at each other like this all day, I don't know if I can handle it," PJ complained.

We laughed. I shyly turned away from Sevante.

"You guys hungry?" I asked. "Mommy made gumbo and peach cobbler."

Sevante nodded while rubbing his hands together and biting on his lower lip. "You know I smelled that goodness walking through the house to get back here. I can't wait."

"Come on. I'll feed you." I grabbed his hand. "You eating, PJ?"

"Of course. I already know Mama Embry did her thang, but I'm going to take mine to go so I can get a little nap in before tonight's shenanigans."

"A nap? You gonna be ready to turn up until the sun comes up."

"That's the only way I know how to do it. Come on, now. You know me." PJ picked up the blanket and walked with Sevante and me.

"You look nice," I said, flashing my bright smile at Sevante.

"Thank you. You always look nice."

"I do what I do," I teased.

"You're something else, Tori." He bit on his lower lip and winked at me.

"Hey, I am who I am. Take it or leave it."

He laughed at me and kept glancing at my smile. "Why you always smile so hard when you're around me?"

"I'm not even smiling hard, and I could say the same thing about you."

Sevante's grin was charming as he replied, "You could. Hey, can we spend some one-on-one time together tonight? After the club? Or are you going to call what's his name?"

Aw, he was jealous. He was too cute.

"I don't have plans with Makani, but let's see how the night goes."

I didn't hide who I was seeing from anyone. Makani and Sevante knew all about each other. It was all about transparency. That way, they wouldn't expect me to jump into a relationship.

"Don't try to take my friend away from me," PJ said. "We already had plans, and I don't need you trying to fuck them up."

PJ was always insanely jealous of anyone who wanted my attention around him.

Sevante nodded. "I got you. I'll be sure to respect your time together."

"PJ, don't be rude to my company," I said. "We're going to the Precinct and have some fun, so don't start tripping."

I didn't have to look back at PJ to know he was rolling his eyes at me. He had some nerve because once he got around his other friends, he would leave me in the dust. As soon as that was going to happen, Sevante and I would get to disappear. For that, I couldn't wait.

Chapter 16

Noble

I couldn't find another way to get money to save my company because I had exhausted all my options. I felt like shit about it. It had been a little over a month since I turned down Alohnzo's ridiculous offer, but I didn't regret my decision. No one was going to take my company from me, and I meant that with my whole heart. I would rather see it closed than with anyone else. Was I so wrong for that? I didn't feel like I was.

Tru and I had barely had a full conversation since because I didn't want to talk about anything other than ways to save Constantine. I tried not to cry over my failure, but I couldn't help it. I was a grown-ass man, and I had never felt this weak and helpless in my life.

Tru walked into the bedroom, and I quickly pretended as if I weren't sulking. I scrolled through Netflix, staring at the selection recommended, but I really wasn't interested.

She sighed loudly as she sat next to me on the bed. Placing her hand on my back, she said, "I know you're hurt, babe, but you got to get over this. You can't keep beating yourself up."

"Tru . . . I opened up that company for my grandma, and I lost it," I mumbled.

"Don't think of it that way. There's so much more to live for, Noble. Everyone makes mistakes, and we had a good run while it lasted. Hey, let's take a break and go on a vacation. I could use a break. Let's take the kids to my mom's in San Diego, and we can go somewhere for a whole week." She rested her face on my chest.

"Where are we getting the money to take a vacation? Can we afford a week-long vacation at a time like this?"

Before she could respond, Noelle walked into the room, yelling, "Mommy, did you make that peanut butter and jelly sandwich for me?"

"Yes, I did. Wait, did you eat those brownies before the sandwich?"

"No, I promise, Mommy."

"Okay. Good girl. Go finish your lunch and tell Junior to help you clean up because your mama is off duty for a few hours."

"Okay." Noelle rushed out of the room.

"Don't worry about how much the vacation will cost, Noble. We'll use my rainy-day fund."

"How many rainy-day funds do you have stashed away?" I wondered aloud.

"Just think of a place, and I'll book it."

"All right."

"Have you talked to Alohnzo yet?" she asked.

"No, and I'm not going to. I already told you that."

"You're really that upset with him?"

I scoffed, "Alohnzo thinks his shit don't stink, and Luca always said he couldn't stand his smug ass. Alohnzo could've helped me out, but, no, he wanted to take my company from me."

"I hate that you think of Alohnzo that way. Luca is dead, and his opinion really shouldn't be your opinion, to be honest. I thought it was a good deal. I would've taken it."

I sat up, which made Tru sit up as well. "Why? You think he could've done something better with my own company? Why don't you say how you been feeling?"

"You know what? I'm going to leave this alone. I get that you're upset that you lost the business, but you don't have to take it out on Alohnzo. From what Tahira tells me, he has moved on and invested in a vineyard. I want to go to the party."

"Well, you're going alone. I have nothing to say to Alohnzo. He should be apologizing to me."

Tru sucked her teeth as she got up from the bed. "He should be apologizing to *you?* For what?"

"For trying to steal my company from under me. If he thought it had such potential, why would he try to cut me out?"

She didn't say another word as she walked out of the bedroom.

I took a deep breath and lay down. Looking up at the ceiling, I placed my hands behind my head. Though I was acting like an asshole, Tru was right about needing to get away, but I still couldn't figure out how she thought we could afford it. I grabbed my iPad and scrolled the internet to see if any deals would give me an idea of where to go. We had already been to Jamaica and Hawaii too many times. My eyes landed on Bali, and I got a little excited. Bali was on my bucket list. I started researching flights and hotels to price out to see if Tru really had the money to do this.

Chapter 17

Tru

When Noble was in a funk, I couldn't stand him. I loved my husband to death, but this thing with him not wanting to talk to Alohnzo was over the top. I didn't want to be at odds with my neighbors, especially not after Tahira shared her news that Alohnzo had proposed. I was mad that I wasn't there to see him get down on his knee. I was happy for Tahira. She deserved every bit of happiness Alohnzo wanted to give her. Alohnzo had found the piece to make his life complete. Why should we miss out because Noble was stupid?

After inspecting the kitchen to see how well the twins cleaned up after their lunch, I had to go behind them and clean because jelly was all over the counter. I thought about calling them down from their rooms to clean it, but I didn't feel like it. Once I was done, I made a batch of blueberry muffins so I could give them to our new neighbor.

While the muffins were baking, I checked my phone, and there was a missed call. I listened to the voicemail from the immigration lawyer.

"Hello, Mrs. Mason. This is Ximena's immigration lawyer, Isabelle Sanchez. Ximena's application for her green card was denied. We submitted for a visa renewal.

I'll be in touch soon. Give me a call at your earliest convenience."

I called her back quickly because I missed Ximena and was ready for her to come home.

"Isabelle Sanchez speaking."

"Hello, Miss Sanchez. This is Tru Mason."

"Hi, did you receive my message?"

"I did. How long will it take for a visa renewal?"

"I expect to have an answer within around ten days from the US Embassy on whether she's been approved."

"Okay. Will you call me to let me know the results?"

"Of course."

"I might be out of the country on vacation with my husband, so if you call and I don't answer, that could be the reason."

"Understood. Thank you for returning my call."

"No problem."

I ended the call and sighed. I wished that I could hear Ximena's voice to know that she was okay. The only thing that comforted me was the fact that she was with her family. I was starting to really miss her.

Noble came down the stairs with his laptop and said, "I found us a reservation at a villa in Bali. All you gotta do is book it."

He placed the laptop on the counter in front of me, and I stared at the prices. It was expensive, but affordable.

"Looks good. I'll pay with it from my personal account right now. You know I've always wanted to go to Bali, so it'll be worth it. Let's leave in three days."

"Tru, how can we afford this *and* law school?" he asked as worry lines appeared in his forehead.

Ignoring him, I said, "Should we drive the kids to San Diego tomorrow? I can call my mom and let her know."

"Yeah . . . I guess so."

I kissed his cheek before I completed the authorization for our trip.

He took a deep breath and exhaled. He wasn't going to get an answer from me. What I had in my personal account was personal. If the bills were paid, he had nothing to worry about.

"You baking?" he asked.

"Yeah. Our new neighbors moved in today, so I want to deliver these muffins as a welcome to Sand Cove. Remind me to bring up the end-of-summer bonfire to see if they would like to come."

"You think we should still have one?" he asked as he opened the refrigerator.

"Yes, it's tradition. That's why you need to let this thing go with Alohnzo. Not to mention, I need to go over to talk to Alistair and Kinsley."

"Alistair and Kinsley? Wait . . . He's with Kinsley? Have I been that out of touch with what's going on around here?"

"You've been too much in your funky-ass mood to notice. Alistair married Kinsley on some island, and they're having a baby. She came back with him when Alohnzo's father had a stroke."

He took out a can of soda and closed the refrigerator. "I knew Amos had a stroke, and Alistair came back for that, but I didn't know he moved back in with Kinsley."

"Yeah, he did, and now I have to be nice to Kinsley. As awkward as the bonfire might be, I'm still going to let them know they're welcome. If they decide that they don't want to come, then that's on them."

"Damn. Okay. Fine. I'll talk to Alohnzo."

"You can wait until after our trip. That way, you'll have a cleared mind to do so."

"I hope so."

"You have to think positively, Noble."

"I know, but it isn't going to happen at the snap of a finger. I lost my company, and I blew the deal with Alohnzo. And now, I don't know how we're going to recover from it."

"Shhhh. Let's not worry about anything until after our vacation." I paused for a few seconds before I said, "The immigration lawyer called, and although Ximena didn't get approved for her green card, she submitted for a visa renewal."

Noble studied me as he asked, "If she gets approved and can come back, can we afford her?"

"I'll talk to her to see if she'll take a little bit of a pay cut. I can always ask Alistair and Kinsley since they're having a baby if they need her. They'll definitely need a nanny."

"Well, let's just see what happens with the visa first, and we'll go from there."

"Okay."

While he drank soda, I checked on the muffins.

Noble and the twins joined me to greet our new neighbor. I carried the basket of muffins that were wrapped in a white cloth napkin. We dressed in coordinating colors. Noble and Junior wore navy slacks, white button-up, short-sleeve shirts, and Noelle and I wore navy and white dresses. We all had on red shoes.

I rang the doorbell.

Shortly, a lady about four foot eleven answered the door with a smile on her face. She was so cute and petite. I recognized her from TV. Tahira didn't say a celebrity had moved in.

"Judge Embry?" I asked.

"Yes."

"Hi, we're the Masons, your neighbors on the other side of you. I'm Tru, and this is my husband, Noble, and our twins Noelle and Noble Jr. We welcome you to Sand Cove. Here's a basket of homemade blueberry muffins I made myself." I handed them to her.

"Oh, how sweet. Thank you. Please call me Sidra. I live here with my 23-year-old daughter, Tori. You'll see her around here with cameras following her. She's filming a reality TV show."

"Really?" I asked. "That's neat. I used to watch your show in the afternoons. Will your daughter's show air soon?"

"Yeah, in about a month or so."

Noble said, "I'll be sure to avoid any background cameos."

She laughed. "I don't blame you. And these muffins look delicious. Thank you again."

"It's no problem," I replied. "We have a bonfire at the end of every summer. Each neighbor take turns hosting. Last year, I hosted my Jamaican theme. Alistair and his wife live in the first house of the row. Have you met them yet?"

"I haven't met Alistair or his wife. I, of course, met Tahira and Alohnzo. The bonfire sounds delightful. I look forward to it all."

"Yes, it's such an amazing time for our small community to bond," I added.

"I like the sound of that. Another great reason to enjoy living here."

"Yes. Well, we won't keep you long. You have a nice evening."

"Thank you so much. You have a beautiful family. Good evening."

"Thank you."

We turned and walked off her porch as she closed the door.

"She was pleasant," Noble said. "I remember you used to watch her show all the time. She used to be so cut-throat with those people. I always wondered if she was really like that. Does it feel weird seeing her in person?"

"A little bit, but it's super cool. Now, I just hope that we'll all gel nicely at the end of summer."

"Don't worry. I'll do my part." Noble sighed as he stared behind him for a moment. "I guess I can talk to Alohnzo before we leave. I'm still pissed about my company, but it's not his fault."

"You know, that was the best thing I've heard you say in a long time," I beamed. "You kids want to go get some ice cream?"

"Yeah," they shouted excitedly and took off running toward the house.

Chapter 18

Alohnzo

Tahira and I jogged along the beach the next morning. The sun was finally shining, and it was the summer's first day of heat. It felt good to feel the rays on my skin. We needed the sunshine. It was becoming too dark and dreary.

"Finally, warm weather. I'm definitely getting in the water tonight," Tahira said with a bright smile.

"I know you can't wait. I'll come out here with you."

"Yeah? That would be nice. You down for a skinny dip?" she asked in a flirty tone.

"Hell yeah."

She laughed.

We ran from our house to the back of the Masons, and as we came back, a camera crew was following Tori and two other young women wearing bikinis. They were walking down from Sidra Embry's deck holding blankets, umbrellas, and a picnic basket.

"What's going on here?" I asked between strides.

"Oh yeah, I meant to tell you that Tori is filming a reality show."

"Like a real one?"

"Yeah."

"So, if we run by, we'll be on the show?"

"Probably so."

"Wow. This is new for Sand Cove. As big a star as Luca was, the only cameras we had to worry about were paparazzi."

"She might have that same problem if her reality show does well."

"I just hope it doesn't bring people trying to get to the beach. This is supposed to be our own private peaceful haven."

"I know. That would be crazy, but Sidra doesn't seem like the type to play those games."

We ran past them, and I glanced behind us. The camera crew wasn't concerned with us at all. The team was too busy filming Tori and her friends laughing and talking. Tori looked like the "it" girl. She was young, and her mother was rich. She reminded me of a Black Kardashian.

We kept our pace until we reached the stairs up to the deck. There, we stopped to breathe before walking up. As soon as we were inside the house, Tahira retrieved bottles of water from the refrigerator.

"That was a nice run," she said.

"Yeah, I needed that. How are you doing on wedding planning?"

"I'm thinking about getting a wedding planner to relieve the stress since we have a date for next April."

"Great idea. That'll be less stressful. You have a venue in mind?" I asked.

"Yes, I do. The vineyard. Ever since Mabel mentioned your parents attended a wedding there, I thought it would be perfect."

"It would be, and it would be free since I own it."

"That's the best part," she said. "How are things coming with the premium rosé?"

"Perfect. We're wrapping up tasting. I need to start looking at bottle samples and branding. We have also decided to have a launch party and grand reopening of the vineyard soon."

She drank the water and nodded. "Sounds like things are lining up the way you guys want."

"Indeed. Were you able to book a gig?"

She shook her head with sad eyes. "Not yet."

"It's okay, babe. I'm sure you'll find something soon. You want to take a shower?" I asked, raising my eyebrows.

"Last one up," she said with a naughty giggle.

She ran toward the stairs, and I chased her.

Chapter 19

Sidra

After my long, warm shower, I dried off while humming a soft made-up tune. I put on my bra and panties, and then picked out a simple yellow summer dress from my closet to wear and laid it on the bed. I sat on the padded bench located at the foot of my bed and applied shea butter to my skin. As I stood to put on my dress, my phone rang. The sound of Grant's ringtone immediately put a smile on my face. I answered as I stood in the window to look down at Tori, her friends, and the film crew on the beach.

"Well, hello, Grant." I smiled.

"Baby, I'm sorry I didn't make it over last night." His voice was low and deep. "How's your morning going?"

I sighed softly as I turned away from the window and lay on the bed. The satin comforter felt good against my skin. "My morning is fantastic, to be honest. I'm thinking about spending a few hours on the beach today. The sun is finally out."

"You finished unpacking?"

"For the most part, yes. I love this house so much that I can't stop smiling every time I enter another part."

"What are you doing right now?"

"I just got out of the shower."

"Are you still naked?"

I bit my lower lip, feeling aroused by his question. "No, I'm wearing a black bra and matching panties."

"Mmmm. I like that."

"I bet you do. What are you doing?"

"I'm running a few errands with Jarrell."

"Oh yeah? How did Jarrell like the gumbo?"

"You know he loved it. I should've packed some more for me too."

"No, you were supposed to come back. Then you would've had more and some peach cobbler."

"You're right. Any left?"

"Yeah, so what time will you be by? I might be out on the beach."

"I should be there soon. Leave the door unlocked, and I'll join you if you're still out there."

"I can definitely do that."

"Okay, baby. I'll see you soon."

"Okay. I love you, Grant."

"I love you more, Sidra," he replied, kissing the phone.

I kissed the phone and ended the call. Then I slipped into my dress, grabbed my sun hat, towel, sunblock, and got ready for my first beach day.

As I walked down the stairs, my phone rang. It was a zoom call. I smiled because the only people who called me on Zoom were Rena and Nina, my daughters. They liked to call me together when they could step away from their busy lives. I answered as I continued to head out of the sliding door to the beach.

"Hey, there," I said, staring into my phone at my beautiful daughters.

"Mommy," Rena said.

"Hi, Mommy," Nina added. "What are you up to?"

"I'm walking to the restricted beach to enjoy the sun. When are you guys coming to check out my new house?"

"Very soon," Rena said. "My schedule should be freeing up, so I can come to check it out. How's Tori doing with her reality show?"

"It's going good. They are out here filming almost every day."

"I talked to Daddy this morning," Nina mentioned.

"Oh yeah? What he up to?" I asked.

I didn't hate their father, but we never got along. Rena and Nina kept in contact with him and visited him. Tori, on the other hand, didn't get along with him at all.

"Nothing. He was asking about Tori and asked me why she never calls him."

I laid out my plaid blanket away from Tori, her friends, and the film crew. I thought about telling Tori her sisters were on the phone but didn't want to interrupt what she had going on.

Sitting down, I replied, "They argue all the time, but I'll tell Tori to call him later. She's in the middle of shooting right now." I turned the camera to show them Tori before turning the camera back on me.

"Mommy, how do you really feel with those cameras around all the time? When you were on TV, you went down to a set," Rena questioned.

"Some days, I'm not in the mood. On those days, I avoid them."

We all laughed.

"When is Tori going to do something else other than trying to be an Instagram and reality TV star?" Nina asked. "She's running around here acting like she's still in high school."

"Leave Tori alone. She just turned 23, and she's still young enough to figure her life out. Don't be so hard on her."

"That's her problem," Rena said. "You always baby her. She needs to be out of your house and making her own money. Don't you get tired of giving her money all the time?"

"No, I don't. When she's ready to move out, she will do just that. There's no rush."

"Okay, Mommy, but if you ever need us to talk to her, just let us know," Rena replied.

"Where's Mr. Grant? You still running away from getting married?" Nina asked, changing the subject.

"I'm not running. Marriage is not the only way people can be together. We see what happened in my first one. I can't stand that fool."

"You got three beautiful girls out of that deal, so it wasn't *all* that bad," Nina said. "You and Grant love one another, so you shouldn't make him pay because of what Daddy did."

"I'm trying to get him and Jarrell to move in. Look at how beautiful this beach is." I turned the camera to face the water as I stood up. I panned the beach and spun around slowly to show the houses.

"Ooooh, that looks so lovely," Rena admired.

"So, you have any weird ghostly stuff happening around the house yet?" Nina quizzed.

"Ghostly like what?" I questioned.

"You know, like are cabinets flying open or doors slamming shut?"

"Oh God, no. I don't believe in that stuff." I turned the camera back on myself.

"I thought a man was killed in that house," Nina said.

"He was, but I don't care anything about that. It feels so peaceful here."

"I'll take your word for it, but don't expect me to sleep over anytime soon," Nina replied.

"Scaredy-cat," Rena teased. "Mommy, I'll stay the night. You make sure the guest room is ready for me."

"It's ready for you anytime."

"Yay. I gotta run. I have to head to a meeting with a client," Rena said.

"And I have to get to my next patient," Nina added.

"Okay, I love you guys. Have a wonderful day. See you soon?"

"Yes, love you, Mommy," Rena said.

"Bye, Mommy."

I blew them a kiss and tapped out of the Zoom call. I placed my phone next to me on the blanket, took my sunblock out of my bag, and started rubbing it on my legs and arms. Then I put on my sunglasses and lay down with my hands behind my head. I drowned out the sounds of Tori being loud with her friends, soaked up the sun, and concentrated on the sounds of the ocean.

Chapter 20

Tori

"Aye, aye, aye," I said, dancing to the music coming from the boom box. "That's how you twerk, Josie. Work it, girl."

Josie was going crazy to a song by Future while Yanni and I danced with her.

Josie turned down the music and said, "We need some menfolk over here. Tori, can you call some men to come through right now? All this sand and pretty water, and we're looking too cute to be out here by ourselves."

"I tried to invite some guys, but they're all working."

"Sev and Makani are probably the only ones working, but what are the other guys you never fucked with doing?" Josie scowled.

"Why would I invite a bunch of dudes over without at least one I'm talking to? That doesn't make any sense," I said.

"For us. Anyway, Ted came over to see Jeon and—" Josie started but stopped because Yanni was waving her right hand in the air to cut her off.

"Hold up. Before you start talking about your baby daddy . . ." Yanni reached into her ice cooler and took out a bottle of Hennessy with three red plastic cups. She poured each of us a drink. Then she gestured for Josie to continue.

"Basically," Josie continued, "he was talking about going on a vacation for a few weeks without our son, but a few weeks? He usually watches him on the weekends. Who am I supposed to get to watch him now?"

"Can your mom watch him?" I asked with a deep frown.

"That's beside the point. Who's he going with if it isn't me?" Josie yelled.

"There it is," I said. "You're making this about *you,* not your son. So, are you guys still together?"

"We're still fucking if that's what you're asking."

I took a sip of the Henn. "Yanni, you bring some cola or something for this? I can't drink this straight."

"No, you got some in the house?"

"Yeah, I'll go get some because I can't do this." I walked toward the house with the cup in my hand and phone in the other. One of the cameramen followed me. Before I reached the stairs, I decided to see what Mommy was doing, looking like a bronze goddess lying in the sun. "Mommy."

She looked up at me through her shades. "Yes, honey?"

"You over here sunbathing?"

"Yes, I sure am. Just for a little while. I just talked to your sisters."

"You did? When are they coming out here?"

"They said they're coming soon. Your daddy asked Nina about you. You should probably call him."

"I'll call him," I said.

"Okay, good. Y'all having a lot of fun over there?"

"A little something. Mommy, can I throw a party soon? It's the perfect spot, and all my friends been asking."

She hesitated before she responded. "Let's get to know our neighbors a bit first. We share this beach with them, and I don't want anyone to get offended."

"How about if I ask them if it's okay? I'll follow any rules and guidelines they want."

"Just wait it out a little bit, baby girl. Give it until the end of summer."

I nodded, but I wasn't happy with her answer. I pouted as I walked into the house to grab three cans of cold Coke from the refrigerator. I wasn't used to Mommy telling me no. She was a homeowner, just like the rest of these people. If we wanted to throw a party, all we had to do was give them a heads-up and do it. I opened a can and poured some into the Hennessy. Then I took a sip and looked at my phone, thinking of Daddy. He got on my last nerve with his judgmental comments about not going to college or being like Rena and Nina. If he was asking Nina about me, that meant he was missing me.

I called him, and it rang quite a few times before his answering message came on.

"You've reached Harper Embry. I cannot answer your call right now, but if you please leave me a message, I will be sure to return your call as soon as I can."

"Hi, Dad. This is Tori. I was just calling to check on you. Give me a call back when you get this message." Dad was calling on the other end. I switched over. "Hey, I was just leaving you a message."

"You were?"

"Yup. Nina said that you asked about me."

"Yeah, I sure did. You haven't called me in a long time. I saw a promotion for your show. How's that going?"

"Going fairly good. How's life treating you?" I asked.

Daddy was a psychiatrist with a home office, and he loved to travel.

"I only work about three days a week now. I want to retire but can't bring myself to leave just yet. I booked my trip to Spain, and I'll be leaving in a week."

"Oh yeah? How long will you be in Spain?"

"Three weeks. It should be nice. How's your mama doing?"

Daddy always asked about Mom. I think he still had love for her, but she was so over it.

"She's good."

"I hear y'all staying in Sand Cove now," he said. "That's a nice piece of property."

"Yeah, we've been here almost a week now."

"You like it?"

"I love it. I want to throw a party, but Mommy wants me to wait until the neighbors get used to us, I guess."

"A party? Girl, you always trying to throw a party. When you going to start college?"

I rolled my eyes. *There he goes with that college talk.* "Daddy, college is not for me. I have no plans on going."

"That's too bad. We're a family of generations of college graduates. The mind cannot grow without knowledge. You cannot do better if you don't know better."

I mouthed the words with him because that was how often he said it. "I love you, Daddy. I gotta go now. I'll call you later."

"Okay. Thanks for calling. I love you too." He kissed the phone.

I kissed it back and ended the call. Then I put the Cokes in a plastic bag and headed back out to the beach to join my friends.

My girls left as the sun was going down. Right as they were leaving, Sev was entering the house to watch the sunset with me. The cameras were done for the day, and I was glad to have a little break from them. He was carrying something bulky in his hands.

"What's that?" I asked.

"A little fire pit."

"Nice. You get that from the workplace?"

When Sev wasn't surfing, he was the owner of a little surfing shop near Venice Beach. They sold many things for beach life and swimming.

"Sure did. I've had it for a little while, though."

"Cool. I'm going to grab something to throw over this bathing suit, and we can go sit on the beach."

"Okay."

I jogged up the stairs to my bedroom, pulled my tunic from my drawer, and tossed it on. I checked my hair in the mirror and smoothed out my ponytail before heading down the stairs. Sev smiled as soon as he stared up at me.

"That was quick."

"Yeah, just didn't want to be cold. I got some blankets out there already."

"That works."

He reached for my hand, and I gave it to him while we walked toward the kitchen to go out the sliding door. We walked in silence down the deck's stairs and through the sand toward the setup I had prepared for his visit.

"You ever watch a sunset on the beach before?" he asked.

"Yeah, plenty of times."

"But you never watched it with me."

"This is true."

He set his little fire pit in the sand. In his bag that was over his shoulder, he had small wood logs and matches. I sat on the blanket while I watched him create a small fire. Once he got it going, he sat behind me so that he could wrap his arms around me. He rested his chin on the top of my head.

"What you do today, beautiful?" he questioned.

"I spent the entire day on this beach filming with Yanni and Josie."

"How'd that go?"

"It was good up until Josie started talking about her kids and baby daddy. Yanni and I can't relate to that. I was like, girl, come on. I'm starting to think my life may be too boring for TV."

He chuckled a little. "Why you say that?"

"I don't have kids or baby daddy drama. I don't have dating drama. I just have friends, and I like to have fun. I almost feel like they wanted to create drama between Yanni and Josie for no reason, so I stopped for the day."

"I see . . . Take a deep breath. Relax. You gotta take some time out for yourself too, you know. I'm glad you wanted me to come to see you without the cameras. We couldn't really be alone after we went clubbing."

"I know. The cameramen can be annoying." I turned to face him while positioning myself on my knees. Wrapping my arms around him, I kissed him.

My lips seemed unable to detach from his. Our passionate kissing grew hungry and fiery, burning the way the fire was from the fire pit. He lay back on the blanket as we continued to kiss, and I was on top of him. We didn't care that we were on the beach, and we didn't care if one of the neighbors would see us. I pulled at his jeans to unbutton and unzip them. He helped me out of my bikini bottom.

"Fuck it," he said with a laugh.

The way he said it turned me on even more. He sucked my neck, and I moaned. I lay on my back so he could fit between my legs. It didn't take long before he was entering inside me. The feel of him made me close my eyes, and my lips slightly parted open so that my pleasure-filled moans could escape. Our bodies felt like one because he fit me so well. Our lust filled the evening air and mixed with the sounds of the waves. He rocked my body with strong and deep movements.

One of his hands squeezed my breasts, and his fingertips found my nipple. Through the tunic, he played with it for a few seconds. He then lowered his hand down my torso until it reached my clit. His thumb rolled my sensitive spot as he stared down at me. I moaned louder.

More in-depth, he pushed himself, and I held on his back, squeezing him.

"Please, don't stop, Sevante."

"I love the way you say my name," he said in a deep voice.

His lips returned to mine, and he didn't stop kissing me until we shared an orgasm. Sex on the beach with the risk of getting caught excited me. What if one of the neighbors caught us? What if my mom caught us? I closed my eyes and tuned everything out. The only thing I concentrated on was the way he made me feel.

Chapter 21

Kinsley

I stood in the kitchen, wearing a white two-piece skirt and crop top. My belly was protruding as I was only a week away from my due date. My hair was neatly brushed up into a high ponytail. The chef made Alistair's coffee and a hot apple cider for me as he cooked breakfast.

Alistair trotted down the stairs in his blue slacks, long-sleeved button-up with suspenders, and his jacket in his hand. He draped it over the back of the bar chair as he said, "Good morning, wife."

"Good morning, husband. I hope you have a wonderful day at work today."

He picked up the coffee and sipped. "It's the first day that Pop has officially decided not to come to the office since the announcement of his retirement. He's there so much, you would think he never said it."

"I bet. Amos has never been the type to sit at home and do nothing."

"I get that, but he needs to find a hobby like golf, fishing, or something. I just don't think he likes being at home with Mama all the time."

"I mean, would you? She nags all the time." I stopped talking before I said too much to make him upset. Alistair hated it when I spoke about Mabel. "Can you believe we only have a week before the baby is here? I'm so happy we were able to get the things we needed."

"It's crunch time. How you feeling? Any contractions?"

"Not really. I feel like I want to clean the entire house. I appreciate you getting the chef and maid to help me out around here."

"That's no problem. I gotta take loving care of you. Today, kick up your feet and relax."

"Okay. You don't have time for breakfast?"

"No, I'll probably grab something on the way to the office. I'm running a little late."

"Okay. Are you planning on taking any time off work when the baby comes?"

"Don't worry. I'll work it out. I'm the boss now."

I fixed his tie and kissed his lips. "That's right, baby. You're my boss. Stay close to your phone."

"I will."

"I can't wait because I don't know if I can take this belly growing any bigger."

Alistair touched my stomach and bent down to say, "Hey, little one. Don't give Mommy any trouble today, you hear me? Daddy loves you."

He kissed my lips before he grabbed his blazer and went to the garage.

I took my cider and went to the window in the living room so I could watch him drive away. He backed out of the driveway and disappeared from my view. Before I could step away from the window, I saw Tru walking up to the door. I frowned, wondering what she was up to.

I opened the door before she could ring the doorbell.

"Hello," she said with what appeared to be a genuine smile.

"Yeah?" I asked with a deep scowl.

"Oh, um, sorry to bother you. I know you've been back for about a month now, and I feel bad because I hadn't had the chance to come and welcome you. Congratulations on the marriage and baby."

I softened a little. That was nice of her. "Thank you, Tru. Um, would you like to come in?"

"Sure," she replied.

I opened the door wider, and Tru walked in. Then I closed the door behind her. "You can have a seat. Would you like some water or coffee? Alistair just left for work."

"No, thank you," she said as she sat down on the white couch. "I saw him leaving, and I meant to come early enough to welcome both of you."

"I'll be sure to let him know."

The sound of pots and pans moving around made Tru look toward the kitchen. "You have company?"

"Oh, that's the chef cooking breakfast. How are Noble and the kids?"

"They're good. We're going on vacation in a few days and taking the kids to San Diego to visit my mom."

"That sounds nice. Where are you guys vacationing if you don't mind me asking?"

"Bali. Have you met our new neighbor, Sidra Embry, yet?"

"No, not yet. I saw a film crew. What's up with that?"

"Her daughter is filming a reality show."

"Oh, wow. That's interesting. Wasn't Sidra on TV before?"

"Yeah, she had a court show. I hope you'll get to meet before the end-of-the-summer bonfire. You guys are invited to join the annual bonfire. Actually, I'm thinking about letting you guys host this one."

Was she kidding? I had the worst time last year. However, things were different now that I was married to Alistair, so it was something I would consider. Were we being accepted in Sand Cove? The thought of it made me feel a little better about returning.

"I'm due any day now, so I'm not sure if we should host this one, but maybe next year. I'll talk it over with Alistair and see if he wants to attend. I'll let you know."

"Great." She stood up. "I don't want to hold you. I hope to see you soon. Let me know when you're having visitors when the baby comes. I love babies. What are you having?"

"We don't know yet. We want it to be a surprise."

"That's sweet. I pray for a healthy delivery. When I was pregnant, I felt that the twins were one of each before they told us, and most mothers say that they know deep down what they're really having. You have any ideas of what it might be?"

"I feel like it's a girl, but I'll be happy with whatever we're blessed with."

"I know that's right. Anyway, it's good to see you and best wishes. Here, take my number in case you need me for anything."

I took my phone out of my pocket and typed in her number.

"I got you locked in." I rocked back and forth until I stood up.

"Oh, I remember those days when I couldn't get up. I was huge with the twins."

"It's getting harder and harder." I walked with her to the door.

"Also, my nanny, Ximena . . . She's in Mexico right now, but we won't need her anymore. I'll be happy to refer her if you need a nanny."

"That's really nice. I'll talk it over with Alistair. Thanks."

"Sure. No problem. Have a good day," she said.

"You too."

After closing and locking the door, I went to the kitchen, where the chef was making a plate for me.

"Everything is ready," he said. "I'll bring a plate to the table for you."

"Smells good. I'm starving." I walked to the table and sat down.

The chef brought a mouth-watering plate. I ate the French toast, egg whites, and Canadian bacon while I scrolled the internet and current events through my phone. The news was crazy with stories about police brutality, and the police shot another Black man. This was getting out of control. My heart instantly felt heavy as anger filled me. America was supposed to be better than this. I wondered if things would ever change.

As I got up from the table, I felt a little trickle as if I were peeing on myself. I started to head for the bathroom as a gush suddenly rushed down both legs.

"Oh no," I said, looking at the chef as he picked up my empty plate. "I think my water just broke."

Chapter 22

Alistair

"I understand your concerns, Mr. Smith. My father worked tirelessly building Amos Kelly Financial Advisors as a reputable brand, and I intend to keep it up," I said as I turned in my leather chair to face the large window behind me. The skyline view of Los Angeles never got old to me. "You have nothing to worry about."

"Alistair," Mr. Smith said and then paused for a second. "I own a chain of bakeries in the city, and I'm a successful man because of your father. He's guided me with a wealth strategy that has proven to work. He's given plenty of investment advice and set up my Trust and Estate Plan. He has advised me for decades. I understand that he has retired, but I'm a little leery. I heard you disappeared and left many clients hanging. Where's Alohnzo?"

"Alohnzo is no longer with the company. He's moved on to a new venture. You have no reason to be leery, Mr. Smith. I have no plans to leave. How about this? Let's get together to talk over lunch tomorrow."

"I will as long as Amos is there."

I rolled my eyes and replied, "Sounds good. I'll be sure to get him there. See you tomorrow."

"Sure thing."

I pressed the button to end the call, removed the headset, and loosened my tie. Getting Pop's clients to feel confident in my skills was much harder than I thought it would be. Mr. Smith wasn't just a client. He was a longtime friend to Pop, and I was hoping that I would be able to maintain that relationship. How would that look if I lost his biggest clients?

The office door opened, and my secretary, Tawny, put half her body in the door frame as she said, "Sorry to interrupt, Alistair. I finished cleaning Alohnzo's office with Farrah, so I'm all yours starting today."

"Thanks, Tawny. Farrah is still helping out the first floor since Alohnzo is gone, right?"

"Yes, HR gave her instructions. Don't forget about your meeting that started five minutes ago."

"Shit." I forgot Pop said I had to lead the morning meeting because he was finally going to let me handle things. My first day in charge, and I was late.

Tawny was Asian with jet-black hair. She was one of two Asian women working for the company. Before I left for the island, she had only been my personal assistant for a few months because my previous assistant quit after five years. Tawny was slim, petite, and looked as if she didn't weigh more than a hundred pounds.

"I'll let them know you're on the way."

"Okay. Thanks. I'll get ready to head to the conference room. Which conference room?"

"The Sierra Room, first floor."

"Got it. Thanks," I said.

"No problem. Make sure to look at your Outlook calendar throughout the day. All your appointments and meetings are on there. If you need me to block out any time for any reason, let me know."

"I will."

She left my office, and I gathered my laptop, then quickly walked down the hall to the elevator and went to the first floor to the Sierra Room. Ten financial advisors were waiting patiently for me, and Pop was sitting there. My heart started beating fast. Pop hated people who weren't punctual. It was the highest form of unprofessionalism in his eyes.

"Hey, Pop. I didn't know you were coming."

"I know. I decided to check on you."

I smiled nervously. I should've known that he would pull something like this. I cleared my throat and said, "Good morning, ladies and gentlemen. I apologize for being a little behind. My phone call ran a little long."

They greeted me in return, "Good morning."

I sat at the head of the conference table and set my laptop down. "As we discussed in the previous meeting, my father is retired, and I have taken his place. Any questions or concerns you might have before we get started?"

"I have a question," Jeff said.

My cell phone rang, and I took it out of my pocket. Kinsley was calling. Pop gave me the craziest look because my ringer was on at the wrong time—another unprofessional pet peeve of his.

"Hold on one second. It's my wife." I walked out of the room and shut the door. I felt flustered and frustrated as I said, "Hey, I'm in the middle of a meeting—"

"My water broke."

"What? Are you sure?"

"Yeah, and contractions hit me hard. I won't be able to wait until you get here, so Tru is taking me to the hospital. Meet me there."

"Okay, okay. I'll be there." I ended the call as I walked back into the conference room. "I apologize, but I have to go. My wife is having a baby. Jeff, hold on to that question, or, matter of fact, everyone send your questions to my email, and I'll answer them as soon as I can."

Some nodded.

A few said, "Congratulations," along with other happy wishes.

I was flustered as I checked my pockets. I remembered my keys were up in my office.

"You are too stressed right now. I'll drive you," Pop said.

"Thanks, Pop. Let's go." I snatched up the laptop, and we rushed out of the building.

When we arrived at the hospital, we checked into the emergency station and were instructed on where to find Labor and Delivery. I was a nervous wreck. I had no idea what to expect when it came to a woman giving birth. Another part of me was excited because the moment I had been waiting for was finally here. I was going to be a father.

We walked into her room, but no one was there—not even her. I went to the desk outside of the room with a look of confusion written all over my face.

"Who are you looking for, sir?" a nurse asked.

"My wife, Kinsley Kelly."

She looked at the board behind her and replied, "She was just wheeled in for a C-section. I'll need to get you prepared to go in there."

"A C-section? Is she okay? What about the baby?" I panicked.

"Don't worry. She's fine. The baby's heartbeat was just dropping too fast, so they had to do this. Follow me."

"Okay."

Pop said, "I'll be right here in the waiting room."

"Okay." I followed the nurse with my heart continuing to race and my head sweating. I had already tossed my tie off in the car.

She gave me a pair of blue scrubs. "Put this over your clothes and the cap on your head and follow me."

I quickly put them on and followed her into a room with bright lights. The doctor was cutting the cord on the baby and handing it to the nurses. Oh no, I missed everything. The baby was already here.

"It's a girl," the doctor said, smiling.

Tru was holding Kinsley's hand as she said, "Kinsley, Alistair is here. Sweetie, he's here. I'm going to step out now. Congratulations."

Tru smiled at me as she exited the room.

I took her place next to Kinsley. Holding her hand, I saw she had tears streaming down her face. I said, "Baby, we have a girl."

"Yeah," she cried. "I want to see her."

I looked over at the nurses cleaning her off. One look at her and I was in love. She was the most beautiful baby I had ever seen. As soon as she was in my arms, I cried. Although she didn't have much color to her, she looked just like me. I held her so Kinsley could see her.

"Hi, pretty girl. Hi. It's Mommy."

"What are we going to name her?" I asked. "I know you like the names Violet and Autumn."

"I really do. I think we should stick with an A name, don't you?"

"Yeah, I like Autumn. Hi, Autumn," I said.

"Rose as her middle name. Autumn Rose."

"I love it," I replied.

"I'll take the baby to run some tests, and we'll bring her to you in the postpartum room," one of the nurses said.

I gave the baby a soft kiss on her hand before handing her off.

"Everything happened so fast," Kinsley said. "It was like once my water broke, there was no way to stop her from coming."

"I see. How did Tru end up bringing you?"

"She came by to welcome us back and to invite us to the end-of-summer bonfire next month. She gave me her number, and she was the only one other than you I thought to call."

"That was nice of her. I guess that's what good neighbors are for."

"I agree. I look at her differently now. I feel like I'm part of the 'in' crowd now."

I nodded, feeling crazy inside. The delivery of our baby didn't go the way I envisioned.

"All right, Mrs. Kelly. We're going to take you to the recovery room for a moment and then to your postpartum room."

I stood up as they started wheeling Kinsley out of the room and down the hall. I followed. Once in the postpartum room, I called Pop.

"Hey," he said, "Everything okay? I'm still in the waiting room."

"Yeah, it's a girl. We named her Autumn Rose," I said proudly. "When we get into the next room, I can have you come in."

"Okay. I'll hang out."

A nurse entered the room, saying, "Mrs. Kelly? Is this Mr. Kelly?"

"Yes?" I asked, with the phone still pressed to my ear.

"Hi. Congratulations on the baby."

"Thank you," Kinsley and I replied.

"A few things here . . . The baby has jaundice and extreme anemia. Since she doesn't have enough healthy blood cells to carry adequate oxygen to her tissues, we suggest a blood transfusion immediately. We were able to get blood when you checked into Labor and Delivery, so we know that Mom is type A positive. Would you mind, Dad, giving some blood to confirm your type?"

"Oh, you don't need to draw my blood or anything. I know my blood type. I'm A positive as well."

The nurse frowned a bit as she replied, "Um, are you sure?"

"Yes, I'm sure."

She went to the computer in the corner and typed for a little bit.

Pop asked through the phone, "Is everything okay?"

"The nurse says the baby needs a blood transfusion or something."

"Who's that?" Kinsley asked, staring at me.

Before I could answer, the nurse said, "The baby has AB negative type blood, and if you two are her biological parents, it's impossible for two A positive blood types to produce an AB negative blood type. If you're her father, you would have a B or AB blood type. You sure you're A positive?"

"I'm A positive, so what the hell does this mean?" I asked, not comprehending.

Everything she said sounded like a foreign language.

"That means that there isn't a possibility that she is yours, Mr. Kelly," she said.

Kinsley's eyes widened with surprise, and my mouth dropped open. My eyes darted over at Kinsley to see her reaction. She had sadness in her eyes as if to say she was hoping the baby would be mine, but she knew there was a possibility that she wasn't. My heart plummeted to my feet.

"Alistair, what room are you in? I'm on my way," Pop said.

Disorientated, I asked, "Miss, what room is this?"

"Recovery C."

"Pop, we're in Recovery C." I ended the call and stared at Kinsley again.

"You guys made a huge mistake," she said. "You sure you got the right baby's blood sample?"

"Blood tests are pretty accurate. Listen, without complicating things, um, we have blood to give her, so no worries. We'll just use that."

"Hold on one second," I said. "My father is in the lobby and on his way to this room."

"Amos is here?" Kinsley questioned with a look of fear in her eyes. "That's who you were talking to?"

I gritted my teeth as I replied, "Yeah, he drove me here."

"I thought he wasn't going to be at the office today."

"Well, you know him. He wanted to pop up and surprise me."

Pop walked into the room, looking cool, calm, and collected.

Kinsley's body tensed up at the sight of him.

Pop didn't look at Kinsley as he said to the nurse, "The baby needs a blood transfusion?"

"Yes, she does. We have blood to give her, but we wanted to check with the parents first."

"What type does she need?" he asked.

"AB negative, A negative, B negative, or O negative. The parents both have A positive, so their blood types will not work . . ."

"I'm B negative. Use my blood."

"Really? You're the paternal grandfather?" the nurse asked with a curious stare.

"I am."

"All right. Come with me." The nurse walked out with Pop.

I clenched my jaw so tight that the muscles danced. I closed my eyes as I tried not to think about what was happening, but I couldn't stop connecting the dots. If Pop had the blood type to create Autumn's blood type, that had to mean that *he* was her biological father—unless she had been with someone else.

Kinsley was hysterically crying into her hands.

"You screw anyone else with type B or AB blood?"

She looked up with tears flowing like a river and said, "Fuck you, Alistair."

Tears threatened to appear in my own eyes, but I fought them hard. "Fuck *me?* Nah, you don't get to say that. You had every opportunity to tell me that she could've been Pop's. Instead, you chose to play me like a fucking fool. I'm out here looking stupid." I rubbed my face, feeling frustrated and hurt to my core. This was bullshit.

She made eye contact with me, but I didn't recognize the way she was looking at me. Her eyes, once filled with purpose and love, were now replaced with guilt and shame. She lowered her eyes to her shaking hands.

"You said you loved me, and I took you at your word," I said, still trying to make sense of her reasoning.

"I *do* love you, Alistair. This doesn't mean that I love you any less. I made a mistake, okay? I didn't know that you would chase after me. What was I supposed to say after you declared your love for me? How could I ruin that?"

"You should've said something the moment you found out you were pregnant. I think Pop knew. The way he looked at me when he asked and talked about you. And Mama, she . . . She tried to warn me."

"Don't tell me anything about Mabel."

"You don't want to hear it because you know everything she says about you is true."

"Everything she says about me is a fucking lie. So, what now, Alistair? You want me to leave your house?"

"I don't know. I need to think about this."

"Humph, well, you don't have to worry about it. Me and the baby will leave."

"If that's what you want to do," I said.

She looked surprised that I responded that way. It wasn't that I was okay with her leaving. I was pissed. I didn't know how to feel or what to do about our relationship at that moment.

"I don't want any of you in her life. We don't need you!" she cried.

Her words cut me like a knife. I imagined that was how she felt when I said she could do what she wanted. Anger and pain were raging inside of me. Even if I wanted to work things out with her, Autumn was my father's child.

Pop poked his head in the door fifteen minutes later and said, "Let's go, Alistair."

"All right." I turned to Kinsley. "Try to get some rest. Let's talk tomorrow."

"Talk about what? I'm done with you," she said.

I nodded as I replied, "Fine."

I walked out of the room, wondering if this was how Kinsley and I would truly end. My chest was heaving, and I felt tears sliding out of my left eye, no matter how hard I was trying to fight it.

"You good?" Pop asked me as soon as we were down the hall.

"No, Pop. I'm not good!" I exploded.

Pop looked at me as if I lost my mind for yelling at him. "You might want to lower your voice."

I looked around as we walked through the hallway. There were quite a bit of people around. I wiped my tears and lowered my voice as I said, "Autumn is *your* baby. I thought she was mine. Why didn't you tell me?"

"I didn't know for sure. She didn't tell me she was pregnant. The last night I spent with her before she ran off to that island, we didn't use protection."

"I know all about that night because she showed up at my house with her dress on backward."

"Look, don't say a word about this to your mother, you hear? I'll figure out a way to tell her when I'm ready."

"Pop, you're insane. I can't believe this shit," I said. "You expect her to raise that baby without you?"

Pop grew silent.

I already knew what that meant. He would never say a word about this to Mama, and he would never be there for Autumn. I wasn't sure what pissed me off more. We continued to walk down the hall to the elevator.

"Why aren't you gonna be there for Autumn?" I asked.

"I don't know what I'm going to do yet, so calm down. She looks just like me."

"Yeah, she definitely does. Did they say she would be okay after the blood transfusion?"

"Yeah, she'll be fine. They're going to make sure she gets iron drop supplements to keep her blood looking good."

We stepped inside the elevator and rode down silently, then continued our silence on the way to the car and on the car ride. I was hurt and angry. I wanted to punch my father in the face so bad. All he had to do was step up to the plate and take responsibility. I loved Kinsley with all my heart, but this situation had me thinking hard about our marriage.

Chapter 23

Alohnzo

As Tahira pulled her car into the driveway, Noble was walking down from our front door. I frowned a little because I hadn't spoken to Noble since the day he told me to get the fuck out of his house. I was wondering when he would stop being stubborn.

Tahira rolled down the window. "Hey, Noble. What are you doing?"

"I came by to talk to Alohnzo. You got a minute?"

"Yeah," I replied and stepped out of the car so Tahira could park in the garage. "What's up?" I walked toward him.

"We're going on vacation to Bali in a few days, but before we leave, I wanted to ask if you could keep an eye on the crib for us."

"Of course. As neighbors, I always got your back, no matter what."

"And, um, I also would like to apologize for what I said to you. I was emotional."

"Understandable. Constantine was and is incredibly special to you."

"No question. I realize that you were only trying to help. My pride and ego got in the way, but it should not reflect on our friendship. We've been close since the day you moved to Sand Cove. I admit that Luca isn't here to save me anymore, you know."

"I get that. Man, no hard feelings. The women we love are too close for us not to get along. We gotta keep the tradition of Sand Cove alive."

"Facts. So, we're good, right?"

"Yeah, man, we're good," I said.

We shook hands and hugged it out.

As we stepped back, Alistair was pulling into his driveway.

"Tru just came home from the hospital. Kinsley had the baby," Noble said.

"Really? Tru went with her?"

"Yeah, Kinsley and Tru talked, and then her water broke. Alistair was at work."

Alistair didn't pull into his garage; instead, he got out and walked over to my driveway.

"Hey, congrats on the baby girl," Noble said.

Alistair rubbed the back of his neck, shaking his head. "Thanks, but, uh, she's not mine."

"How you know so fast?" I asked, wondering if he requested an instant DNA test.

"The baby needed a blood transfusion, and my blood type didn't match. Pop's did, though, so he gave blood."

I shook my head because this was a mess. Pop was the father?

"Damn," Noble said. "So, the baby is your sister?"

Alistair nodded, looking at me. "What you think about that, little big bro?"

"I don't think anything," I replied honestly. "I mean, I hate that this is happening because I know you care and love Kinsley. The question is, what are *you* going to do now?"

"She doesn't want to be with me anymore. She wants to leave. Pop doesn't seem to care too much unless he's just acting tough for me. He doesn't want me to say anything to Mama. It makes me wonder if he's ever going to tell her."

"Not our problem, and Kinsley shouldn't be your problem anymore if she doesn't want to work things out. You want to work things out with her?"

"She's still my wife, but if she doesn't want to move on from this, I may have to go back to the island to get a divorce or annulment."

"Good luck with that," Noble said. "Well, I'm going to head home. Good talking to you, Alohnzo. I'll holler when I return."

"No problem. Thanks for coming over."

Noble walked down the street.

"I don't want to see her again," he said. "I bought the baby a ton of stuff, which she can keep. Even if I wanted to work things out, I don't know how to get over the betrayal."

"Well, look at it this way, all the things you did for the baby are big brother gifts," I joked.

"Hey, now isn't the time to kid around."

"I know, but it's kind of a funny situation. You had to have had doubts, though, right?"

"Nah, I trusted her. I was so busy trying to love her, you know? I guess I was looking for true love myself."

"Yeah, but she had been with Pop unprotected apparently. To see you fall for her so hard and fast surprised me. I wanted to believe she could do right by you, but it was like she had done too much already."

"Kinsley didn't know what real love felt like, and I wanted to give that to her."

"And you did. There are plenty of other women, big little brother," I said, holding out my arms to hug him.

He accepted, and we gave each other a big Martin Lawrence-type of deep breathing and exhaling hug.

"Thanks, bro," he said.

"Listen, I'm here for you. I got you. How are things going at the office?"

Alistair blew out air while looking up at the sky. "Much harder than I thought. Pop has been there almost every day."

"I could've told you that."

"This shit with Kinsley got me thinking about leaving the company. It's like I can't even look at Pop without thinking about her and the baby."

"I remember he mentioned that he knew where she was this whole time."

"Yeah," Alistair nodded. "The thing that fucks with me is that he should've contacted her before all of this. Hell, he could've contacted *me*. I wouldn't have had to wait nine months to find out the baby wasn't mine."

"Yeah, it would be hard to work around him. I think you should let this breathe and give it some time. Pop needs you."

"I'm going to take another leave of absence and chill out. I gotta box up Kinsley and the baby's things. If she doesn't want any of this stuff, I'll donate it."

"Let me know if you need any help."

"I will. I appreciate that. I'll talk to you later."

"All right. Try to have a good night," I said.

Alistair opened the garage, got into his car, and drove inside.

I walked into my garage and closed it. When I got into the house, Tahira was watching TV from the couch.

"Look, there's a quick little sighting of us running on the beach for the promo of Tori's reality show," she said.

"What?" I asked, looking at the TV.

It was so weird seeing myself in the background. It was blurry, and you couldn't make out our faces, but we were there.

I chuckled, sitting next to her. "That's too funny."

"Everything okay with you and Noble now?"

"Yeah, he apologized."

"Good. I saw Alistair from the window. How's Kinsley and the baby?"

"The baby needed a blood transfusion, and Alistair couldn't give blood because his blood type didn't match. Long story short, Alistair isn't the father, but Pop is."

"What?" Tahira asked with wide eyes. "That's crazy. How is Alistair taking it?"

"Not too well. He loves the hell out of Kinsley, and he feels betrayed by her *and* Pop."

"Yeah, I would too. Poor Alistair. What's going to happen now? Are they going to work it out?"

I shrugged. "Alistair says Kinsley wants to leave with the baby."

"She's just saying that because she's embarrassed. She probably didn't think it would be Amos's baby. Well, regardless of the crazy situation, that baby is still your guys' family."

I nodded. "Very true. I'm sure Alistair will do what's best."

"What would you do if you were in that situation?"

"Well, I would never be in that situation."

"I know, but let's just play what-if for a moment, Alohnzo."

I thought about it, and I couldn't think of what I would do. "To be honest, I don't know what I would do. I would be heated if Kinsley were my woman and didn't be straight up the moment she found out she was pregnant. What if the baby didn't need a blood transfusion? Would she have gone on with life as if Alistair were the father?"

"God, this is so messed up," she said.

I leaned back on the couch with my arms stretched out along the back of it. Tahira rested against my chest as she kept her eyes on the TV. I rubbed her back.

Chapter 24

Noble

I couldn't help but keep taking deep breaths as the scent of the ocean filled my lungs. It smelled so fresh, and I was ready for it all. Little small droplets of the sea splashed on my face as the yacht quickly approached the shore. The flight had been long, but the short yacht trip to the island was refreshing, and it was just what I needed to let go of that jet-lagged feeling.

We stepped off the yacht and walked down the bamboo planks toward the walkway. A bellhop immediately took our luggage. Amid the serene rice paddies of southwestern Bali and less than a mile from Berawa Beach was one of only five elite Dea Villa Balinese vacation homes. We couldn't wait to put our luggage away to enjoy the amenities, which included chef service and a personal butler. Tingles shot up and down my spine.

The other guests in the villa were walking around and seemed so happy and full of life. This villa hosted six guests with three private sleeping quarters. The look of the villa captivated me—the tropical motif with lava-stone steps surrounded by ponds that connected the estate's three separate pavilions. The main pavilion was open with ornate and majestic pillars giving it a regal feel. To keep the privacy of each pavilion, tall plants grew on each side of them.

I could picture us poolside underneath the bale day-beds with cocktails and seafood.

A man near the main pavilion said, "Welcome to Bali. If you ever need a ride around the island, I'm your man." He handed us a card.

"Thanks for the offer. We'll keep that in mind," I said.

"There's a party on Berawa Beach in two hours. Enjoy."

"Ooooh," Tru cooed. "I know you're feeling jet-lagged, baby, but, please, can we go to the beach party? We have to."

"Okay, sure. Let's do it."

I stared at Tru as we walked into the main pavilion to check-in, and she looked gorgeous. Seeing her look so happy made me feel good about taking this much-needed vacation.

We got our key after we checked in. As we walked toward our pavilion, I admired the swimming pool, waterfall, terrace with a lounge area, and poolside bales. Our room was adorned with fascinating Indonesian objects of art surrounding our king-sized bed. The bathroom was en suite with a rain shower and a stone tub carved out of river rocks. I walked over to the window that was draped in sheer white curtains and stared out at the black sand and powerful waves. It was more beautiful than it looked on the website.

I didn't feel like going to the party. All I wanted to do was relax.

The bellhop set our luggage by the closet.

Tru fell back on the bed and said, "Yes, we are kid-free, and this bed is heavenly."

I went to bed and lay on top of her. "Finally."

She wrapped her arms around me as we kissed. "It's really just you and me. When was the last time we could say that?"

"It's been too long."

"We're alone. No kids."

"Yes, baby. We are alone." I kissed her nice and slow.

She moaned as I squeezed her.

Suddenly, there was a knock on the door.

Tru asked with a scowl, "Who's that?"

I shrugged and got up to answer the door.

Two ladies were standing there with towels.

"Yes?"

"You ordered massage?" one asked.

I closed my eyes because I completely forgot that I booked massages upon our arrival.

"Oh yes, come in."

They walked in and slid open the divider. Then they stepped down into the area where two tables were already set up.

"Ooooh, massages," Tru said. "Will we have time to go to the party?"

"The massages will be for an hour, and that will give us more than enough time to go to the party."

"Undress and put these on," the same lady said.

Tru got out of the bed, and I took the robes. I handed one to Tru. We got out of our clothes in the bathroom and put on the robes. By the time we came out of the bathroom, the ladies were ready to massage us. We lay on the tables facedown, the robes were removed, and a thin sheet was placed on our bottom half. As soon the woman's oily hands touched my back, I was knocked out. I snored loudly and even woke myself up a few times during the massage, but I was asleep. When the massage was over, and the ladies left our suite, I stared at Tru.

"I fell asleep," she said.

"I did too."

"I wanted to go to the party, but now I'm too relaxed. That massage took me out. Thank you, baby. I really needed it."

"Me too."

"You want to order some room service and stay in tonight?" she asked.

I was glad she said it because I wasn't feeling partying at all. "I'm down. I also want to get in this shower and rub all over your naked body."

"Yes, baby. You know I'm all about that."

Chapter 25

Sidra

Grant entered my home. As soon as I was in his arms, I kissed his neck and lips tenderly. Instead of being mad at him for not showing up for a couple of days, I said, "Hey, baby, I thought you would never make it."

"I know. I'm sorry. I got caught up at work for the last few days. I'm so sorry I haven't been able to get over to you. You know I'll make it up."

"I know. I also know how busy things can be at work. Luckily for you, I put up some peach cobbler before Tori and her friends devoured it."

"Thank the Lord," he said, looking up at the ceiling. "I do feel bad for making you wait for me like this, but can I get some of that peach cobbler right now?"

I took his hand and led him to the kitchen to heat it for him. "You want some vanilla ice cream on top of that?"

"Yeah, you already know how I like it, baby. I love it when you talk to me like that."

I giggled. Grant always made me feel giddy when he was around.

When we first met, he expressed he was a remarkably busy man. As a project manager, he didn't have time for dating. Over the years, we dated, and I was happy to take whatever time he could make for me. I figured that if we lived together, we would be able to see each other more often. Sometimes, I wondered if he stayed away because I wouldn't marry him.

He sat at the island and watched while I heated his dessert and put a scoop of vanilla ice cream on top.

"Guess what?" he said.

"What?"

"I'm spending the night tonight."

"Oh, are you?"

"Yes, indeed."

"Where's your overnight bag?" I asked, looking at his empty hands.

"In the trunk."

"Why didn't you bring it in?" I quizzed.

"It would've been obvious if I brought it to the door. I wanted it to be a surprise. I'll get it before we go upstairs. Guess what else?"

"Another surprise?"

"There's more. I don't have to work tomorrow. We can enjoy the beach and each other."

I put up the ice cream and slid the bowl with a spoon toward him. "Now, *that* is the best surprise."

He took a spoonful and hummed. "Damn. It seems like it tastes better after a few days. Either that or I just haven't had it in a while."

"Combination of both. Letting it set gives it time to let those flavors marinate."

"You know this is my favorite right here. This was how you won me over."

"I know that for sure," I laughed.

"What made it even better is how incredibly beautiful you are."

"Thank you, honey," I gushed.

"Where's Tori and the camera crew?"

I rolled my eyes with a heavy sigh. "They took that mess down to a restaurant today. I can finally have some peace and quiet. You know she had the nerve to ask me if she can throw a beach party. She is crazy. I don't need the neighbors complaining about trash and noise. These are good people."

Grant nodded. "That was a good call. You don't want those problems already. Hey, is that a walk-in pantry right there?"

"Yes, it sure is."

Grant got up from the stool and walked into it. He turned on the light and eyed how carefully I stacked my canned goods and organized my flours, sugars, and snacks.

"You're one of the most organized women I know. I love that about you too. What's this right here? It looks like the wall is cracked in the corner. I might have to touch this up with some paint." He pushed on the shelf-less wall gently and noticed it moved a little. He used a bit more force, and it opened the way a door would. "What is this?" He pushed it open some more and walked in.

I followed in after him with a look of confusion. "I don't know. What is it?"

He flicked the light switch, and my mouth flew open.

We were standing in a tiny private room. Nothing was hanging on the white walls. On the desk were three monitors of live surveillance of the kitchen, back deck, and the front door.

"Tahira didn't mention anything about a hidden camera room unless I missed that part of the tour."

Grant and I walked toward the desk.

"Looks like this equipment has a recording system." He moved the mouse and clicked around until he found how to rewind. When he clicked *play,* it played Grant and me in the kitchen a moment ago. He clicked rewind for a little bit and then clicked *play* again. "Looks like it only records motion. It doesn't seem like there was much to record over the past couple of months if you look at these time gaps."

"Tahira said she was in London for about eight months, so there probably isn't much."

He clicked *rewind* and *play* again.

Footage played of Tahira and Alohnzo kissing near the sliding door to the deck before he walked down the steps. The date was September 30th of the previous year. When he rewound again, an older lady was cooking in the kitchen, and Tahira was sitting at the island watching her.

"How can this thing keep this much footage?" Grant pulled out the black leather chair and sat to take a deeper look at the equipment. He whistled as he said, "Storage clusters."

"You're talking that geek language. What does that mean?"

"Storage clusters are separate from the DVR/NVR, and what they do is they communicate across the IP network so that it can hold a lot of data. Looks like whoever set this up planned on having more than 1,000 TBs easily. This thing has serious bandwidth."

"Grant, baby, I don't understand anything you are saying. Can you break it down just a little bit better?"

"These storage clusters allow recording for longer durations. Most security cameras and surveillance can only hold up to ninety days of footage. I've never seen anything like this." He walked out of the pantry into the kitchen, and I followed him. He ran his hand below the upper cabinets and removed something. He held a tiny black thing between his thumb and pointer finger.

"What is that?" I asked.

He inspected it. "This is a mini magnetic wireless 1080P HD IP WIFI camera that supports night vision and motion detection."

"It's so tiny."

"Perfect so that no one can see it. I'm amazed that it can see up to 150-degree super wide angles. Let me think here. Tahira was gone for eight months, these cameras only record when motion is detected, there's more than enough bandwidth, so there may be footage on here from over a year ago. Shit, whoever set this up spent a pretty penny for home security. With all that storage, they could keep up to two years of continuous recording and still only hit 6 TB."

I took my phone out of my dress pocket and looked up the date Luca was murdered. My curiosity about these cameras had been piqued.

I held my heart as I said, "Luca Moretti was murdered on September twenty-seventh. I wonder if we can see who killed him."

"Now, *that* would be crazy. Wait, how'd he die? I don't want to witness no gory shit."

"He was poisoned. Try to rewind to see how far this goes back."

We walked back into the pantry. Grant sat in the chair and pressed *rewind* until it stopped. Grant clicked *play,* and the date was June 9th, which was exactly a year ago. The screen changed to the front door camera, showing a mailman dropping off a package, then to the deck of a white cat jumping on a chair, and then to the kitchen of a maid cleaning.

"There are three cameras so far that I can see."

"I think I should call Agent Stanton," I said, feeling nervous about seeing a murder happen right before my eyes. "He's a good friend of mine, and I know he was working this case."

"You don't want to look at it first to see if we see anything before calling? What if nothing is on here? Can you bring my peach cobbler here? Let's see what I can find."

I left the room, grabbed his cobbler from the counter, and returned. I handed it to him.

"Thanks, babe," he said.

Grant fast-forwarded and stopped. Luca and Tahira were coming in and out of the home. He fast-forwarded some more. Tahira looked as if she was home alone a lot. Grant stopped when he saw Luca letting in some woman on July fifteenth. Then another woman a few hours later.

"Old dude was busy," Grant said with a snicker.

"I heard he was quite the playboy."

Grant fast-forwarded until he got to the morning of his death. Someone wearing a black hood entered through the sliding door. The person took what looked like a bottle dropper out of the bag and put a few drops into the coffeepot. Watching over their back, the person quickly exited through the sliding door. The maid walked into the kitchen, poured coffee into a mug, and walked down the hall.

"Wait. Go back to the person coming in that sliding door. Can we zoom in on the person's face? Did that look like a man or a woman to you?"

"I don't know," he said as he pressed rewind.

He stopped the video at the person entering again. He froze it and zoomed in. I got closer to the screen and squinted my eyes.

"Holy shit," I uttered in astonishment.

"You know who that is?" Grant asked.

I nodded as I immediately dialed Agent Stanton.

Chapter 26

Stephanie

"Hey, Stanton, what's up?" I asked as I washed and rinsed the plates from dinner.

"You'll never believe this," he said with excitement in his voice.

"I'll never believe what?"

"Judge Sidra Embry bought Luca Moretti's beach house, and she found some secret room."

"Really?" My ears perked up.

"She and her boyfriend also discovered hidden camera footage. The recordings go back a year."

I turned off the water. "Are you serious?"

"Yup, and she says we can come over first thing in the morning to look at it."

I was excited that this could be the break I had been looking for, but I wanted to make sure we were good to start right away. We had been down too many rabbit holes in the past. What if there wasn't anything on there at all? But then again, what if this would solve the case?

"Don't tell Director Thomas about this yet," I said. "You know how he feels about reopening cold cases without hard evidence."

"Okay. We don't have to put it on his radar yet. You do know who Judge Sidra Embry is, don't you?"

"No, I never heard of her."

"Even after her reality court show?"

"No, never."

"Oh, okay. It doesn't matter. She has a great track record. I'll probably head over there around eight or so."

"Perfect," I said, yawning. "I'm going to get some sleep, get up bright and early, and let's see how this goes."

"Great. I'll pick you up."

I set my phone down on the counter and took a deep breath. What if this was the break we had been waiting for? The FBI was still my dream, and ever since this case, I hadn't felt like myself because I couldn't solve what seemed to be unsolvable. I took a deep breath and hoped this wouldn't be a waste of time. As much as I hated thinking about going back to Sand Cove, I was anxious to see what Judge Embry found.

"Mom," Chloe said with the broadest grin on her face as she entered the kitchen.

"Yeah?"

"Dad just texted and paid the deposit on my apartment."

"That's good, honey. You need anything from me? Some furniture or dishes or anything?"

"Yeah," she said with a twinkle in her eye. "Every little bit helps."

"Congratulations on your new place, Chloe Bear." I hugged her. I was happy for her.

Her brown hair was pulled up into a messy high ponytail. She still liked to wear oversized sweatshirts, but now with her college name on them, and a pair of denim jeans with rips in them.

I walked to the family room and lay on the couch. I wasn't going to be able to sleep from the anticipation I felt.

"Mom, why do you look so serious?"

I looked up at her and replied, "I'm just thinking. That's all. I have so much on my mind, work and stuff."

"I got you something."

"You did?" I asked.

"Yup. I got us two tickets to see the Los Angeles Clippers playoff game." She held them up and waved them in my face.

I sat up. "Aw, Chloe Bear. How'd you get these?"

She handed them to me. "I saved up from my job. I knew when I came home for the summer that you might want to go to a game, have some beers, and eat hot dogs and nachos while rooting for your favorite team."

I smiled, feeling so lucky to be this kid's mother. I hugged her, and she sat down on my lap. She could hardly fit anymore, but I held her.

"I'm happy you enjoyed your first year of college," I said.

"Me too. Dad has been so cool, and my baby brother is adorbs."

"That makes me happy, as well. You got plans tonight?"

"I plan to go with Jessica to the movies."

"That sounds like fun."

"Yeah, we have so much to catch up on. We might also go get something to eat afterward."

"Just be sure to be back at a decent time. I don't like hearing my door open late. I'm paranoid."

"I know. If it ends up being too late, I'll just come back in the morning."

"Thank you."

She kissed my cheek and hopped off my lap. I watched her skip out of the family room and up the stairs. It was good to have her back home. I was starting to get lonely without her. I thought about getting a dog to keep me company when she wasn't here, but I didn't have time for the responsibility that came with having a pet. I closed my tired eyes and fell asleep.

Chapter 27

Tahira

Alohnzo and I laughed as we walked along the shore. It was late in the evening, and we had finished our swim. It was still warm out, but once out of the water, we felt cold. We held on to our towels to warm us up while managing to hold hands.

"You ready to go inside and have some wine?" he asked as he shivered.

"Yes, please."

We walked, barefoot, away from the shore, toward our house.

"Tahira? Alohnzo?" Sidra called from her deck.

We looked at her as she waved at us.

"Hey," I yelled toward her.

"Come here for a moment, please."

We looked at each other, and Alohnzo shrugged before we headed toward her. We walked up her stairs.

"Hey, Sidra. How are you tonight?" I asked.

"I'm well. Do you mind coming in for a moment? I have something to show you."

"Sure," I replied, looking at Alohnzo.

I noticed the new Jacuzzi hot tub sitting on her deck. I hadn't thought of getting one of those, but it was a nice touch.

As soon as we were inside the sliding door, she closed it. "Follow me." She walked inside the food pantry.

I had been inside of that pantry a million times, so I wasn't sure what she wanted me to see. Was a rodent in there? If so, what was I supposed to do about it? I never had issues with pests in the house before, but there were plenty of pest control options on the internet.

She pushed on the wall, and it opened. "Did you know this was here?"

"What in the world?" I asked. "No, um, how'd the wall move like that?"

She stepped inside and motioned for us to continue to follow her.

We walked into the small room, and I was speechless for a moment as I stared at a gentleman sitting in front of monitors at a desk.

"What's all this?" Alohnzo asked.

"This is a secret room with surveillance of some hidden cameras. If you didn't know anything about it, Tahira, then I'll assume that Luca placed it here. Do you know where the hidden cameras are, Tahira?"

"No. He never talked about any extra security. We already had a full home security system that was monitored from the library. Not sure why he would need hidden cameras, especially if he hadn't told me about them."

"Hmmm," she said. "Seems like Luca may have used it to spy on you."

"On me? Oh God. He was the one who did all the cheating, and he wanted to spy on *me?* Incredible."

"He purchased enough storage, so his killer might be on here. Let me ask you, Tahira, do you drink coffee?"

"No, I'm not much of a coffee drinker at all."

"So, Luca was the only one in the house who drank coffee?"

"Yes. He loved coffee, espresso, and cold brews. Why?" I replied.

Alohnzo shifted uncomfortably while my heart started beating so loudly that it was hard for me to concentrate.

"Luca's coffee was poisoned, and there's footage of it. I'm sure you're familiar with Agent Stanton as he was assigned to this case. He's my good friend, and I want him to have a look at the footage since he may be more of an expert on this matter, but I was wondering if you would look at it first."

I stared at Alohnzo, and he stared at me. Neither one of us knew what to say as the guy clicked *play*. An image of someone walking up the deck and entering the sliding door with a hoodie on appeared. We watched the person as they walked in, removed something from a bag, dropped a few drops into Luca's coffeepot, and left.

My breath felt caught in my throat. I didn't need the man to zoom in on the person to know who it was. I took a deep breath and exhaled, feeling faint. I felt weak in the knees. This couldn't be happening, I thought.

"Is that—" Alohnzo paused as he gave me an intense look.

I swallowed the hard lump in my throat as tears came to my eyes.

"Why would . . ." Alohnzo started to ask but stopped himself.

My mind was racing because I couldn't believe that it was Tru on that video. "Tru said she didn't know about Noble's gambling and money issues with the company, but what if she did?"

"She said she had no idea until the FBI showed up with questions, so why would she lie?" Alohnzo asked.

"To cover her tracks . . . She must've known."

Alohnzo dropped his head and uttered under his breath, "Dammit, Tru."

"Let me in on what you're talking about," Sidra said.

"Noble had a huge gambling problem and borrowed millions from Luca to save his house and company. Luca threatened to kill him if he didn't receive the money when Noble fell behind on payments," I said.

"Getting rid of Luca meant saving her husband from having to pay it back," Alohnzo added.

"Tru killed Luca to protect her family from losing everything," Sidra said. "Hmmm . . . I wonder how this slipped through the cracks. Did Tru have an alibi?"

I shrugged. "I don't know. This is horrible. She's our friend. Look, Sidra, please don't go to Agent Stanton with this yet. Let me talk to Tru and see what she has to say. I want to hear it from her. She owes that to me."

Sidra thought for a moment before she replied, "I've represented many killers. I've looked them square in the eye. I've turned down the pathological killers and ruthless, coldhearted people because I wasn't going to go to hell defending them. I've also defended people who deserved second chances. Tru doesn't strike me as a pathological killer, but she killed that man. Listen, I know I'm new to the community, and this is not how I would like to be remembered, but we must do what's right here."

"Luca was an awful person to most people. He was a cheater, liar, manipulator, intimidator—"

"And he was spying on you like you were some criminal. I find that part to be sick," Sidra interrupted.

"Do you think he deserved to be killed?" the man at the desk asked.

"I don't want to justify her actions. I just think that maybe there is a way we can handle this ourselves and not do something to ruin the community," I said. "Sand Cove has been through so much surrounding my husband's death. Just let me talk to her."

Sidra asked, "Do you think her husband is in on it?"

"I don't think so," Alohnzo responded. "He and Luca were close regardless of what it looks like. Alohnzo took Luca's death hard. I can't imagine him knowing."

I loved Tru. She was the only real friend I had. The fact that she murdered my husband and pretended as if she knew nothing had me feeling confused, but the thought of seeing her handcuffed and put in the back of a police car hurt my heart.

"I know how bad this looks, but can you give us some time to talk it over with Tru? I know you called Agent Stanton, but, please, can you give us some time?"

Sidra narrowed her eyes as she stared through Alohnzo and me. In her silence, I didn't know if she would hold off on things until we at least talked to our friend.

I continued, "I would like to talk to her. I'm sorry you had to find this. God, I wish I knew this was here. I thought I would feel some relief once I knew who killed him, but I can't believe this."

The man clicked *play* to reveal the maid pouring a cup of coffee and walking out of the kitchen with it.

I inhaled through my mouth and exhaled through my nose silently. Luca had to have his morning cup of coffee to get his day started. My stomach was in knots, and I felt a little nauseated.

"Can you call her to come by right now?" Sidra questioned. "That way, we can try to work something out before I speak with the agent."

"She's in Bali on vacation with her husband, but I can try to call her when we get home. Then I can let you know what she said."

"Let me know before the night is over."

"Thanks, Sidra," I said as I walked out of the pantry.

Alohnzo was right behind me. We walked out of the sliding door and down the stairs. As we walked to our home, a chill swept over my body, and it wasn't just the breeze.

"What you going to say when you call her?" Alohnzo asked.

I wiped the tears from my eyes and shrugged. "I don't know yet. I can't believe this. This isn't right, Alohnzo."

Alohnzo hugged me before we could walk up to our deck. "Let's go inside and talk this out before we call her."

As soon as we were inside, we headed upstairs to shower.

"I don't want to say this, but I don't think she should go to jail," Alohnzo said. "Noelle and Noble Junior need their mother. If she's remorseful and sorry about it, then I don't think she should go down."

"So, you're okay with her getting away with murder?" I asked with curious eyes.

"I'm not saying that. Look, we can all now have peace knowing who killed him, but Tru is still one of our friends," Alohnzo answered. "What if this is all one big misunderstanding? She's not a malicious person."

"Will we really have peace knowing what she did? I don't know if I can ever have peace with that." I said those words, but I couldn't imagine sending Tru to jail.

Luca had been horrible to everyone, but did that mean he deserved to die? We couldn't play God.

"We may not ever really have peace. Even if we send her to jail, we won't have peace knowing the twins will grow up without their mother," Alohnzo said.

"Can we go on pretending as if we have no clue? Sidra used to be a judge. It doesn't matter what Tru says. She called her agent friend, and they're going to arrest her."

"We don't know that. Let's hear what Tru has to say. She might feel the need to turn herself in. Noble might even want her to."

"I wonder if she'll admit it to us," I said, sighing. "I've never had to confront Tru with anything, so this is hard for me."

"You want me to talk to her? What time is it in Bali right now?"

I shrugged as we washed and rinsed off. As soon as we were dry, I grabbed my phone and accessed my world clock. "It should be 2:00 p.m. tomorrow over there."

"I can call her."

"No, it's okay. I should be the one to do it."

With shaking hands, I called her. While it rang on speakerphone, I sat on the bed with the towel wrapped around me. Alohnzo put on his underwear and T-shirt before sitting next to me.

"Hello," Tru answered in a chipper tone.

"Hey, Tru. How's Bali?"

"Girl, Bali is amazing. I'm so happy we are here. What're you and Alohnzo up to?"

"Um, nothing. Well, I wanted to talk to you. Is now a good time to talk?"

"Yeah, we're in the hotel room having cocktails. What's up?"

"Well, Sidra discovered hidden cameras in the house and some secret room behind the pantry . . ." I paused to gather my thoughts.

"Really? You didn't know about it?"

"No, it appears Luca used it to spy on me."

"That does not surprise me one bit. Good ol' Luca. Noble, Sidra found hidden cameras and a secret room Luca used to spy on Tahira."

I could hear Noble in the background, saying, "His ass was crazy."

"How do you feel about it?" Tru asked. "That has to make you feel some kind of way."

"Not sure yet. She, um, discovered that there is footage up to a year. We saw someone on the morning of Luca's murder enter the house through the sliding door of the kitchen and drop something into his coffee."

Tru became so silent that I thought she had hung up.

I looked at Alohnzo, and he nodded for me to keep talking.

"We saw you, Tru."

We heard Tru drop the phone.

Noble asked Tru, "What's the matter?"

"Tru, are you there?"

Noble picked up the phone. "This is Noble. Tahira, what's going on?"

"Noble, I'm not sure what you could hear, but Sidra found footage in that secret room. We saw Tru enter the house the morning Luca was found unresponsive. She dropped foxglove in his coffee. I just want to know why."

"She did *what?* No . . . Tru, what is Tahira talking about?"

"I'm sorry. I'm so sorry," Tru cried. "I didn't think anyone would ever find out. Luca was threatening to take everything we worked so hard for, and I couldn't have that. I couldn't stand to see him treat Tahira like that. She didn't deserve that. He was a disgusting piece of shit."

"Oh my God, babe. Why?" Noble asked.

"I just told you why."

"So, what's going to happen now? Did Sidra call the cops? Is Tru going to jail?" Noble panicked.

"She's good friends with Agent Stanton, but she hasn't shown the video to him yet. She mentioned he would be there first thing in the morning."

"Oh my God. Baby, please tell me you didn't do it," Noble pleaded.

"Just put me in jail," she sobbed. "I don't deserve to be free after what I did."

It hurt my stomach to hear her talk that way. I couldn't hold it in. I was crying with her.

Noble said, "Does Sidra want Tru to turn herself in?"

"She didn't say," Alohnzo answered.

"Tru, I wish you would've talked to me first," I cried.

"I should've, but I just felt so much anger. I hated him."

"We all hated him," Alohnzo said.

"I didn't hate him," Noble said, "but he was tough to deal with at times."

"I'm so sorry, you guys. It wasn't right for me to take his life. I've never wanted to hurt any of you. I love you guys. You're my family," Tru said.

Alohnzo looked sad and in pain as he listened to Tru cry. "What if we talk to Sidra?"

"And say what?" I asked.

"There has to be an alternative like some kind of deal," Alohnzo said.

"And why would she do that for us?" Noble asked.

"We won't know until we talk to her," Alohnzo replied.

"Can you give Tru and me a little bit to talk this through?" Noble asked.

"Yeah, but you only have a few hours. We have to talk to Sidra tonight before she shows Agent Stanton that video," Alohnzo said.

I stared blankly at the wall, taking deep breaths and exhaling through my tears.

Chapter 28

Tru

Luca threatened my husband way too many times, and I was in full protection mode. No one was going to threaten my family and get away with it. I saw the nasty emails. I heard the private conversations. I saw the money disappear and reappear. I wasn't stupid. Noble thought I was stupid, or at least he hoped that I was. What he failed to realize was that I was simply waiting for him to be honest, but that didn't happen until the FBI exposed him. Did I think the cops would discover Noble's gambling issues and make him a suspect? Absolutely. I had my answers ready when they came to question him.

I recalled the day Agents Tyler and Stanton entered our living room.

Agent Tyler said with a straight face. "As you know, we're investigating Luca Moretti's murder. He was poisoned with a drug called foxglove or digitalis."

"Never heard of it," I said, which wasn't the truth.

I did some research and found the drug on the black market. I knew exactly what it did and how long it would take for it to work. After I dropped it into his coffee before getting ready for work that day, I threw the small bottle out with the morning trash, which was picked up by waste management twenty minutes later.

Agent Tyler went into her folder and pulled out some photos. "Have you seen these?" She showed us pictures, one by one, of Tahira and Alohnzo naked on his deck.

I nodded. "Yes, on social media."

"I saw them on the news today while at work," Noble admitted. "You think Alohnzo killed him? He has a motive, you know."

I hit him on his arm because I knew Alohnzo didn't do it, and I didn't need him to be falsely charged with anything. "You don't know that. He doesn't know that. Alohnzo would never kill Luca."

Agent Tyler continued, "Did you know about Tahira and Alohnzo's affair before it was leaked to TMZ?"

"Yes, but it's not what you think," I replied quickly.

"You don't know what I think," Agent Tyler fired back. "Where were the two of you on Monday morning?"

"We were both at work," I said.

Stanton didn't say anything as he eyed us.

"And you are both entrepreneurs. You started your own cosmetic and fragrance corporation a few years ago, made a nice piece of change, bought this big fancy beach house. I must say Sand Cove is very nice. I bet it was hard to grab a piece of this real estate without having good friends in high places, considering you didn't have the credit for it."

I fluttered my eyelashes because she was trying to imply that as Black people, we couldn't afford property worth over $10 million. "What exactly are you trying to imply, Agent Tyler? My husband and I have worked hard for everything we have. We didn't need a hookup to buy this home. Everything we have, we worked hard to get it."

"You sure about that?"

I looked at Noble, even though I knew he didn't have the credit. He lied about his score from the day we met. I liked doing background checks on guys I was interested in. My score was perfect, but when you were a married couple, the bad score affected the perfect one.

"Isn't it true that Luca helped you get the loan for this house?" Agent Tyler questioned.

"No," I answered even though I knew that too. "He was the one who told us about Sand Cove. We moved in a few months after he did, but he didn't help us get the loan."

"Mr. Mason, is it true Luca Moretti helped you get the loan?"

"Kind of. Luca was good friends with the real estate and lending company, and he put in a good word for us because I had a few issues on my credit."

To be dramatic, I whipped my head in his direction. I knew everything. I knew about his outstanding loans before we got married. My husband didn't hide his gambling problem well, but I had to pretend as if I didn't have a clue.

"What does this have to do with his death? I don't see what our house loan has to do with his death," Noble replied.

"How long have you owed Luca money, Mr. Mason?" She handed him a copy of a few emails from Moretti's email address to his, and his to Luca's.

I leaned over to see what he was reading, even though I had already seen it. I had his passwords. I had access to everything.

"I think you're confused, Agent. My husband and I aren't in debt, and we sure don't owe Luca any money. Right, Noble?" I continued to pretend.

Noble looked at it and blinked in disbelief. He was acting guilty.

"You look surprised, Mr. Mason," Agent Tyler said with a hint of evil in her smile. "I take it you don't pay much attention to your finances, Mrs. Mason. I guess you don't know that your company is on the cusp of going bankrupt."

I kept glaring at the side of Noble's face, so the detectives wouldn't be able to catch on to me.

"Your husband had a habit of borrowing large sums of money from Luca time and time again. In one of these emails, Luca is threatening your husband that if he didn't pay him back the money, there would be consequences. How much money do you owe him, Mr. Mason? Do you know?"

"That's none of your business," Noble replied.

"I'm afraid that is my business. Now that he's dead, you don't owe him anything, right?"

"When did you borrow money from Luca, Noble?" I asked.

"I was paying him back in installments," he replied quickly.

"What? How much do you owe him?" I put on my best acting voice and shrieked.

"Am I a suspect, Agent?" Noble asked.

I felt like punching him in the face with that question. If they thought he was a suspect, he would've already been in handcuffs.

"It's my job to find out who killed Luca Moretti. As of right now, you're not a suspect, but we know everything about your financial situation."

This agent was on to us, so I had to think of something.

I acted mad as I yelled, "Noble, you better tell me how much you owed him, and you need to tell them too."

Noble refused to answer.

"The thing is, Mrs. Mason, we already know how much he owes. I want to see if Noble will tell us the truth. This is all about your character. If you lie to me, I know what kind of person you are."

"I don't really know how much," he replied.

"Since you don't know, would you like me to tell you? Maybe you lost track or count, but I highly doubt that. With your house and your company on the line, I find it hard to believe that you don't know how much money you owe someone you call your best friend. In Mr. Moretti's safe was a book he kept full of how much money he gave out to others. This book dates to 2001. He was much like a loan shark. His interest rates were ridiculous, yet you still borrowed money from him. You first borrowed money from him in 2013 to start your business. You paid him back well before the year was up, but then you borrowed more. The amounts got bigger. The interests had grown so much that you owe him two million dollars."

"Two million dollars? Why would you need that much money?" Again, more pretending from me.

"Your wife doesn't know that you have a gambling problem?"

He shook his head slowly.

"Gambling? You never said you liked to gamble. Is that what you do down at that Cigar Lounge?" My voice cracked.

"I have an app on my phone."

"Oh God. You have an app?" Now, that part, I didn't know.

Agent Tyler interrupted us. "Why weren't you able to pay him back before he started threatening you?"

"I didn't have the money. I thought I would be able to win it all back, but I've been losing. My last few bets, I lost big." He paused. *"I owe him, yes, but I would never kill him."*

"How did you feel when he said he would bury you in the desert if you didn't pay him back in full?"

That was the line that got to me when I read it in the email. Luca Moretti had threatened to bury my husband in the fucking desert if he didn't pay it back in full in a few weeks. A few weeks? We didn't have that kind of money. I felt rage, fury, and anger all over again, hearing the agent say it aloud.

Noble answered, *"I was afraid, but not to the point where I had to watch my back. I made sure to pay in installments so that he would know I was trying."*

Agent Tyler looked over at Agent Stanton. He nodded at her.

"Here's my card. I'll be checking out your alibi." The agent handed me the card and walked to the front door with the other agent. *"You all have a good night. Beautiful family, by the way."*

I walked her out.

My flashback washed away with my tears. I never expected anyone to find out about what I had done.

"Tru," Noble said after he wiped his tears, "can you tell me what you were thinking?"

"Luca Moretti was one evil son of a bitch. He pretended to be your friend, but he didn't respect you. He would've put your black ass in the dirt in a heartbeat. Was I just supposed to sit back and watch it happen? And what about Tahira? She didn't deserve any of the verbal abuse or the cheating. She's so beautiful, intelligent, and funny. Why couldn't he do right by her?"

Noble took a good look at me before he reluctantly asked, "Are you in love with Tahira? I mean, I know you love her as your best friend, but I also know how you feel about women . . ."

What! Was this the day to confess all my sins? Falling for Tahira was weird at first, but every day, I fell in love with the idea of being with her. My feelings were unpredictable at times, but I hid them well. I was guilty of pretending Ximena was Tahira when we had our encounter. Tahira could never know about my feelings because she wasn't gay. I wasn't sure if I was even gay. I just knew that I was attracted to beautiful women.

"I find her attractive, and at times, yes, I feel like I've fallen in love with her."

"So, how do you really feel about her and Alohnzo?"

"Seeing her happy makes me happy because she's being loved the way she deserves to be loved. At times, I wish it were me who could love her but . . . I know how to turn off my feelings for her because of my love for you."

"You expect me to keep taking all your secrets, Tru? Is *that* what you want me to do?"

"Yes, because I've accepted yours. All your flaws, Noble, and I still love you. Please stop judging me with your eyes."

"I'm not judging you, but I'm hurt. I'm hurt because you're with me, but this is the second woman that you've fallen for while married. What if I fell in love with an-other woman who I called my 'friend'?"

I shook my head. "It's not the same thing."

"It is—and you murdered my friend!"

"Listen, I took care of our problem. No, it didn't save the company, but you're alive, and we still have our home, and our kids are safe. No one will ever be able to put us in that position ever again. I made sure of that. You've learned your lesson, and we're moving on."

"You think it should be that easy, huh?" Noble stared at me as if suddenly, I were a stranger to him.

"Listen, baby. It's that easy. What I did was crazy, and, of course, I have regrets, but what if we never came up with the money to pay him back? Would he have killed you? What would he have done to me for knowing he killed you? You ever think about *that?*"

Noble stared off into space as he slowly shook his head. "I know Luca has admitted to whacking people before, but seriously, he wouldn't have done that to me."

I chuckled a little while looking at the water over the balcony. "I guess I should've kept him alive to find out, huh?"

"Maybe . . . Listen, if Luca were still alive, I would still have my company."

"Oh, is that right? You think he would've loaned you another two million to save your company? You're delusional if you believe that."

"I would've asked him to partner with me before hitting rock bottom."

"If Alohnzo thought it was a bad idea to partner with you, what you think Luca would've thought?"

"You know what? I'm going for a walk. When I get back, I'll have two answers for you. One, do I want to be married to you, and two, do I want to remain at Sand Cove." Noble got up from the lounge chair and walked into the hotel suite.

The hotel door closed, and so did my eyes. Not only did I feel like shit, but I was also embarrassed. Noble wasn't going to want to stay in Sand Cove with everyone aware of what I did. His pride wasn't going to allow him to go through that. I wasn't sure he would want to be married to me anymore, either.

What I had done was awful, and I worked so hard to justify and cover up my actions. No one was going to feed our kids if I sat back and lost everything we had. No one was going to step up and pay these bills if we weren't breathing. I did what I had to do. Now, my friends knew it all, and my guilt was sitting on my chest and in my head. What I did, I couldn't undo. If they didn't discover it, I would've never confessed. I spoke to God and begged for his mercy already. I didn't deserve the love of Jesus, but I clung to my faith and hung on to the shreds of the sanity I had left. I prayed that one day, I would feel removed from my sin, washed clean of it, but that guilt was going to be a stain, an ugly-ass scar. I had to believe in redemption to move on.

Chapter 29

Alistair

The birds were chirping ceaselessly outside early in the morning. I groaned. I hadn't slept well, and I drank too much silver tequila when I got home from the hospital. I looked at the clock on my nightstand. It was a little after 7:00 a.m. There was no need to get up because I wasn't going to work. I decided to quit. I hadn't told Pop yet, and I wasn't sure I needed to. He could go back to running his business the way he wanted to anyway. For the first time in a long time, I woke up alone. At that moment, I missed my cat. When I moved to find Kinsley, I gave her up to a shelter. I wished I hadn't.

I replayed what happened at the hospital in my head. I wished there were a button to shut it off. I was tired of thinking about it. Then my phone rang. I let it ring a few times before I grabbed it from the nightstand. It was Mama.

"Hello?" I answered.

"Good morning, Alistair. How come you didn't call me and tell me Kinsley had the baby?"

"Oh, I apologize."

"So, what she have, a boy or a girl?"

"A girl." I cleared my throat and sat up.

"You sound like I woke you up."

"I was already up, but I'm not out of bed yet."

"Okay," she said. "Your father told me that she's a beautiful baby."

"Oh yeah? Did he?" I smirked.

"He sure did. I was wondering where he was as I had been calling him, and he finally answered and said he drove you to the hospital. I can't believe that I'm a grandmother."

I knew Pop didn't dare to tell her everything. Just like him to withhold vital information. Since he told me not to say anything, I gritted my teeth and replied, "Yeah, it's crazy."

"Do you think I'll be able to go to the hospital to see her today?"

"No, the baby has jaundice, and Kinsley had a C-section. You should let her rest. I'll let you know when it's okay."

"All right, well, let me know when she and the baby get home so I can see her. What kinds of things does she need? I feel like shopping."

"I'm not sure," I replied, frowning at how happy she sounded. "Get whatever you want."

"You get rest too because you sound exhausted. I love you."

"I love you too."

She hung up, and I set the phone down. I couldn't believe how much of a coward Pop was. I had to pretend to Mama like the baby was mine until he was ready to let his secret out. I wasn't feeling that one bit. Mama sounded a little weird, and she was never that happy. I wasn't sure what was going on and why she was suddenly glad to have a grandchild. I wondered how shit was going to hit the fan once she discovered Autumn wasn't her grandbaby.

I hopped out of bed and went to the bathroom. After I relieved my bladder, I washed my hands. Then I went to the garage to see if I had any boxes to pack up Kinsley's things, but I didn't have anything. I went back upstairs and grabbed my MacBook. I searched the internet for a packing company to help me out.

Chapter 30

Noble

I walked around the villas, drinking piña coladas. Once I finished the second one, I went to the bar for something stronger. I ordered a shot of rum. Tru's confession was heavy, and it wasn't a game to me. My wife murdered Luca right under my nose, and I hadn't suspected a thing. I felt like I didn't know who my wife was. I didn't think she would be capable of something like this. I couldn't think about looking her in the face, touching her, loving her, or kissing her when she had deceived me.

She watched me go through hell over Luca's death without showing any sign of remorse. I heard her explanation, but it didn't make sense. My wife killed my best friend, and what was I supposed to do about it? Turn her in—and then what? What would I tell our kids?

I gulped down the rum and tried my best to wrap my head around what she was thinking. Tru was loving. She cared about me, and she cared about our family. That woman risked getting rid of a man to protect us. If I were in her shoes, would I have done the same thing? If Luca had threatened Tru or the kids, would I have wanted to kill him? I wasn't sure, but I didn't play around when it came to my family. I understood why when I thought about it, but I didn't like it.

I called Alohnzo from my cell, using the international card so that I wouldn't accrue extra charges.

"Hello?" he answered.

"Hey . . . I know this may sound crazy, but I can't see my wife go to jail. How can we make this issue disappear?" I slurred my words.

"Noble, are you drinking?"

"Yup, but it's okay. I'm good."

"You sure?" he asked.

"Listen to me, Alohnzo. My wife made a mistake, and I want to erase it all. I guess the big dark secret is out now, huh? We gotta stick together on this and get Sidra to change her mind. I need you guys like I never needed you before. Please do this favor for us."

Alohnzo replied without hesitation, "We'll talk to Sidra."

"Thanks, man. I appreciate that. I just wish Tru didn't do what she did. Things between Luca and I would've panned out. I mean, come on. Did you take his threat against you seriously?"

"Not really. I was going to talk it out with him. He pissed me off with the text messages, but he was just talking to me. When he told us the stories about what he did to people who fucked with him, I never saw him do anything crazy like that."

"Exactly. I would've never done Luca dirty for him to hurt me. I was going to pay him back, but it might not have been all at once as he wanted. Damn, I'm just fucked up. I'm going to try not to be so hard on Tru. I'm sure she's hard enough on herself."

"At the end of the day, Noble, she's your wife. You love her. We're here for you guys if you need us. Be safe out there, and don't drink too much."

"Too late. Have a good night. Let me know what Sidra says." I ended the call and raised my glass for the bartender to give me another drink.

I lost count of how many shots of rum I downed. I was shocked that I remembered how to get back to the room. When I stumbled in, Tru was pacing back and forth in front of the bed. We locked eyes, and I dropped to my knees in tears. My emotions were uncontrollable.

Tru got on her knees instantly with me as her own tears slid down her cheeks.

"Baby, are you drunk?" she asked, putting her hands on my tears.

"A little bit."

"Are you going to be okay?"

"Looks like I don't have a choice but to be okay."

Tru shook her head. "No, baby, you always have a choice. If you don't want to be with me anymore, you don't have to be. I don't want to see you live in pain just to force yourself to be okay."

I looked up into her eyes. My heart pounded. I didn't want to see my wife spend the rest of her life in prison. When I stared into her eyes, all the memories flooded me like a tidal wave. Through the good, the bad, and the ugly, we took vows that we would love each other for better or for worse, but where was I supposed to draw the line? Was this my deal breaker? My answer was no. I loved Tru too much to lose her.

"I'm not going anywhere, Tru. I love you too much to let go."

She cradled my head against her chest as we cried together.

"I'm sorry, Noble," she said sincerely. "I don't deserve your forgiveness, and I can't go back and change what

I did, but I want us to have a better future. I'll go to therapy and do whatever I need to do. I'll even give up law school."

"No," I roared. "Don't do that."

I didn't remember what happened next because I passed out in her arms on the floor.

I woke up the next morning in bed. I looked over at Tru as she slept on her side away from me, and my head was pounding. Holding my forehead, I looked over and saw some Tylenol, bottled water, and a Gatorade stood on the nightstand. Tru had it ready because, with as much as I drank, a hangover was guaranteed.

I sat up and took the Tylenol with the water. As I opened the Gatorade to drink, Tru stirred. Gulping the Gatorade, I stared at her until she turned over and looked at me.

"Good morning," she said.

"Good morning."

"How are you?" she asked.

"Hungover." I got out of the bed and relieved my bladder. Then I washed my hands and returned to bed. "I think that we should act like we never received that call last night. I'm going to forget about what happened altogether. I don't ever want to talk about it again. Agreed?"

"Agreed. What's on the itinerary today? I know you planned something."

"I did. I hope this headache goes away in time for the Sekumpul Waterfall and Temple Private Tour, and end with an Ubud Paon cooking class."

"Those sound incredibly fun, but I think you should nurse your hangover and just relax today. Then if you're feeling better, we can improvise. I want to go with the flow and not have to stick to doing certain things at a certain time. How does that sound?"

"Sounds good."

"Okay, good. I'm going to shower, call the kids, and see about breakfast."

She got out of bed and went into the bathroom.

One thing was for sure: I wanted my wife. I might not have known what I was going to do for work, but I wanted to be with Tru.

Chapter 31

Kinsley

I stayed in the hospital an extra day due to having a C-section. Autumn was treated for her jaundice, and her blood transfusion was successful. The doctor recommended that I not fly for at least a week and to have help because a C-section recovery was a process. I didn't know who to call to pick me up or anyone I could stay with. Staying in a hotel would've been okay if I still didn't need help with getting in and out of bed. I had a few hours before my release to figure it out.

One of the nurses gathered diapers, wipes, and sample formulas. Alistair dropped off her car seat, some clothes, more diapers, and wipes at the front desk without my having to ask him. Though he didn't stay or speak to me, I appreciated that he didn't leave me trying to figure that part out alone.

I was going to call Tru, but I remembered she was in Bali. My mind was racing. Who could I call? I had burned so many bridges. Then it came to me. I could call Kairo. Kairo was my older sister, but we hadn't spoken in a few years. We fell out over a stupid argument. It was so stupid that I didn't remember why we even got into it. When our mother died of a heroin overdose, we were placed in a foster home. Although our adoptive family was hardworking middle-class Black people, we were nothing but a check to them. On Kairo's eighteenth birthday, they kicked her out, and I went with her. We were homeless but learned quickly that we could make money messing around with older men. That was how we survived.

I prayed her number was the same as I dialed.

She picked up on the second ring. "Hello?"

"Kairo, this is Kinsley. Please don't hang up. Can you come to the Malibu General Hospital? I really need your help. I'm in room 211 on the fourth floor. Please say that you can come."

"Kinsley? Is everything all right?"

"Yeah, I'm fine, but I don't have anyone. I'll explain once you get here."

"Okay, I'll be driving from Long Beach, so it will take about an hour or so if there isn't much traffic. Is that a baby I hear?"

"Yes, I had a baby. I'll explain everything when you get here."

"Okay. I'm on my way."

I ended the call and tried to get comfortable, but I was in a lot of pain.

The nurse placed the pacifier in Autumn's mouth to quiet her. It worked.

"Nurse, can I get some pain medication? My sister won't be here for another hour, and I feel the pain coming back."

"Okay, I'll be back."

I looked at the bassinet from the bed to see if Autumn was okay. She was sucking away at that pacifier with her eyes closed. Just as I closed my eyes because the pain was so bad, the nurse came in with some codeine. She handed me two pills and brought the cup of ice water with a straw from the tray to my lips. I took the pills and drank the water.

"Thank you," I said.

"You're welcome. Did you sign your discharge papers yet?"

"No, not yet."

"Okay, I'll check on those for you and have you sign them. We also will walk you to the car to see that the baby is strapped into the car seat correctly."

"That's no problem."

The nurse walked out of the room, and I closed my eyes to wait for the medication to work.

A few hard knocks on the door woke me up from attempting to doze for a little bit. Mabel walked in, and I tried to sit up, but the pain was too much.

"Relax," she said, walking over to the bassinet. "You might not want to bust out of your tape. Wouldn't want them to have to sew you up again."

"Who told you I was here?" I fussed.

Mabel smirked as she looked down at the baby. She removed the pacifier to take a good look at her. "What a cute little girl. Hi, honey. Aren't you beautiful? So precious."

"Don't touch my baby, Mabel!"

Mabel put the pacifier back and took a deep breath before she glared at me. "I asked Alistair about you and this baby, and he couldn't bring himself to tell me that the baby wasn't his. I know one of the head nurses here, and she called me as soon as you checked in. The name Kelly isn't exceedingly common, so she figured you had to be kin. The baby was born with jaundice, and she needed a blood transfusion. It was the perfect way to determine DNA."

"What are you talking about?"

"Blood types are very telling, as you now know. Did I know my husband would be here with Alistair? No, but it must've been the divine works of the universe because not only did we prove this beautiful little baby is not my son's, but we proved that she's my husband's."

"Are you fucking serious?" I asked as my blood quickly boiled. "Mabel, the things that you do are just so damn evil. Why? You didn't have to do that."

"Yes, I did. I asked the men in my life not to lie to me anymore, and they came home from this hospital, still lying to my face. Alistair allowed me to call the baby his, and he didn't correct me or tell me what happened. His father asked him not to say a word, and he did what he was told, so I'm not completely mad with him about it."

"Your issues with your son and husband are your problems, not mine. You don't have to worry about Autumn and me because as soon as I'm good to fly, we'll be leaving the United States for good this time."

She pointed at me with her stiff, crooked finger, and said, "You better make sure you do. You've already gotten enough money from him, so if you think to come to him for child support, we have the documentation of the check, which has now been classified as a payoff. You and your baby need to stay out of our lives."

I rolled my eyes. "Whatever. Just get out. You made your point. You broke your son's heart too."

"No, *you* broke my son's heart. He wanted to believe in you so badly. You had him under a spell. It's not his fault. You must have some good twat between your legs to make him dumb as fuck, but you're not as smart as you think you are. You could learn a thing or two from a woman like me."

Shaking my head quickly, I replied, "Don't worry about what I got between my legs. It wasn't a spell. It was love. Sorry to break it to you, sweetie, but he loved me, regardless of my past."

"Yeah? Well, it's too bad it couldn't stay that way." She approached the hospital bed. "You better be glad that I'm done with raising children, or else I would have my husband take her from you."

"Oh, I'm *so* lucky."

Mabel sauntered out of the hospital room wearing her smug grin, and I felt the tears emerge. I wanted to find out who her friend was in this hospital because they deceived me into doing something unethical. If Alistair wanted to question paternity, she should've left that up to him.

I grabbed my phone and called Alistair.

"Hello?" he answered.

"Alistair, your mother just left here."

"What? Why?"

"She has a friend who works here, and since the baby needed a blood transfusion, your mother and her friend decided to use that as a way to find out the baby wasn't yours."

Alistair took a deep breath and sighed into the phone. "Man, seriously?"

"Yeah, and she basically told me to make sure I stay gone this time."

Alistair didn't respond.

"Hello?" I asked.

"Yeah, I'm here," he replied, sounding uninterested.

"Aren't you upset about what she did?"

"Look, Kinsley, I've cried about this situation since it happened, and I won't cry anymore. If I didn't find out at that moment, when would you have told me? Her eighteenth birthday?"

"No, I wouldn't have done that to you."

"But you didn't know who you were pregnant by, and you never said that so . . ."

"Wow, so you just going to ignore the fact that I'm telling you what your mother did?"

"My mother did what she felt was necessary. She knows her husband ain't shit, but she's a rider. She's rocking and rolling with him until the wheels fall off. That's her right to be that way. She felt that you weren't honest, and, no, I don't agree with the way she did it, but I'm not mad at her either. I'm shipping all your things to the island, so you won't need to come here. I wish you and my little sister the best."

He hung up on me.

Shaking my head, I gave up trying to talk to him. I owned my error, but these people were crazy. I couldn't wait for my sister to hurry up to get me out of there.

Chapter 32

Sidra

I spoke with Alohnzo and Tahira for at least an hour. They let me know how Noble and Tru were feeling, and Alohnzo wanted me to come up with an alternative or work out a deal for Tru. There wasn't a DA alive that would give her less than twenty years for what she did. I admired how they were trying to work together to support her, even though she did a terrible thing. They didn't come right out and ask me to cover up the murder, which I would've never allowed them to ask, but after some convincing, there was something about the way they felt for one another that led me to believe that something like this would never happen in Sand Cove again. Being a part of their community meant the world to me because I waited so long to have this house.

I thought about what they hoped for, and I considered all the options. As a lawyer, I had represented and defended guilty people, but there wasn't any hard evidence to prove they were guilty, so I got them off. In this case, there *was* hard evidence. Tru murdered Luca Moretti because he threatened to kill her husband, and she believed him. I thought long and hard on what I could do to get her less time or get her completely out of this situation. I could hardly sleep, hoping I was making the right decision and was not going against every moral I believed in. Every time I thought of Tru being away from her husband and children, I thought about my family. I felt for her and those kids.

Grant and I got dressed to prepare for Stanton's arrival. I couldn't tell Stanton never mind and that it was nothing, so I kept my appointment with him and filled Grant in on my plan.

"Did you completely erase the footage of Tru?" I asked him.

"Yes. I deleted it from the NVR/DVR and copied it to a brand-new SD card. I hacked into the system since I'm not the admin, and it was protected with a password, but I was able to get into the camera settings. I also got rid of the footage of Tahira and Alohnzo coming in here last night. Everything is all good."

"Okay."

"How do you feel about what we're doing?" he asked.

"Well, I don't know Tru that well, but she seems like a good-hearted person. She admitted she was wrong to Alohnzo and Tahira, and they say she's remorseful, so for that, I won't judge her. This isn't my courtroom. I feel like I acted prematurely in calling Stanton, so now, I just need to make sure he doesn't suspect anything."

"Relax. You reacted because this is murder we're talking about. After hearing them out, I don't blame you for changing your mind. He can take what we give him back to his station or wherever, and he will see there is nothing on here to worry about."

The doorbell rang as he buttoned up his shirt. I straightened out my skirt in the mirror, and we headed downstairs.

I took a deep breath and exhaled before opening the door. Stanton was standing there with a white woman in a business suit with her hair slicked back into a bun. He didn't say anything about bringing his partner. A fake smile appeared on my face anyway so that I wouldn't look surprised.

"Good morning. Come in," I said.

Stanton hugged me. "It's nice to see you, Sidra."

"It's good to see you as well, Stanton. This is my boyfriend, Grant."

Stanton and Grant shook hands.

"Nice to meet you," Stanton said.

"Same here," Grant replied.

"This is my partner, Agent Tyler. She was on the case with me before it turned cold."

"Hello, Agent Tyler," I said.

"Nice to meet you, Miss Embry. I like what you've done to the place."

"Thank you. I put some of my personal touches to it."

"It looks so different in here," she replied. "Can you show us this secret room?"

"Yes, no problem. It's right this way, in the kitchen." I led them to the kitchen and through the pantry.

Agent Tyler shook her head once inside. "How did we miss this?"

"Probably because the only person who knew about it is dead. Tahira didn't even know it was here. I was showing Grant the pantry, and he noticed that the wall looked weird, so he pushed it."

"Have you told Tahira about it?" Agent Tyler asked.

"I asked her if she knew there was a hidden room behind the pantry, and she said no. I didn't mention anything about the hidden cameras or surveillance, and she didn't ask any other questions. She said the house still gives her the creeps, so I didn't want to bother her about it."

Grant pointed to the NVR/DVR system. "Due to the storage clusters, this system can hold up to one year of recording. The cameras are motion-detected, so you will only see footage of movement from the three cameras. Tahira was out of the country for nearly a year, so there was hardly anything to record for eight months."

"We are more concerned about the morning before Luca Moretti was found," Agent Tyler said. "What did you see?"

"I didn't see anything," I replied.

"When you called me, Sidra, you mentioned that you believed you saw the killer on here," Stanton said.

"No, I didn't say that," I answered because that wasn't what I said. "What I told you was that I looked up the date of Luca's murder and put two and two together. I didn't actually see anyone. Just dates. I thought you should look at it since you're the expert."

"Did you look at any of the footage?" Agent Tyler asked.

"We tried, but we weren't too good at working this thing. We clicked around and saw us standing in the kitchen. That was what made us click rewind. We just kept going until the beginning," I responded. "I hope it's helpful to the case."

Agent Tyler gave me a hard look as she said, "We have gone around in so many circles. So many lies were told. No one had ever heard of digitalis, but in my gut, I felt that one of them was lying. Let me ask you, do you think someone from Sand Cove murdered Luca Moretti?"

"No," I replied.

"Why not?"

"From what I remember about this case, none of them were suspects, right?"

"It's not that they weren't suspects," Agent Tyler replied. "We just couldn't prove anything."

"But all of their alibis checked out."

"All checked out except for one," Stanton said, and Agent Tyler nodded in agreement. "We couldn't make that stick because there wasn't a motive."

"Whose alibi didn't check out?" I questioned.

"Tru Mason's."

"Really? That's interesting. What about the alibi didn't check out?" I asked with curiosity.

"She said that she was at work when she was still at home at the time he was poisoned. She was on her way to work by the time the ambulance arrived. Our director wouldn't let us grill her because her husband was the one with a strong motive. Director Thomas didn't have any interest in Tru," Agent Stanton answered.

I hummed, feeling slightly nervous, but I shook it off. "I met Tru. She's such a sweet lady, and those twins, ah, just adorable. I met Noble and the rest of the neighbors as well. They've welcomed my family and me with open arms. You know I've met a lot of murderers in my life, and I don't get those vibes from them."

"You've known them all for what? A few weeks?" Agent Tyler said. "The people of Sand Cove are hard to read, and they think they've outsmarted us. They know something. I just hope these recordings are the link we need."

"Anything else worth mentioning?" Stanton quizzed, writing in his notebook.

"Nope," I replied.

I motioned for Grant to eject the SD card. He ejected it and handed it to Agent Tyler.

Agent Stanton looked up at me with a puzzled expression. "Do you mind if we speak in private?"

"Sure."

Agent Stanton and I went out of the pantry and into the kitchen.

"Sidra, now, when you called me last night, you sounded like you had seen something."

"Other than dates, no, I didn't see anything. I don't really know what I was looking at, but I figured you guys worked closely on this case and could make a better judgment call than I could."

"Okay, I appreciate you. Do any of the neighbors know about this?"

"Not at all."

"Good," he replied. "Don't say a word. All right, Tyler, let's head out."

Agent Tyler walked out of the pantry, and Grant followed. We walked them to the door.

"Good luck," I said as I let them out.

"Thanks again," Stanton said.

I closed the door and looked at Grant. "Did she ask you anything?"

"She asked me questions like if I lived here and how long we've been dating. What did Stanton ask you?"

"He asked me about calling him like I had seen something. I told him I felt it would be better if he looked at it because I'm not a detective."

"You think they bought it?" he asked.

"God, I hope so. If not, Tru may go down for this."

"Well, you did what you felt was right."

"Yeah, and I hope I won't regret it."

Chapter 33

Stephanie

"Something's not right here, but I can't put my finger on it," I said to Stanton as he started up the car. "Coming back to this place gives me the chills. I can't stand it here."

"Being back in that house felt weird, but she's doing a wonderful job with making it her own."

"You felt comfortable?" I asked with a deep scowl.

"Maybe because I know Sidra. She has that warm Southern hospitality. What did you observe?"

"First thing, Sidra mentioned that Tahira didn't know about the room, which means that she asked her about it."

"Yeah, but she also said Tahira didn't ask any questions."

"Why wouldn't Tahira want to know about a room her husband had full of surveillance, clearly from hidden cameras? If I were her, I would want to know more or at least see it for myself," I said. "That's just weird."

"Do you think Sidra showed it to Tahira when she asked her about it? She could've called her and asked."

"I don't know. I can't explain it. That whole interaction with Sidra and Grant was strange. Not to mention, when I brought up the fact that Tru Mason's alibi didn't clear, Sidra didn't blink, but she immediately responded with questions and added some sugary bullshit about Tru being so sweet. It was a little over the top, don't you think?"

"No, I think you're reading her wrong. I've known Sidra Embry for years. She has a great reputation for doing what's right, especially when it comes to the law."

"Stanton, she represented and defended cold-blooded killers before she became a judge. When she became a judge, she didn't handle cases like these. She stuck to small claims for her TV show. I did a little research on her last night."

As he drove down the street, he replied, "What would she have to gain by covering for any of them? She doesn't know them like that."

"She doesn't have to know them. Did you know she was on the waiting list to buy a home in Sand Cove for two years? She must've wanted to live here pretty bad."

"Look, I'll remove my bias because she's a good friend of mine. Let's get to the station and see what we can find," he stated.

Stanton and I looked through the footage and focused on what happened before Luca's murder up until two days after. It took hours of rewinding and playing. All we could see was Luca's affairs, Tahira, and staff coming in and out of the house. Nothing seemed out of the ordinary. Nothing jumped out and grabbed us, not even on the day of his murder. Stanton went back to the morning of his murder to see if anyone came in or out of the house. The only movement the camera recorded that morning was the maid making coffee, the chef preparing breakfast shortly after, and staff doing their regular routines.

"We questioned everyone on this video. Their stories stayed consistent, and as we can see in the footage, they were working as they usually did," Stanton said. "There's nothing here."

"Damn," I said, feeling frustrated.

"We gave it one last shot," he said. "Sidra tried to help."

"Yeah, I guess you're right, but why does my gut still feel like something is wrong?"

"Your gut has been feeling that way since we first started this case, Stephanie. If you want to take this with you to look it over again, you can," he added. "But I'm done with it."

"Let me take it with me."

"Your hunch has always been a trip on this one," Stanton said, shaking his head.

"My hunches are usually always right. You'll see. What's done in the dark always becomes known."

"All right, well, let me know what you find. I support you in any way I can."

This case had irked my nerves for the last time. I didn't want to waste any more time. I had already spent too many days and nights obsessing over finding Luca's killer. He had a shitload of enemies. People he black-mailed. People he used and manipulated. He had power. He had money. Any one of those people could've done this, but they didn't. Somebody from Sand Cove killed him, and I was going to nail that sucker to a pole.

Chapter 34

Noble

When we returned from Bali, we laughed, we cried, and we tried to prolong what was left of our vacation. We weren't the same, but we had bonded in ways we didn't think we could. We were life partners, bound by our secrets, but had enough respect and love for each other to never use those secrets against the other again. Tru revealed a lot in Bali, but it was all right because we were going to work through it. Tru's mom wanted to keep the kids for another week in San Diego, so we left them with her, and she would drive them home when she was ready for them to return.

We walked into the house, setting our luggage by the door. Tru flicked on the lights. I sighed contentedly because although we needed the vacation, I was glad to be home. I walked up the stairs to the master bedroom, feeling jet-lagged. I didn't bother with changing into something comfortable as I flopped down on the bed.

"You that tired?" Tru asked as she went into the bath-room.

"Yeah, I am."

I fell asleep immediately while Tru showered.

When she got out of the shower, the doorbell rang, which woke me up.

"You expecting company?" she asked.

"Yeah. I forgot I told everyone we would be back to-night, so we all could talk."

"Everyone—all as in who?"

"Me, you, Tahira, Alohnzo, and Sidra, so put some clothes on."

"What you tell them to come over for?" she asked with a frown.

"It's nothing bad." I got up from the bed and walked down the stairs and opened the door to see our neighbors. "Come in. Let's have a seat at the dining table. Tru will be down in a minute. She's getting dressed."

"Did you just get home?" Sidra asked.

"Yeah." I hugged them all before sitting at the table.

Tru came down the stairs in a pair of purple sweats. She tried to make eye contact, but it was hard for her. "Hey, guys."

"Hey, Tru," everyone said.

"Let me start by saying thank you all for everything. You didn't have to do what you did, but you did, and for that, I'm grateful. With that said, we need your reassurance that no matter what, this can never get out to anyone," I said.

"You have my word," Alohnzo replied.

"Mine too," Tahira added.

"As well as mine," Sidra replied.

"Anything happened that we should be on guard about, Sidra?" I asked.

"Grant made sure to delete the parts that needed to be deleted. The visit from the agents was pretty straight-forward, but I do want you guys to know that Tru's alibi never checked out, but since they couldn't figure out a motive, they couldn't do anything about it."

Tru looked as if she'd seen a ghost. "There was a problem with my alibi?"

"Yeah," Sidra said. "But if they had any proof, they would've arrested you by now."

Tru nodded. "I won't worry about it then, but I'm thankful. I feel bad about what I did. . . . I do. I just don't want any of you to look at me differently."

"We don't," Tahira replied. "You're still and always will be our friend."

"When we have the annual end-of-summer bonfire next month, we'll celebrate as a unified community. Nothing will threaten to ruin our bond ever again. Sidra, you're new, but you're a part of this community too," I said. "Your support in this means the world to us. I'm sure you struggled with doing it because of who you are."

"I did, but I'm not losing any sleep over it. I'm happy to be here."

"Would you mind hosting this year? I know you're not familiar, but I can let you know what we did previous years," Tru said. "It was supposed to be Alistair's turn, but I haven't spoken to him since what happened between him and Kinsley. Have you talked to him, Alohnzo?"

"Yeah, but he's not in the mood. He might feel better at the end of summer, but I wouldn't count on him to host, though."

"No worries. Sidra, you got this year. Next year will be Alistair, if he's still here, and then Alohnzo, then us," Tru confirmed.

We all nodded in agreement.

"How's your daughter's reality show coming along?" I asked, wondering if any cameramen might've been around when she found the room.

"It's coming along. They haven't been filming at the house too much lately. Tori says they've been filming at restaurants."

"Was the camera crew there the night you found the hidden room?" I quizzed, making sure all loose ends were tied up.

"No, they were filming at a restaurant in L.A. I have a contractor coming tomorrow to help me toss out the surveillance equipment and knock down the wall in the pantry to turn the room into an even bigger pantry," Sidra said.

"Perfect. Well, then, we're all good," I said.

"Wait, can I get everyone's phone numbers?" Sidra asked.

She passed her phone around, and we all saved our numbers into it.

"Thank you," she said.

"I'm going to get some rest," I said.

Everyone stood up.

"Well, that was short and sweet," Sidra said with a hearty laugh.

"Yeah, no need to drag anything out. Have a good night, everyone," I said. "Thank you for your time."

Tru and I hugged our neighbors and walked them to the door.

Then Tru sat on the couch silently with her head lowered a little.

"You okay?" I asked.

"Not really. How come I wasn't told that my alibi didn't clear?"

"For whatever reason, you weren't a suspect, so you shouldn't worry about it."

"What if the agents start putting things together?" Tru started to panic. "Luca and his damn hidden cameras."

"Babe, listen, everything is okay. Since Sidra knows Agent Stanton, she would be the first to tell us if she heard anything."

"I don't know, Noble. Sidra should've never called her agent friend in the first place. If it came down to choosing a side, why would she have loyalty to us over him?"

I put my arms around her, and she rested her head against my chest. "Listen, she gave us her word. We must trust her. What else are we going to do?"

"I think we should move. Get out of Sand Cove."

"What? And move where?" I asked.

"Let's go to San Diego with my mom while I finish school."

"Hell no, Tru. I can't live in your mama's house. Sand Cove is our home . . . well, at least for another year or so if our savings permit. You gotta relax."

"God, I hope you're right."

I hugged her tightly. "Let's go to bed. We need it."

"Okay."

Tru was going to have to shake her funny feelings and go back to not caring about what happened because if she didn't, this could all blow up in our faces.

Chapter 35

Tahira

When Alohnzo told me that his mother wanted to meet with me to have a pedicure, I thought he was joking. The way that woman looked at me, there was no way she liked me. I immediately suspected she had something up her sleeve. Alohnzo, on the other hand, seemed to think her invite was genuine. That was the only reason I agreed to go. I was nervous, but I told myself that if she said one crazy thing, I was going to leave.

I walked into the Beverly Hills upscale spa a little early and found Mabel already there, speaking to the woman at the reception desk. She was wearing a cute green-and-white striped summer dress with matching sandals.

"Here she is right now, my future daughter-in-law," Mabel said to the receptionist in the sweetest voice. "Tahira, pick a color you want right there on the wall for your toes."

I nodded, feeling even more nervous now that she was being extra nice and scanned the wall of nail polishes. When I looked back over at Mabel, she was staring at what I was wearing from head to toe. Her voice might've been sweet, but her stare made me want to leave.

I was curious about the invite, though, so I picked a sparkling purple and followed Mabel to the pedicure spa chairs where the nail techs were waiting for us. Removing my sandals, I sat. The tech put peppermint- and citrus-smelling powder into both basins of bubbling water. Mabel got comfortable in the chair next to me as she placed her feet into the water. The air between us was a little tight, but I decided to thank her.

"Thanks for inviting me, Mabel."

"It's no problem. Contrary to what you may think about me, I don't hate you, Tahira."

I looked over at her, and we made eye contact. I couldn't tell if she was sincere or not.

"I don't think you hate me. I just think you're very protective of your family. For that, I don't blame you."

"I've never been able to connect with the women my sons choose. Since Amos is a compulsive liar and cheater, I have a challenging time trusting people. My sons had to grow up seeing his nonsense, and I prayed that they wouldn't become womanizers. You are different than the rest, so I want to give you a chance and get to know you."

"I appreciate that. I would like to get to know you as well."

"We all have issues. . . ." Her voice drifted off. "My husband has made my life a living hell, and I've never opened up to anyone about it, not even family members. When Alohnzo shared at dinner what you went through with Luca, I wanted to cry for you. Sometimes, I wish Amos would never wake up, but that's not right."

"I understand what you mean. I'm glad Alohnzo is nothing like Luca. He would never do or say any of the things Luca did. You gotta feel proud that you raised your boys to become great men. You're a strong woman to endure all that you have."

Mabel shook her head slowly. "I like to think of myself as resilient, but there are times where I feel like an idiot."

"I have my moments as well."

"I'm quite sure you heard about Kinsley's child."

"Yes, Alohnzo told me. That had to be a tricky thing for everyone."

"Sad to say, but I had a feeling the child wasn't my son's. I hate that Alistair got hurt in the process."

"Me too."

"You know, Kinsley wasn't the first woman to get pregnant by Amos. Now, whether she's the last, that's something we'll just have to see about."

"Does Amos have other children?"

"After I had a little 'talk' with the women, they chose not to go through with their pregnancies. Kinsley only went through with it because she hoped it was Alistair's."

Her story saddened me. Why would a beautiful, wealthy woman put up with such bullshit?

"You ever think about leaving Amos?"

"Every day, but then I think about our boys and how tied up our finances are. The ranch belonged to my father, and I could kick him out at any time, but I can't explain why I stay. It just is what it is."

I observed the sadness in her voice and her eyes as I asked, "Are you a little happy? Is that why you stay?"

Mabel started to answer but then paused before she responded. "No one has ever asked me that before. I love my boys. I love Amos. I do plenty of things to make life enjoyable. I'm not miserable, but I want the disrespect to stop. That's what I want."

"I wish I had advice to give. I was in the middle of filing for divorce and had moved out when Luca was murdered."

"So, you were going to divorce him?"

"Yes. I had an attorney and everything. When I caught him in his trailer with that actress, I couldn't do it anymore. The years of lying, cheating, and verbal abuse made me so unhappy."

Mabel shook her head and sucked her tongue. "I'm sorry you had to go through that. I admire you for doing something I never dared to do. I threatened Amos so many times with a divorce he probably wouldn't believe me if I went through with it."

She stared at the nail tech who started scrubbing her feet with a sugar scrub before she leaned back and closed her eyes. I followed her lead and closed my eyes as well.

"Would you like hot rocks?" my nail tech asked me.

"Yes, give us the works," Mabel answered for me. "I'm paying, Tahira."

"Okay," I replied. "You don't have to. I—"

"I insist. I want to make up for my behavior."

"Lovely of you, Mabel."

Mabel smiled, and it seemed genuine. "It's been a long time since I've been able to connect with another woman. You have plans after this?"

"No, my calendar is free."

"Would you like to join me for lunch?" she asked.

I smiled at her. "Okay."

If Mabel had any intention of doing anything nasty or saying anything out of line, I couldn't tell. I had heard all the stories about how she treated other women. With my professional career not being where I hoped it would be, this was a pleasant change.

Chapter 36

Alistair

Alohnzo invited me to the Portofino Marina for lunch, and it felt good to be around him without any kind of tension for a change. We laughed about old times, I told some jokes, and he said some corny ones. I needed this male bonding time with my brother.

"It's nice and warm out today," Alohnzo said. "Perfect weather for yachting."

"Little brother is extra, extra fancy now. Your new business must be lucrative. Now, you're adding boats to your planes. Are you finally going to tell me what you invested in?"

"I bought the Pinnacle Vineyard."

"Damn. By yourself?"

"No, with a partner," he said.

"Nice. You going to be moving to billionaire status soon if you keep it up."

"That's the plan, but I'm not quite there yet. I rented this yacht for the day."

I nodded. "Maybe I should buy a yacht."

Alohnzo chuckled. "There you go."

"I can't let little brother outshine the big brother. Anyway, I can't tell you the last time I had a simple lunch like this. Kinsley always wanted to eat fancy shit like truffles, lobster thermidor, and filet mignon."

I took a bite of a lemon pepper flat wing. Alohnzo ordered a few different chicken wings with seasoned fries. Felt good to be simple. I brought the cold beers.

"I know what you mean. I'm happy that Tahira is simple. She wakes up in the middle of the night and makes peanut butter and jelly sandwiches."

I smiled at him. The way his eyes sparkled when he talked about her was extraordinary. It was something I had never seen in him before.

"What?" he asked as I stared.

"Nothing. It's just your eyes light all up when you talk about her."

Alohnzo nodded. "She's the best thing that could've ever happened to me, bro."

I could tell he was serious, and it was refreshing to see. Alohnzo was the type never to catch deep feelings, so to see him speak about a woman he was going to marry made me feel happy for him. For the first time in our lives, I didn't want the woman he had. I learned my lesson with Kinsley.

"That's a beautiful thing," I said. "I hung out at the ranch yesterday. Felt good to ride the horses and tend to them."

"I bet. How's Mama and Pop doing?"

"They're them," I said with a short laugh. "Mama was pissed about the baby, but she's still with him, so . . ."

"The story of their lives."

"Exactly. I don't know why she puts up with it. I know he's Pop, but she should've left a long time ago."

"I feel the same way. Mama deserves better," Alohnzo said. "You hear from Kinsley?"

"Nah. I shipped her stuff to the island. I wonder about her and the baby from time to time. Man, I don't get how women like her don't have a fucked-up conscience."

"She's a force to be reckoned with. You going to divorce her?"

"I might have to."

"You plan on staying in Sand Cove?"

"Yeah. Where else am I going? Sand Cove is home now. It's time for me to mix and mingle with the neighbors. I got some golf clubs the other day, and I'm going to start playing golf. I might even join a golf club, who knows."

"That sounds like fun, actually."

"You should join me and ask Noble if he wants to come. That could be the time we spend together," I suggested.

"I wouldn't mind that at all. I'm sure Noble would be down. We also should ask Grant."

"That's Sidra's boyfriend, right?"

"Yeah."

"I was going to the mailbox yesterday, and I got a chance to meet Sidra, Grant, and Jarrell. They were coming home from a movie."

"Nice," Alohnzo said after he took a sip of beer. "What you think Pop is going to do with the company now?"

"Run it until he can't run it anymore. Then Mama's going to run it."

We both had a good laugh over that. I pictured Mama running the business, firing all the women.

When we stopped laughing, Alohnzo said, "I'm getting married, and I need a best man. Can you hold me down and be my best man?"

I nodded. "Yeah, bro. I got you."

"Thanks, man. That means a lot to me. Have you figured out what you want to do now that you're not filling Pop's shoes?"

I had given it a lot of thought. "I'm going to take the prancing horses, get them in shape, and start doing competitions again. The staff has been keeping them healthy while I've been away."

"You always did love those horses."

"Yeah. I guess you can say I'm an animal lover. I miss my cat, so I got a puppy."

"Mr. Pet Lover over here," Alohnzo said with a head nod. "That would be good company for you. What's the puppy's name?"

"She's a French bulldog. I named her Bella."

"Cute. I gotta come see her," Alohnzo said.

"Yeah, anytime. She took over what would've been the baby's nursery."

"How you really feel about that? I know you were looking forward to being a father."

"I was pumped to be a father, but it's just not my time. I was hurt. I cried like a big-ass baby. I'm good now. I won't dwell on it anymore."

"I hear you. You thinking about dating soon?"

"Man, hell no. You know, normally, I would've already had another woman by now, but Kinsley changed the way I'm going to move from now on. No more impulsive decisions. I don't trust anyone."

"I can't say I blame you. The right one will come at a time when you least expect it."

"I'm not worried about it," I said with a shrug. "Hurt people hurt people, and I'm good on all that. I'm just chilling."

Alohnzo raised his beer toward me and drank. "Listen to big bro. Maturity looks good on you."

"I appreciate that." I gulped some beer.

Staring out at the water, I thought my new beginnings sounded good to hear aloud.

Chapter 37

Tori

Sev was trying to turn up the pressure and get me to be exclusive. He kept texting that he wanted to meet up to talk. I ignored him. The best way to not think about what he wanted from me was to call Makani and invite him over. Correct, both would be featured on my reality show, and the world would be able to see my relationships with them. They both would see my relationship with the other, but I wasn't worried about it at all. It made a good storyline for good television.

Makani was relaxing in the spa on the deck, waiting for me to get in with him. I had known Makani since elementary school. I wouldn't say he was a childhood crush. He was more like the friend that turned into flirting once we reached our senior year of high school.

He licked his lips seductively as he watched me stand in front of him.

"You thirsty?" I asked, but then laughed because I was referring to getting him something to drink, and not the way he was staring at me.

"Kind of. It's hot out here, and you got me in this hot-ass spa, bruh."

"Stop complaining. What do you want to drink?"

"I'll take water if you got it."

"We got it. I'll be right back."

I slid open the sliding door and walked inside.

Mommy looked up at me from chopping onions. "What's that young man's name? I don't want to call him the wrong name."

"Mama, you remember Makani from school, right?"

"No. I can't keep up. You got too many friends. So, you dating him *and* Sev?"

"Yeah," I replied while shrugging. "Weren't you the one who told me to be single and enjoy life?"

"Yeah, but it looks like to me you got yourself two boyfriends. The way Sevante appears without you inviting him, and this one so touchy-feely, what you think he's going to say when he sees Makani or vice versa?"

"Mommy, chill," I said as I grabbed two bottles of water out of the refrigerator. "They know about each other. They know that I'm not ready for a relationship, even though Sevante really, really wants one."

"I can look in his eyes and see that he's in love with you. He's respectful, and he speaks to me. This one strolled through here and didn't say one word. How do you step foot in someone's home and don't say one word?"

"Times are different now, but I'll check Makani about that. I don't like anyone disrespecting my mama."

"Yeah, because that's plain rude, but go on about your business. Today, I'm cooking and feeling too good to be bothered one bit about your crazy love life."

I walked out of the kitchen with the waters and slid the door closed behind me. I handed Makani water and eased into the spa with him. My phone was still vibrating like crazy.

"Your other boyfriend been blowing you up the whole time you been in the house," he said, looking over at my phone, resting on a towel.

"Correction, neither one of you are my boyfriend . . . so . . ." I opened the top of the water and drank it.

"You're not going to answer your phone?"

"Nope."

"Why not?"

"Because I don't want to."

"So, if that were me blowing up your phone, you would ignore me too?"

"Depends on what you were talking about. I don't want to hear or read what he's saying. Why didn't you speak to my mom when you came into the house?"

"I didn't speak? I thought I did."

"She said you didn't."

"My bad. I'll be sure to speak on my way out."

My phone vibrated again.

He drank his water and put the bottle on the side of the spa. He came to me so that we were looking at each other face-to-face. I admired the tiny freckles on his nose before he put his hands around me. As he kissed my lips, I wrapped my arms around his neck.

"When we gonna . . ." he paused, realizing he was about to ask for sex with the cameras watching.

I giggled, gently pushing his hands away.

He grabbed me again. "Come here." He palmed my ass with both hands. "You know I want to be your man, right?"

I showed no sign of surprise, though I wasn't expecting him to say that. "Oh, is that right?"

"So, what's up? Why you playing games with me? You've been running and playing since high school."

"I don't play games, sir. I just don't like being in a committed relationship. I like having fun. Relationships lead to heartbreak, and heartbreak ain't for me."

"Who was the guy that broke your heart?" he asked, staring intensely into my eyes.

"Why do you assume someone broke my heart for me to know what I want?"

"I apologize for assuming, but I tell you what. When you're ready, I'll be here. I'm not going anywhere."

I hugged him as he planted kisses on my neck. He knew that was my spot.

"You better quit," I whispered into his ear. "You know what that does to me."

"I know all about that," he cooed into my ear.

"Do you?" I teased.

"You know that." His tongue flicked against my neck.

Holding his curly hair in both hands, I moaned, "You feel so good."

"Let's go to my place and have dinner," he said.

"Okay."

Makani ordered Chinese food, and our eaten plates were on the floor along with our empty glasses of wine at the foot of the bed. It was almost 10:00 p.m. when the camera crew decided to call it a night. When they left, we talked as I lay on Makani's bare chest. He played in my hair, and I enjoyed the feeling of lying comfortably in his arms. Our conversations were always as intimate as our touching, but that was how things always were between us. We reminisced about high school and the people we either loved or hated. As a football player, Makani still had lots of ladies, but when it came to me, it was like he was willing to give up his player ways if I gave him a chance.

Makani pulled me up to kiss me. His kisses moved from my neck to my collarbone. His kisses were gentle and wet. I gripped his curly hair as he traveled down between my breasts and my navel. My toes curled as he licked my belly button. Suddenly, he flipped me over, kissing my back, and I moaned. When I felt him trying to remove my panties, the first thing that crossed my mind was to stop him. I couldn't have sex with two men in the same week. That wasn't my style.

"Wait . . ."

"What?" he asked, looking confused. "Why're you stopping me?"

"Because I'm on my period," I lied.

That was the only excuse I knew that worked with men. Any other excuse wasn't going to work.

He smacked his lips. "How? We were just in the spa."

"Water stops the bleeding temporarily, but then it starts again. You want to feel my tampon string?"

He scowled and replied, "Nah, I'm good. Damn, I thought this would be the night I finally get to have you."

I kissed him on his cheek. "Don't worry. As soon as it's over, it's on. I'm worth the wait."

"I've been waiting for over ten years. I guess I can wait a little longer."

"That's the beauty of our friendship, Makani. Being lovers is something that will come in time."

He nodded and lay on his back. "I'm just glad that you're here with me." He motioned for me to return to his arms.

I went back into his arms, and he rubbed my back. I played with the tiny hairs on his chest. The whole time I wondered if Sevante was still blowing up my phone. I hadn't heard it vibrate, but it was put away in my purse

on the floor. I felt proud of myself because I didn't sleep
with Makani. As much as he wanted to, I couldn't go out
like that. We lay that way until we fell asleep.

When I woke up first thing in the morning, I looked
over to see Makani's sleeping face. I smiled before
getting up and adjusting my dress. He looked as adorable
as a sweet angel. I slipped into my flip-flops and picked
up my purse from the floor. Then I quickly checked for
missed calls and texts on my phone. Sevante had stopped
texting after I hadn't responded all day. I hoped he wasn't
mad at me. I took my keys out of my purse and tiptoed
down the stairs.

I opened the front door, locked the bottom lock, and
closed the door. I walked to my car and hit the button to
lower the top. I loved riding with the top down when the
weather was good.

"Good morning to you too, with your sneaky ass,"
Makani said from his bedroom balcony. "Why you
sneaking up out of here?"

I looked up at him with a smile as I replied, "Good
morning. I gotta shoot early today. Thanks for last night. I
had a good time. I'll talk to you later, okay?"

He shook his head, saying, "Yeah, a'ight. Hit me when
you get a chance. I'm going back to sleep."

I jumped in my car and drove off with the wind blowing in my messy hair. When I came to a red light, I decided to call Sevante. He was already up and at work. I
hoped he wasn't too mad at me. I was preparing to lay on
the sweetest voice I could.

"You're alive," he said with a slight laugh.

"I am very much alive. Sorry about yesterday. I got
so busy with filming and everything that I didn't have a
chance to step away and talk to you."

"It's all good. I'm sorry if I hit your line too many times. I was blowing you up and figured, okay, I'll stop." He laughed an awkward laugh, which made me think he had never sweated someone as hard as he sweated me.

I smiled, thinking I was the luckiest woman in the world to have two fine-ass men yearning for my attention. "You got plans for tonight? I think we should hit the spot downtown."

"What's going on downtown?" he asked curiously.

"Nothing in particular. I want to go dancing or something, just you and me."

I wanted to make up for the day before. I was feeling guilty about avoiding him while around Makani.

He paused for a moment as if he were thinking about it. I almost thought he hung up, but he replied, "Sure, I'm with it. I don't have plans. I usually like to be the one to ask you out, but this is a nice change of pace."

"I like to change things up from time to time." I felt relieved that he still wanted to hang out.

"Okay. That's cool with me."

"Perfect. I'll see you later?"

"Yeah, I'll meet you at your house. I get off around five, but I need to go home and take a shower first," he said.

"That works, so around seven?"

"Yeah, I'll be there."

"Okay. I can't wait to see you. Bye."

"Same here. Bye," he said.

I ended the call and headed home. Juggling these two was getting harder, especially with both wanting more of my time. I shook off the guilty feeling I was starting to have. I was having way too much fun.

Chapter 38

Sidra

I maneuvered around my kitchen the way a professional chef did as I prepared dinner. While I listened to jazz from the Blue Note era, I carefully washed the greens. Every few minutes, I would glance through the window at Tori filming on the deck with Makani. One thing was for sure . . . She liked guys with beautiful smiles. I pretended as if they weren't there and focused on cooking my dinner.

Grant was giving Jarrell the tour of the house after showing him the beach.

I hummed to the jazz music as I moved the clean greens from the big bowl to the boiling water with a ham hock on the stove. Then I threw in some garlic powder, creole seasoning, and pepper. Finished with that, I washed my hands and dried them with the towel.

A doorbell ring interrupted me. As I walked to the front door, I tightened up the tie of my apron behind my back. Then I looked through the peephole and saw Agent Tyler. I frowned because I wasn't expecting her. My heart started racing as I hoped this wouldn't be an unpleasant visit.

I opened the door and said, "Agent Tyler. What do I owe you for this visit?"

She was dressed down in dark blue jeans and a white top, instead of the suit she had worn before as she walked in.

"Good afternoon, Sidra. You mind if we talk for a moment?" she asked.

"About what?" I said, lifting my eyebrow.

"I thought I'd stop by and see how things are going for you in Sand Cove."

"I feel right at home. Listen, I'm in the middle of cooking dinner, so if you don't mind, I'd—"

"Smells delicious." Agent Tyler walked toward my kitchen.

I closed the door and walked briskly in front of her.

Who did she think she was just walking through my house?

She pulled out a stool and sat at the counter as if I asked her to.

I did my best to keep my composure as I said, "Would you like some sweet tea or ice water?"

"Some sweet tea would be fine. It's a sweltering day today."

I took a tall glass out of the cabinet, filled it halfway with crushed ice from the refrigerator, and poured freshly brewed sweet tea.

"I'm glad the weather is nice. We got a late start to summer weather this year," I said, handing it to her.

Agent Tyler drank some tea. "This is incredibly good. You make this yourself?"

"I sure did. It's definitely not store-bought."

She drank some more as her eyes scanned the kitchen. She seemed particularly interested in the pantry since it now looked different. The contractors did an excellent job of giving me the pantry of my dreams with a glass door.

"I extended the pantry to get rid of that little room. Now I can stock all my goodies. Being retired has allowed me to cook more, so I want to start making jellies and preserves."

Agent Tyler nodded as if she was instantly irritated. "I'm not going to pretend like I was in the neighborhood as we both know Sand Cove is nowhere near my neighborhood."

"Okay, so, why'd you come here?"

"I studied the recordings with Agent Stanton, and we didn't find anything, so I took the footage home and took a deeper look alone. I took my time and studied it hard."

"You find something you could use?"

"No."

"Aw, shucks. That's too bad."

"You want to know why I didn't find anything, Sidra?"

"Not really, but I'm sure you'll tell me anyway."

"You're right. I'm going to tell you. Some pieces are missing because it was edited. Why was it edited?"

I turned to the stove to flip the chicken because it was going to burn if I didn't. "Edited?" I asked, feeling a little nervous, but I didn't show it. "That's strange. We gave it to you straight from the equipment."

"You sure about that?"

I turned to look at her, and she was glaring at me.

"You have some nerve coming over here like this when *I* was the one who called Stanton in the first place. Stanton knows me better than you do. You might want to talk to him."

"That's the thing, Sidra. He knows you, so he has his biased opinion. What he thinks doesn't matter here. If you know anything, it would be in your best interest to come clean right now."

"I wouldn't have called Stanton at all if I knew about anything other than what I already told you."

"Either you really don't know, or you're pulling that courtroom poker face on me. Come on, *Judge* Sidra Embry, you're better than this. You called Stanton that night because you saw something."

"If it were edited, I had nothing to do with it. It could've been done before I moved here. Have you thought of *that* theory?"

"Smells like a cover-up to me."

I countered, "Why would I do something like that?"

"To protect whoever killed Luca Moretti."

"And why would I do that?"

"I don't know. You tell me. I've worked tirelessly on this case, and this could be my opportunity to get justice for Luca Moretti. Don't ruin this for me. Tell me what you saw, Sidra."

"I didn't see a damn thing. Now, if you'll excuse me, I got my daughter and camera crew outside filming her reality show, and my boyfriend and his son are visiting. I'm making dinner, and I don't have time for this right now. I'll see you out."

Agent Tyler finished her tea and looked at me as if she were disappointed. I walked her to the door.

"Thank you for your time. If you see or hear anything, let Stanton know."

"Will do." I closed and locked the door behind her.

Grant came down the stairs with Jarrell. Seeing them made me wish they would never leave. I wanted Grant and Jarrell to stay forever.

I put my arm around Jarrell's shoulder. "How'd you like the tour?"

"This a cool house, Mama Embry. Can I stay the night? I really want to play the game in the entertainment room."

"Of course, you can. You can stay as long as you like. Plus, I'm making your favorite, banana pudding."

"Thank you, thank you, thank you." He ran up the stairs to the entertainment room.

Grant wore a smile on his face, though I could tell by the bags under his eyes that he was tired from working long hours. He wrapped his arm around my waist and leaned down to kiss my lips. He pecked me continuously as he said, "You had that entertainment room set up just for him, didn't you?"

"I'm guilty. What can I say? Jarrell has a special place in my heart." I turned to enter the kitchen.

He smacked me hard on the ass, and I felt my behind shake as I walked.

"Wait now. You must've forgotten that we aren't in the bedroom," I said.

"Nah, I ain't forget. . . . Hey, I'm ready."

"You ready for what?"

"To move in. Me and Jarrell."

My eyes widened with surprise. "Even before we're married?"

"So, you're going to marry me?" he asked with both eyebrows raised.

He had gotten on his knee two times with a beautiful ring during our relationship, and I said no each time. Yet, he didn't give up on asking. He was serious. The thought of marrying him crossed my mind many times, and lately, I had been considering it. If the man wanted more than anything to marry me, how come I couldn't give him what he wanted? He had never been married before, and my previous failed marriage wasn't his fault. Since he was giving me what I wanted, I was going to give him what he wanted.

"You still got that ring?" I asked.

"Of course, I do." He winked at me. "You going to wear it, or do I have to get on bended knee for the third time?"

"I'll wear it."

"Will you marry me?"

"Yes, I'll marry you, Grant." I laughed in delight, but I turned serious as I said in a lowered voice, "Agent Tyler just left here."

"She did? What she want?"

"She said the video looks edited."

"Shit. Are you serious? I put that thing together best I could."

"I know. Listen, I told her I didn't know what she was talking about. She really shouldn't be bothering me about it anymore. I get that she's suspicious, but I don't like her poking around. Now, my guard is up."

"Let me know what you need me to do."

"Let's not talk about it anymore."

"Okay," he said.

Tori came through the sliding door, saying, "Mommy, I'm going to Makani's for dinner. I'll be back later."

"Okay, sweetie. Have fun. Your film crew going with you?"

"Of course," she replied, walking briskly out of the kitchen toward the staircase.

As I checked on the food, I prayed Agent Tyler wouldn't be able to prove that we edited that footage.

Chapter 39

Tahira

"How did the pedicure go with Mom?" Alohnzo asked, coming into the bathroom as he watched me brush my wet hair.

"Surprisingly, we had a wonderful time. We went to this cute and fancy nail spa in Beverly Hills. Then we had lunch and did a little shopping."

"Really? Did you have fun?"

"I did. We talked about her favorite movies and places she's traveled. Mabel is not bad at all. I still think she feels no one will ever be good enough for her sons, but that's natural. If I had a son, who knows how I would feel about the women he's dating."

"I like that you're connecting with her."

"Me too. She took me to the stables. I helped her feed the horses and clean out the stalls. Your family has some beautiful stallions."

"Thanks. That was how my grandparents on my mother's side came into their money. They bred horses for a living."

"She was telling me about that. How was lunch on the marina with Alistair?"

"We did some brother bonding for once."

"How sweet. Bonding time is precious. Be happy you have a sibling. As the only child, I have no one to lean on, but that's why Mum and I are so close. Mabel is looking forward to meeting Mum before the wedding, if possible."

"We can make that happen."

"I'll see what Mum's calendar is looking like and if she's up to a visit to California." I slicked my hair into a high bun and secured it.

As I put on my earrings, Alohnzo said, "What you and Tru got planned this evening?"

"We're going to a food truck festival in the Valley."

"That sounds like fun. You should've invited Noble and me."

"We were going to, but we decided on just having girls' time."

He nodded with understanding. "Okay. Be safe out there."

"We will. Tru should be pulling up any minute so we can ride out."

"You look good," he said with the naughtiest grin as he rubbed his hands together.

"Thank you."

I was wearing high-waist white jeans with the knees cut out, a red tank top, and a pair of red sandals that tied around my ankles. I was still getting used to having a man compliment me instead of pointing out my flaws. Every time Alohnzo told me I was beautiful, I believed it.

Tru honked her horn, and Alohnzo went to the bedroom window to look out. "She's here."

I turned off the bathroom light and grabbed my red purse. Then I kissed Alohnzo on his lips.

"Have fun," he said.

"I will. I'll text you when we leave to see if you might want me to bring you something."

"That works for me."

I walked out of the bedroom, down the stairs, and out the front door. Then I got into Tru's car and smiled.

"You look cute," she said.

"You look gorgeous as always, my dear friend. I can't wait to try some delicious food. I saved my appetite just for this." I took my lip gloss out of my purse and applied it.

Tru found a valet parking lot right next door to the event for five dollars. Fifteen food trucks were set up in a "U" shape around the lot with lots of room and tables for seating. The crowd was good sized but not too packed to make it uncomfortable. A DJ was spinning good '90s music. From young to old, and people with or without families, it was the perfect atmosphere for gourmet food truck fans. The plan was to walk and look and decide which ones we wanted to try.

Tru said the names as we passed them. "No Tomatoes, Mango Tango, Bistro à la Carte, The Greasy Weiner, Shrimp Pimp, Patty Wagon, The Maine Event, Anjou . . ."

"I can't choose. They all look and smell so good."

"Can we get some peach Italian ice from Mango Tango first? It's so hot out here. I'm starting to sweat," Tru said.

"That sounds amazing right now."

We stood in the small line for Mango Tango, and when it was our turn, we ordered two peach flavors.

"This is yummy," I said. "Nice and cold."

"I like the peach chunks. I'm cooling down already," Tru added.

"So, what's going on with Ximena? Any word from the immigration lawyer?" I asked.

"No. The last time I heard from the lawyer was right before we went to Bali. She said Ximena applied for a visa renewal, and she would let me know the results, but she hasn't gotten back to me—" Suddenly, Tru froze as if she saw something troubling.

"What's the matter?" I asked, reading her worried expression.

"The agent who questioned us is here. I can't think of her name right now."

"Where?" I asked, looking around.

"Don't make it obvious. She's standing next to the Shrimp Pimp truck, and she's staring right at us."

I slowly looked over at the truck and saw Agent Tyler. We locked eyes, but I turned around quickly. "Bloody hell, that's her—Agent Tyler. What is *she* doing here?"

"You think she followed us?" Tru asked with a deep scowl.

"I hope not. Let's eat this yummy goodness and check out some food. Last time I checked, it wasn't a crime to do that."

"It sure isn't a crime. But how did she know we were here?"

"I did mention on my social media that we would be here today."

"That's right." Tru bit her lower lip as she stared at Agent Tyler.

"Don't worry about her. You want to leave?"

"No, we drove all the way over here. Let's check out Shrimp Pimp," she said.

"You think that's a good idea?"

It was too late. Tru was heading that way. I wondered if Agent Tyler would acknowledge that we knew she was there.

I tried to concentrate on the menu, but it was hard because Agent Tyler was only about six feet away. Every time I looked at her, she didn't move her stare. As the line moved up, we got closer to her.

"Those drunken shrimp tacos look good, Tru," I said.

"They do. . . . Excuse me," Tru said, turning to the agent. "Aren't you Agent Tyler?"

"I am," she answered.

"What brings you out to the festival today?" Tru asked.

"I heard about it on the radio this morning and figured I would check it out. Glad I did because I'm a huge foodie."

"You sure that's the *real* reason why you're here?" Tru replied with her nostrils flared.

I swallowed the lump that was forming in my throat. Now was *not* the time for Tru to act defensively. The tension between her and us was palpable.

The agent's body was stiff as she stepped closer to reply, "Why else would I be here, Mrs. Mason? It's a beautiful day for a food truck festival."

"Cut the bullshit. Are you watching us?"

"Tru," I said, grabbing her arm, "let's order some food."

"You sure are acting a little defensive, Mrs. Mason. Is there something you want to tell me?"

"Let me tell you—"

"Come on, Tru," I quickly interrupted her and pulled her arm to walk away.

"Is there anything you want to tell me, Mrs. Moretti?"

"Have a lovely day, Agent Tyler," I replied, turning away from her.

Agent Tyler didn't seem interested in the trucks at all as she continued to watch us walk off. I refused to look back at her. When Tru turned to look, I stopped her.

"Don't look back at her, Tru. You can't act like that."

"I know. I know." She seemed flustered and shaken up.

"Let's just go home."

"No, no. Let's stay. Ooooh, lobster rolls."

She walked toward the Maine Event, and I followed her, hoping Agent Tyler would go away so Tru wouldn't wind up saying something she would regret. After we ordered and received our lobster rolls, we walked and didn't see any further signs of the detective.

"That was bullshit, and you know it," Tru said. "That bitch was following us. I think she's trying to catch me."

"If she had anything on you, you would already be in handcuffs. She's trying to intimidate us and make us nervous. Don't sweat her."

"She wasn't even trying to be inconspicuous, and *that's* what's bothering me."

We walked, eating our food.

"I swear these are the best lobster rolls ever," I declared.

Tru nodded as she used a napkin to wipe her mouth as she glanced around, looking for any sign of Detective Tyler.

A few kids ran by.

"How're the twins enjoying San Diego?" I asked, trying to get her back to having fun.

"They love it out there. My mom spoils them to pieces."

I rocked to the music while I finished my roll and peach ice.

"You still don't have any rhythm, my poor friend," she said.

I shrugged because I didn't care. I kept moving the best I could to the music. "If Luca were here, he'd say . . ." I stopped myself because I didn't know why I said it. It was hard for me not to miss him at certain times.

We were silent as we enjoyed the sun, the soft breeze, and the music. By the time evening came, we had eaten more food than we could handle.

Chapter 40

Tru

After dropping Tahira off at home, I decided to stop by Sidra's. The run-in with Agent Tyler had me paranoid. This problem wasn't going anywhere, and I needed to know what I could do to get her to go away for good.

I parked in front of her house and hopped out of my car. Walking up, I rang the doorbell and waited for someone to answer the door.

Grant's son opened the door.

"Hey, Jarrell . . . Is Miss Sidra here?" I asked.

"Yes," he said, leaving the door to get her.

It didn't take long for Sidra to appear. "Hey, Tru. You okay? Come in."

She opened the door wider for me to step inside.

Once the door was closed, I said, "I'm a little shaken up."

"Let's sit on the couch."

We walked into the living room and sat.

"What's gotten you so shaken up?" she asked.

"Well, Tahira and I were at the Truck Festival, and we were having a good time. Then I spotted Agent Tyler watching us. We were standing in line for food at a truck she was standing by, and I decided to let her know we saw her by saying hello and asked what brought her to the festival because it was weird that she was there. Could've been a coincidence, but I doubt it. She said she heard about it on the radio and decided to check it out. I didn't buy it, so I asked if she followed us. She asked me if I had a problem and said a few other words. I can't remember. It got heated so fast. I was so upset. Anyway, Tahira pulled me away to stop me from losing my cool."

"She's out of line. I had a feeling she wouldn't stop digging. She came by here the other day and was curious about the footage. She said it looked edited, but don't worry because I stuck to my story. Listen, she cannot harass you. You can definitely complain. This is what I want you to do. I need you to call this number tomorrow morning." Sidra scrolled through her phone and sent me a text. "That number I just texted you is the number to her director. File a complaint with him, and trust me, she won't bother you ever again. Make sure you mention that Tahira was a witness and that you will sue if the harassment continues. You got it?"

I took my phone out of my purse and saw the text message. "Yes. Thank you so much, Sidra."

"Don't hesitate to call me about anything, no matter how big or small. Even if you just want to vent, I'm here."

"I appreciate it."

We stood up, and Sidra walked me to the door. I hugged her before I left. She didn't have to do anything that she was doing for me, but she did. I was so grateful for her.

As I was pulling into my garage, a taxi pulled up to the curb. When I got out of my car, I waited to see who it was. Ximena stepped out of the car with her luggage. I was so surprised to see her. I hadn't heard from the lawyer, so I wasn't sure if she would ever get a chance to return.

"Ximena?" I asked as if my own eyes were deceiving me.

"It's me, señora," she said.

I went to her, and we hugged.

"Oh my God. How did you . . .?"

"My visa renewal went through. I should've stayed on top of it, but it slipped my mind. I'm sorry about being gone longer than expected, but I am here to work now."

I was so happy she was home, but then I remembered that we did not have the money we needed to pay her.

"Constantine is no longer an operating business. We had to shut it down. Currently, we don't have enough money to pay you. I was hoping that Alistair and Kinsley would need a nanny and hire you, but things changed."

"No worries. I'll work for free until I find something. Is that okay?"

"Of course, it's okay, but I would never let you work for free. Come in and let me talk with Noble. I'm so glad you're here."

"Me too." She followed me into the garage to enter the house.

Chapter 41

Kinsley

"Come on, baby. Latch on for me, please," I pleaded with Autumn early in the morning.

Autumn fussed and refused to latch on to breast-feed. I felt helpless. I had been at it every two hours, and she was getting hungrier and madder at me. I was delirious and wanted to go to sleep so badly. She had kept me up most of the night. I was fighting with my own eyes to remain open.

My sister entered the bedroom with a warmed bottle and took Autumn from me. Kairo and I looked a lot alike except she was about twenty pounds heavier and slightly taller. She didn't enhance her sandy-red hair with hair color the way I did, and she didn't cover the freckles on her nose with foundation.

"Let me see her," Kairo said. "What you going to do with this baby?"

I spent three days at my sister's house, and she tried not to interfere much, but I guess hearing the baby cry so much, she couldn't take it any longer. Kairo had two beautiful munchkins of her own, so she naturally knew what to do. I felt like I didn't know what the hell I was doing. Autumn cried every time I held her, and I was starting to feel like she didn't like me.

"Why don't you keep her in the room with you?" I said, feeling overwhelmed.

"Because she's *your* baby, and *you* need to get used to her."

Autumn stopped crying as she sucked that bottle.

"How am I supposed to get used to her when she doesn't like me? I live on a secluded island with no family, and it's going to be only her and me soon. What do I do if she won't stop crying?"

"Don't go back. Stay here."

"With you?" I scoffed. I loved my sister, but I couldn't live her mediocre life. She might've been okay with just getting by, but it wasn't my style.

"Not necessarily with me," she said, rolling her eyes. "Find you a place in Long Beach so that you'll be close to me. I'll help you with her. Sometimes, it takes a village to raise a child. So, what's up with her father and his family? You haven't said a word about who he is or where he is."

"Because it doesn't matter. I didn't come up in here and ask about your children's father, did I?"

"You could've. Roderick's in the military and deployed now."

"You guys are together?"

"Yes, absolutely. He's a great father to our boys."

"Well, that's good for you, Kairo."

"Don't tell me you are still plotting and messing around with men you shouldn't be fooling with. Is *that* what's going on?"

"Don't go there, dear sister. You haven't always been a saint yourself, so don't fucking judge me. Autumn's father doesn't want anything to do with her. That's all you need to know."

"Why, though?"

I felt like crying, but I didn't dare do it in front of her. "I want to go home. I don't want to be a burden to you and your kids any longer."

"You're not a burden, Kinsley. The doctor said to wait a few weeks. You can't get on a plane when you can barely walk on your own."

"I've messed up my life enough, and I don't need anyone making me feel worse than I already do. I'll just take my pain medication and do what I must do. We'll be gone by morning."

"No, Kinsley. Look, I'm sorry. I didn't mean to upset you. I'm just concerned, that's all. I don't want to fall out again with you. What about your follow-up appointment?"

"I have my own doctor at home. I'll do my follow-up with him."

"Okay, but you gotta stay long enough to heal. The last thing you want is to go to the hospital because your incision is leaking."

Kairo sat in the rocking chair as she continued to feed Autumn. The whole time, I stared with envy. Autumn's tiny fingers curled around Kairo's pinky as her legs kicked in a little jagged motion. Why didn't my baby like me? I didn't want her to have a bottle, but that was the only way she was going to eat. This was not going anything like I imagined. Alistair and I were supposed to be staring blissfully at our daughter on our island. He promised I could have a nanny, one who would help so that I could get some rest.

"You know, I can go get some more formula so you can feed her with a bottle. You're not eating enough to breast-feed her."

"I don't really have an appetite."

"So, how do you expect her to want what you got? You have to take your vitamins and eat well-balanced meals," Kairo said.

I tried to get out of bed so I could use the bathroom. I was struggling to hold the pillow to help me stand up, but I didn't want Kairo to see that I couldn't do it, so I fought through the pain. Sliding both feet, one at a time, I made it to the bathroom. Once inside with the door closed, I cried silently. I felt so alone. Nobody wanted me. It was like Autumn was already siding with her Kelly family. I wasn't going to be able to do this anymore. I brushed my tears with the back of my hand, wiped my pee with tissue, and adjusted my gown. Then I washed my hands and went back to bed.

"You need any pain medication?" Kairo asked, looking at me.

"In a little bit. I just need a good nap. I can't think straight."

"I'll bring you something to eat and medicine when you wake up. In the meantime, I'll take the baby in my room so you can nap, okay?"

"Thanks."

I got as comfortable as I could as she took the baby out of the room. I closed my eyes and started dreaming about lying on a float in a vast infinity pool. A shirtless, muscular chocolate man appeared with sangria on a tray. He walked into the pool and handed it to me. I smiled as I fell asleep.

When I woke up, it was dark in the room and dark outside. My sister's house was quiet. I didn't even hear the television or video games my nephews loved to play. I wondered how long I had been asleep. Looking at my phone, I saw that it was ten o'clock at night. I had slept all day.

On the nightstand was a sandwich wrapped in a napkin, pain pills, and a bottle of sparkling water. I ate the sandwich, took medicine, and drank the water. Pain hit my entire body as I tried to get out of bed, but I had to do it. I walked out of the bedroom and down the hall to Kairo's bedroom. Her bedroom door was wide open, but she, the boys, and the baby were sleeping peacefully. Instantly, I thought of leaving. I didn't belong here.

I tiptoed back to the bedroom, and thoughts of how to escape without her knowing filled my mind. I dressed as quietly as I could in the maternity clothes I wore to the hospital, grabbed my purse, the pills, and my phone. Then I tiptoed quickly out of the house and walked around the corner. While walking in the warm night in the unfamiliar neighborhood, I couldn't shake my dark thoughts. What was going on inside of me was difficult, but it was for the best. Since the pain pills were starting to work, I walked a little farther than I thought I could. Standing in front of a stranger's home, I used my app for a Lyft. I paused because I didn't know where I was going to go. A hotel was the first thing that popped up in my mind. What hotel would have vacancies at this time of night? I launched Safari to bookhotels.com and found a vacancy at the Hyatt in Los Angeles. I booked the room and entered the address into Lyft.

It seemed as if running and leaving were the most natural things for me to do. I always did it. My heart felt like it was going to stop beating because I knew it was wrong to leave Autumn, but I didn't know how to adjust. I couldn't be a good mother to her. I just couldn't. She deserved so much more than what I could give her. I was terrified of being a single mother, struggling, and raising her alone without a father for her. I had money, but what was I going to do when the money ran out? At least if she stayed with my sister, she would have my nephews as big brothers to protect her. I was going to disappoint Kairo, and she was going to be mad at me, but it was okay. I had no plans on returning to find out how upset she would be.

The Lyft didn't take longer than five minutes to arrive. I kept looking behind me to see if Kairo had discovered I left, but she didn't appear. While on the ride to the hotel, I threw my cell phone out of the window. I didn't want to be contacted, I wasn't going to return to the island, and I wasn't going to worry about Autumn. I couldn't. No matter what, she would be taken care of.

Chapter 42

Alistair

"Come on, Bella," I said to the puppy after I picked up her poop with a disposable bag.

I was enjoying our morning walks at the front of the house. She was the cutest little thing. I picked her up since she didn't like walking with the leash on. As I started to step inside the house, a police officer drove on our street, made a U-turn near Tru and Noble's house, and stopped beside.

The white officer rolled down the window and asked, "Are you Alistair Kelly?"

"Yes, sir. What can I do for you?"

He got out of his car and walked around the front of it before he stood by me. "Are you married to Kinsley Smallwood Kelly?"

"Yes."

"Is she here?" he questioned.

"No. We're going through a divorce."

"Do you know where she is?"

"The last I checked, she was at the hospital getting ready to discharge after having a baby."

"We received a call from her sister, and it appears she has abandoned her child. It's been over twenty-four hours, and she's missing."

"What? She told me she doesn't get along with her sister. Are you sure it was her sister who called?" I asked.

"Her name is Kairo Smallwood. She says she's Kinsley's older sister."

"I haven't seen or heard from Kinsley. I dropped off the baby's car seat a couple of days ago, but that was it."

"You're the baby's father, right?"

I shook my head. "No, sir, I'm not."

He looked a little confused as he looked at his notepad. "Kairo said she found hospital papers with your name listed as the father."

"That was probably paperwork she filled out before she found out that the baby wasn't mine."

"Kairo says that if Kinsley doesn't return, she's not capable of taking care of her. The baby may end up in foster care."

I sighed. What was Kinsley thinking? I took my cell out of my pocket and tried to call her. It immediately went to voicemail.

"Kinsley, this is Alistair. Give me a call as soon as you get a chance." I pressed *end* and said, "It went straight to voicemail."

"Kairo didn't have a number for her since Kinsley called her from the hospital originally. If you do hear from her, give me a call." He handed me his card.

"Thank you, Officer. Do you have a number for Kairo?"

"How about I take your number and give it to her? That way, she can give you a call."

I recited my number to the officer, and he wrote it down on his pad.

"Thanks. Cute puppy. Have a good afternoon."

As Bella and I walked up the walkway and stairs to the front door, I had the weirdest feeling. The fact that

Kinsley left Autumn with her sister without telling her where she was going or for how long she would be gone didn't sit well with me at all. I wanted to hear from Kinsley's sister to find out what happened. As I was hoping to receive a call, my phone rang. I put the puppy down and answered.

"Hello?"

"Hi. Is this Alistair Kelly?"

"It is. Who am I speaking with?"

"Hi. You don't know me, but I'm Kinsley's sister, Kairo. The officer gave me your number, and I wanted to call right away. I don't know what to do. I know my sister, and she does this running away when things get hard for her. I don't think she's coming back to get the baby. I really want to be able to take care of her, but I'm struggling to take care of my own children."

"I understand. Did Kinsley leave a note or anything?"

"No note. No money. Nothing. I had the baby in my room for a few hours because Kinsley was having issues with breast-feeding and knowing how to take care of her. While I was sleeping with the baby, she took off. I could kill her, I'm so mad."

Shaking my head, feeling pissed myself, I replied, "I'm not sure how much you know about my relationship with Kinsley, but—"

"She didn't tell me anything. I found papers here from the hospital with your name on them listed as the baby's father."

"She's my wife, but the baby isn't mine. The baby belongs to my pop, Amos."

"Amos Kelly? The rich trick who used to pick her up and take her to fancy hotels back in the day? Didn't she wind up working for him at his big corporation?"

"Yeah," I replied, feeling embarrassed about how my father met Kinsley. "It's complicated. My pop wants nothing to do with the baby, and that may be because my mother won't accept her. None of this is the baby's fault. Autumn is my sister, my blood. I don't want you putting her in the system. What's your address? I'll pick her up now if that's okay with you."

"That's fine. I bought her some formula and things. She's a good baby. Kinsley didn't give her a chance."

"Text me your address, and I'll be on my way."

"Okay."

I picked up the puppy as she ran around my legs and put her in her kennel. As I grabbed my car keys, Kairo sent me the text. I clicked on the address, and it opened Google Maps. It would take fifty-five minutes to travel along CA-1 and then the I-405 south to get to Long Beach. I didn't know how I was going to take care of a baby, but I didn't want the baby to have to suffer in life because her mother decided she didn't want her anymore.

After the drive, I pulled up to the house and got out of the car. I rang Kairo's doorbell. When she came to the door, I found her resemblance to Kinsley eerily similar. I almost thought Kinsley had returned, but Kairo's hair wasn't as red, and she was a little thicker in the hips.

"Hi. Kairo?"

"Yes," she replied. "The baby is back here, sleeping. I packed a few things. Come in."

Two young boys around the ages of 6 and 7 were playing a video game in the family room. I followed her to the first bedroom on the right.

"I can't believe Kinsley—well, actually, I can. She hasn't changed one bit. She still only thinks about herself."

I sighed a little, almost feeling as if I acted impulsively by coming to get the baby, but one look at her sleeping, and my heart wouldn't allow me to abandon her like her mother did.

"I'm sorry she did this. She broke my heart when I found out the baby wasn't mine. I loved Kinsley, but she hurt me deeply."

"Trust me; I've heard this story before. Kinsley's fucked up in the head. I get that we had a rough upbringing, and we didn't know love like that, but this is wrong. I think she might've gone back to some island she kept talking about."

I nodded. "Maybe. Is this all the baby's things?"

"Yeah, the car seat, diaper bag, and grocery bag right there. That's it."

"Okay. Would you mind showing me how to put Autumn in the car seat?" I asked.

"No problem."

Kairo picked up the baby and placed her in the car seat. She strapped her in, and the baby remained sleeping.

"Her pacifier is clasped on to her onesie, as you can see. She is full and burped. Her diaper is dry because I just changed her. She should be good on your ride home. I'll walk you to the car."

I picked up the car seat, and she carried the bags. We walked out of the room and out of the house to my car. I strapped her in the back, the way I saw on YouTube videos, making sure the base was secure.

"Thank you for doing this. You didn't have to, especially since she's not yours, you know."

"Autumn is my family, no matter how she came to be that way. Keep my number, so anytime you want to come and visit, let me know."

Kairo nodded with tears in her eyes. "I will."

"Have a good night." I got into my car and drove away from the curb.

I made my way to the freeway and decided to take Autumn to Sugarcreek Estate.

Without knocking on my parents' door, I walked inside with the baby in her carrier. To my surprise, she was still sleeping. My parents always kept the door unlocked during the day. I could hear my parents' laughter coming from the theater room. I turned toward that direction. When I walked in, I turned on the light to interrupt the *Kings of Comedy* on the big screen. Pop and Mama loved watching that comedy special. They had already watched it a billion times and laughed as if it were their first time viewing it. They turned to see me standing there with the baby.

Pop pressed *pause* from his remote. "Hey, Alistair. What are you doing here? Is that—"

"Yes, this is Autumn Rose."

"What you doing with her?" Mama asked, standing up from her recliner.

"Listen, before you guys jump down my throat, I came here to tell you that Kinsley abandoned the baby at her sister's house, and she disappeared. Nobody knows where she is. The police came to my house this morning and told me, so I drove to Long Beach to pick her up."

"What? You want to drop her off here?" Mama asked.

"No. I already know that Pop wants nothing to do with her because of you."

"That's not true," Pop spoke up. "I never said I didn't want anything to do with her. I didn't want anything to do with Kinsley."

"So, you're going to be a father to her and raise her?" I asked.

Pop paused to think about it while Mama stared him down. "Well . . ."

"If you must hesitate, then your answer is no. Look, I don't care about what you have to say at all. I'm not here to drop her off. I am here to tell you face-to-face that Autumn will know me and *only me* as her father. You two are her grandparents. Period. By the time she's old enough to know the truth, the two of you will be too old, or who knows if you'll still be alive. Kinsley will never ever be allowed to see her again."

Mama looked at me, shocked, but she didn't have a rebuttal, to my surprise. While driving there, I prepared for the worst responses from them. I didn't expect them to agree with what I had chosen to do, but I wanted them to respect it.

Pop said, "You sure you want to do that? Raising a child is a huge responsibility, and I mean, she's not yours."

"Doesn't matter unless you want to do it."

Pop stared at Mama, but she kept her eyes on me.

"Look, I'm not going to twist your arm to be her father. I'm up for the challenge. I'm opening up the stable to breed horses again. I'll be taking the stallions back to expos too."

"Sounds like you have a plan," Mama said. "You're not returning to the corporation?"

"No. Pop can get someone else to take his place when he's actually ready to retire for real."

"I didn't think you still had an interest in the horses," Mama replied. "I was feeling like I should let them go because I'm getting too old to maintain them."

"No. Grandpa wouldn't want that. One more thing before I leave. You'll treat Autumn no differently than anyone else in this family."

"Of course," Pop replied.

"I would never mistreat her," Mama added. "She has nothing to do with how I feel about her mother."

"So, you don't want her to know that I'm her father?" Pop questioned, looking confused.

"Mama, do you want Autumn to know Pop is her father?"

"I think your plan sounds better," she answered.

I knew it was Mama who didn't want Pop to be a father to his own daughter. I wasn't there to make them feel bad about the situation—I was there to solve the problem. Kinsley abandoned the baby, and I was stepping up to the plate because Pop couldn't.

"Well, I'm not going to interrupt your quality time. We're going home."

"Before you go, I want to say something," Mama said.

"Yes?"

"We'll be her grandparents," she said, "but what will we tell her if she ever asks about her mother?"

"We'll cross that bridge when that time comes," I said. "Y'all have a good night."

If my parents didn't want to have anything to do with Autumn, I was still going to raise her as my child.

Chapter 43

Tori

I couldn't believe this was happening. I couldn't find anything to wear, and I was already running late.

"PJ, I'll be there a little late. I'm trying to find something to wear," I said, frantically looking in my closet.

"Just as long as you get here before people start making donations, you're all good. Don't let me down, girl."

"I won't. I'll be there." I ended the call and sighed.

PJ was hosting his first human rights campaign party, which advocated for LGBTQ equality, so it was a big deal that I be there.

Someone knocked on my bedroom door.

"Come in," I said.

"Is everything all right in here?" Mom asked as she opened the door. "I was coming up to tell you that your friend is here, and I could hear you fumbling around in here."

"I can't find the right outfit for PJ's event."

"Will this be filmed?"

"Yeah. The crew is already at the venue."

"Tori, you have all these clothes, and you can't find *anything?*"

"Mommy, I can't just look any ole kind of way with Sevante."

"I hear you, but I'm sure Sevante will love anything you're wearing. He's so in love with you." She walked into my closet and started looking. "What about this dress?"

She pulled out a black and blue sequined dress.

"Oh, I forgot about that dress. I haven't worn it yet. Thanks, Mommy."

"Okay. Hurry up because Sevante is already downstairs waiting."

"Tell him that I'll be down in about twenty minutes."

"Okay." She walked out of the closet and my bedroom.

I quickly took a shower, dried off, and put on lotion and perfume. After that, I put on my panties, bra, and dress and applied my foundation, eye shadow, liner, and mascara before taking the curler rods out of my hair. I slid into my heels and grabbed my clutch out of the top drawer in my closet. Finally, I checked myself before going downstairs.

"I'm ready," I sang as Sevante got up from the couch.

He was wearing a dark blue button-up, black slacks, and black dress shoes. His hair was freshly cut with a deep line on the side, going toward the back of his head. We were matching and hadn't planned it.

He whistled before he brandished that handsome grin. "You look so beautiful."

"Thank you. You lookin' good there."

"Thank you, boo. Damn, we're matching."

"I had that same thought in my head. Bye, Mommy," I called up the stairs. "I'm gone."

I didn't hear a response, so I walked toward the front door.

"We taking your car or mine?" I asked.

"I'll drive. We can save the drop-top ride for another night." As we walked toward his car parked along
the curb, he asked, "Why do you ignore my calls all the
time? It's like you only talk to me when you want to talk
to me. I'm not really feeling that anymore."

"Sev, I don't like to be rude when I'm chilling with my
friends. I always call you back when I can. In fact, you're
like the first person I get back to."

"You know what, I'm going to drop it because you did
tell me from the beginning that you're busy and don't
have time for relationships, so I'll fall back."

The way he said he would fall back made my heart
thump. I didn't want him to quit seeing me. I was worried
that was what he meant. All I wanted was to do me
without any pressure.

"You still plan to see me, though, right?"

"Yeah," he said as he opened the door for me to get in.

He waited until I was inside before he closed the door.
As he walked around the front of his car to get into the
passenger side, I checked my phone because PJ texted:
Where are you?

I texted back: On my way right now.

Sevante got in and started up the car.

"You have the address?" I asked.

"Yup," he replied.

"That's PJ now, wondering if we were on our way."

"Oh, okay."

I couldn't help but notice his short answers.

"Are you going to have short responses for the rest of
the night?"

"I hope not," he replied, glancing over at me for a
second before looking back at the road.

"I hope not, either." I stared at him.

He grew quiet as he pulled away from the curb. This was not the way I wanted our night to start. I turned on some music from my phone using his Bluetooth connection to drown out our silence. I nodded my head and snapped my fingers. We continued to ride in silence until we reached the venue. He opened the door for me, and I got out so he could have a valet park his car.

He held his arm out for me to hold it.

The camera crew was already at PJ's event to film behind the scenes. PJ was too thrilled because he would have his opportunity to shine on my show. I didn't mind because he was entertaining, and people would love him.

Jumbo rainbow balloon arches decorated the walkway, and we were greeted with a program that included charity information and how to donate. Once we stepped inside, the cameras were all over us. As soon as PJ saw us, he rushed over in a pink three-piece suit. His hair was blond and finger waved.

"Excuse us," PJ said, grabbing my hand, pulling me away from Sevante. "Hey, gorgeous. You finally made it."

"I'm here. You look like a million bucks, bestie," I replied, adoring his latest look.

"Thank you, doll."

I looked behind me to see the disappointment on Sevante's face, but I couldn't pull away from PJ. PJ took me into a sea of people who immediately swamped me.

"Tori, you look cute," I heard someone say.

"Thank you."

"Bitch, you finally got here," Josie said after she gulped a flute of champagne.

I hugged her and Yanni. The crew was in the building. The music was pumping, and people were everywhere I turned.

Out the corner of my eye, I saw Makani walking toward me. My heart dropped to my feet. What the hell was *he* doing here? I had been avoiding his calls and texts for the last couple of days without returning any of them. He was getting on my nerves with his crying and whining for some pussy. I didn't like having sex with multiple men at one time. Since I was having sex with Sevante, I was trying my best to keep Makani on ice.

"I thought you said this was invitation only?" I asked PJ, eyeing him suspiciously.

"It was, but then I thought it would be a great idea to invite him. His parents have deep pockets, and I need all the donations I can get."

I shook my head, feeling ambushed. PJ was playing right into what the producers had been asking for all along. Since they couldn't get Yanni and Josie to go at it with a fake storyline, putting me in a sticky situation was the next best thing. The last thing I wanted was for Sevante and Makani to come face-to-face when I wasn't expecting it. Before I could think of a way to avoid this drama, Makani was already standing in front of me, looking at me from head to toe.

"Damn, Tori. You look good as hell tonight. I've been calling you all day," he said, reaching out to hug me. "Why haven't you called me back?"

I tried my best to pull away from him, but he didn't want to let go, so I slightly pushed him away.

He frowned, looking like I lost my mind.

I wasn't worried about him whatsoever. I was looking to see if Sevante was watching what was going on. When I looked to the right, Sevante was staring with his right eyebrow raised. He was watching everything. This wasn't about to be good. I swallowed the hard lump forming in my throat and tried my best not to break out in a sweat. The room was suddenly hot, and I felt like I couldn't breathe.

"Makani, I didn't know you would be here. Why didn't you tell me?"

"You would've known if you had answered your phone, but I see you came with ol' boy. Is he your date or something? Is that why you haven't answered me? I guess you do me the way you do him when I'm around."

"Don't start this right now. I'm glad you're here to support PJ, so that's all that matters. This is not the time or the place to jam me up about phone calls and text messages."

"Well, step outside with me then so that we can talk." He reached for my arm.

I snatched back before he could touch me. "Not right now."

"Is everything all right?" Sevante asked me as he stood at my side.

Fuck, I said in my head. I prayed that this wouldn't be the moment that they fight over me.

"Yup," Makani replied quickly, looking him up and down.

"Sev, this is my friend, Makani. Makani, this is my friend, Sev," I introduced.

They didn't shake hands as they continued to stare at each other. They both looked hurt that I called each of them my 'friend.' What was I supposed to call them?

"Tori, can I please speak to you outside?" Makani asked. "We really need to talk."

"About what?"

"About you dodging me. You won't fuck me because you're fucking him."

"Really?" I asked with a frown. "I don't have to explain anything to you. I'm *not* your woman."

"Oh, you're not? You stay calling me when he's not available," Makani said, trying to pull my hand.

I noticed he was slurring his words a little bit. Taking a good look at him, I didn't know how I didn't see that he had been drinking.

"Are you drunk?" I asked, pushing him back.

"I had a few drinks. So what? I'm in love with you, Tori. You know that, and I've been in love with you since we were in high school. You have been playing these games with me forever. Wait. Are you fucking him? You must be because you're not fucking me." He laughed as if that were the funniest thing in the world.

I rolled my eyes and turned away from him. PJ, Yanni, and Josie were right there, making sure to get all the tea.

"Ugh," I groaned. "You're so disrespectful. You don't need to worry about what I do with anybody because I'm single. I belong to me. Why can't you get the hint?"

Makani bit his lower lip, and his head dropped as he stared at the ground. My statement punched him in the gut. I didn't care if he was hurt because he was trying to embarrass me. I turned away from him to see if Sevante was still standing there. He wasn't.

Sevante was walking out the door. I started to run after him, but I felt Makani touch my shoulder gently.

"Baby, I'm sorry," he pleaded. "I don't mean to yell at you. Can we please just go outside and talk this out?"

I took my phone out of my purse to text Sevante. "We'll talk later, Makani."

"It's like that?" he asked.

"Can you please stop filming me? Stop filming," I ordered, pushing the cameraman. "Get out of my face!"

I rushed to the door to see if I could catch Sev, but I couldn't get to him fast enough. He had managed to get his car out of valet and was driving away.

Me: **Sev, I'm sorry. Please, come back. I'll leave with you if you come back. I don't want to be here anymore.**

I waited for him to reply, but he didn't.

PJ came outside. "Tori, come back in. Why are you chasing after him?"

"PJ, I can't believe you did that," I said, clutching my stomach.

"I didn't do anything. Makani is my friend too," he said.

I shook my head, my chest heaving up and down. "Just leave me alone, PJ. This is a hot-ass mess, and for what? For some stupid-ass drama? I don't do drama."

I looked up, and the cameras were still rolling even though I told them to stop. I was so embarrassed. This wasn't how my show, or my life, was supposed to be. I didn't feel good at all. I needed to get home. I pulled up the app to order a Lyft.

"You're really about to leave?" PJ asked as Josie and Yanni came outside. "She's about to leave, y'all."

"No, sugar, don't leave," Yanni said.

"Yeah, don't leave. We'll make Makani leave, and we all can turn up for the rest of the night. Girl, fuck these men," Josie added.

I rolled my eyes and gave them all the middle finger. Then I walked down the street and waited for my Lyft to arrive.

Chapter 44

Stephanie

"Stephanie Tyler, this is the craziest shit I've ever heard you say," Stanton said after taking a drink of Starbucks coffee while standing at his desk.

I told him the story about following Tru Mason and Tahira Moretti to the food truck festival, and he didn't understand why I did it.

"I really wanted to see their reactions, see if they would act guilty. My gut is telling me that they know about this footage, and they know what happened to the missing pieces. When they saw me, the look they gave me was like they saw a ghost. Guilt was all over Tru. She seemed nervous and guarded."

"Why didn't you tell me you thought the footage was edited? Why didn't you show me?"

"I can still show you. I also went to Sidra's and questioned her."

"You did *what?*" Stanton asked with a scowl.

"I went to Sidra's and asked her if she knew anything about this footage being edited. When I questioned her about it, she tried to pretend as if she had no idea what I was talking about. She's lying."

"How can you be so sure she was lying? I should've been there. I know her better than you do, Tyler."

"Listen to me, Stanton. The footage jumps a bit on the morning of his murder, like a piece is missing. The camera only records when there is movement, so the time stamp skips a lot, but you gotta see it. I know it sounds crazy, but I think if I keep applying pressure, I'll end up with something. Why can't you back me up on this?"

"Because you'll drive yourself batshit crazy the way you have for nearly a year since. We know that someone killed him, but without hard evidence, we can't do anything about it."

"Stanton! Tyler!" the director called from his office. "In my office *now*."

We walked into his office and closed the door, then sat in front of his desk. Our boss was as red as a fire hydrant, and the little bit of hair he had left on his head was sticking straight up.

"Tell me why I just received a formal complaint from Tru Mason and Tahira Moretti for harassment? They say that you followed them to a food truck festival, Agent Tyler, and you harassed them."

"I didn't harass them, sir."

"So, it's not true that you followed them to the festival?"

"I did, but I didn't harass them," I replied. "I was there, making observations."

"Tru Mason says that you made quite the scene. She said she was humiliated and embarrassed."

"Sir, I did not cause a scene. She's the one who got all defensive. She acted guilty as hell. Are there any witnesses?"

"Yes, Tahira Moretti."

"They're lying."

"You tell me what happened then."

"I followed Mrs. Mason and Mrs. Moretti to the festival because Stanton got a tip about some footage of the morning Luca Moretti was murdered from some hidden cameras in the home. Though we did not find anything on the footage we could use as evidence, what we were given seemed to be edited. I was trying to figure out why it would be edited and what was missing. The ladies saw me, and they walked over to where I was standing. Tru approached me and asked me what I was doing there. Then she got angry because I didn't admit that I followed them. They walked away, and I got some food and left. That was all that happened."

"Wait one damn minute. You're telling me that someone gave you footage, and you're *just now* saying something about it? Who gave it to you?"

"The current owner of the home, Sidra Embry."

"Judge Sidra Embry?" Director Thomas asked.

"Yes," Stanton said. "She's a good friend of mine, so when she called for me to see if the recordings could be useful, I didn't hesitate. I didn't want to tell you about it in case it didn't work out."

"Okay, and you didn't find anything, so then, you, Agent Tyler, decided to follow and harass them?"

"I didn't harass them."

Stanton replied, "Sir, Tyler believes the footage has been edited."

"This is what I want both of you to do since you seem to be so obsessed with this shit; let it go. Do *not* go near Sand Cove. Do *not* harass Tru Mason or any of the residents. You got that? I'm in deep shit right now over this, and this is a lawsuit waiting to happen."

"Yes, sir," I said through gritted teeth.

"Good. Now get out of my office. I have other things to do. Luca Moretti's case is closed. That's it."

Stanton was the first to stand, and I followed him out the door.

"Fuck," I said as soon as we reached his desk. "So, that's it? Tru makes a false report, Tahira backs her up, and we let it go? Can't he see that she's doing this because she's trying really hard to cover up the fact that she murdered Luca Moretti? She's the only one with a sketchy alibi."

"You don't know any of that. Plus, what would her motive be? We don't have one for her."

"Luca threatened to kill her husband over a gambling debt, money they didn't have to pay back. That's motive enough."

"Sorry, Stephanie. I know how badly you wanted this, and I wanted it too, but it's time to let it all go." He patted me on the back. "I'm going to get started on this case that just landed on my desk."

I shook my head as I walked away—*Sand Cove for the win*. If Tru Mason murdered Luca Moretti, she had better hope that it would never come to light. If it ever did, I hoped to be the first person to watch her sneaky ass go down.

Chapter 45

Sidra

"Thank you, Sidra. I think our problem is resolved," Tru said over the phone while I watched Grant hang up his clothes in his side of the enormous walk-in closet. "Director Thomas was extremely apologetic."

"It's never a problem," I replied. "You won't have anything to worry about ever again."

"I feel so much better now. It's been hard for me to sleep, wondering if they'll show up at the house and arrest me in front of my children."

"You don't have to worry about any of that. You have my word on that. If you see Stanton or Tyler anywhere near you again, you let me know."

"I will. Have a good night," she said.

"You too. Talk to you later." I set my phone on the dresser.

"Sidra Embry, the fixer," Grant said with a smile.

"Agent Tyler had no business following Tru and Tahira like that." I decided to change the subject. "Hey, Jarrell really likes his room, huh?"

"He does. It's much bigger than the one we had at my place."

"I'm so happy you guys are here for good now."

Grant came out of the closet and kissed me on the cheek. "Me too. I feel like I don't have enough clothes to fit in here."

I laughed. "We can fix that."

He shook his head. "Nope. I don't need you buying me a bunch of clothes I'll never wear just to take up space."

"You know I'm going to do what I want, right?"

"Yes, woman, I do know that. Where's Tori and her crew?"

"She's in her room. She was saying something earlier about the production being on hold. She doesn't like the direction of the show. They want more drama between her and her friends. I hope she doesn't give them what they want just to be on TV. I don't want that mess around here. Next thing you know, they'll be fighting and doing too much."

"Reality TV can be a hot mess. I don't watch it, but I hear people talk about it at work. She needs to stick to her guns on not wanting drama. If they try to push her, she can quit. It was starting to get weird with the cameras around all the time anyway. I'm sure the residents can't wait to have their beach back. I feel like they don't come out as much when the cameras are rolling."

A knock on my bedroom door interrupted our conversation.

"Come in," I said.

"Mama," Tori replied as she opened the door.

"Yes, baby?"

"Can I talk to you for a moment?" she asked.

"Yeah."

"I'll go check on Jarrell to see if he needs anything," Grant said, leaving the bedroom.

"Come sit on the bed," I said, staring at her sad eyes.

We sat at the end of the bed together. I waited for her to talk, but she seemed to struggle with finding a way to say something.

"What's the matter?" I asked, taking a good look at her. Tori was pale and didn't look too good. "You feeling all right?"

"Not really. The network dropped the show. It won't air anymore after this season. Does this mean I failed?" she asked as her tears slid down her cheeks.

I put my arm around her and rubbed her shoulder. "No, baby. It doesn't mean that at all. You mentioned something about them wanting more drama, right? You and your friends couldn't make up something? That's what everyone else does."

"Yeah, I mean, I could've, but I don't want to hurt my friends. I don't want the backlash from fans and people picking sides. The producer tried to make Sev and Makani confront each other at PJ's charity event. I care a lot about all my friends. I mean, I really wanted the show to work out without having to sell out. I didn't mean to hurt Makani or Sev. Now they're both mad at me because I won't choose."

"I don't want to get in your business, baby girl, but do you think you should choose one?"

"Honestly, after the way Makani was drunk and acted like an ass, I'm not feeling him anymore. He was so drunk and embarrassed me. When Sev walked away and left the party, I felt like my heart broke into a million pieces. I can't eat, and I couldn't sleep last night, thinking about him. He won't return my calls today."

"Don't worry. He'll come around."

"I feel like I messed everything up with Sevante. I'm afraid that it's too late."

"All you can do is tell him how you feel, baby. From there, it's his choice if he wants to be with you."

I rubbed her head as she rested on my shoulder. Tori was grown, but she was still my baby girl. I wondered what she was going to do with her life now that her reality gig was a done deal.

"Why don't you call Sev and ask to see him face-to-face so you can talk? None of the text messaging crap, you hear me? Tell him how you feel."

"What if he says he doesn't want anything to do with me?"

"Then you give him time to do what he needs to do. You played with those men long enough. Now, that isn't a reason for him to not be there for you, but you must allow him time to process. If you want my honest opinion, Sevante doesn't seem like the type to abandon you."

Tori got up from the bed and said, "Thanks, Mommy. I'll go call him right now."

"Good. I'm going to help Grant finish putting his clothes in this closet. Let me know if you need anything from me. I'm here for you, baby girl."

She walked out of the bedroom. I took a deep breath and exhaled. I was partly glad the reality show was over because I didn't have to look over my shoulder anymore.

Chapter 46

Tori

Mommy was right. It was time for me to stop playing games, especially when I knew I was in love with Sevante. From the moment I laid eyes on him in that surfer outfit, it felt like he was supposed to be mine. My own selfish ways and behavior clouded my judgment. I should've broken things off with Makani once Sevante and I started kicking it more.

I paced my bedroom with my phone in my hand. I almost hit Sevante's number but paused. How was I going to say this to him? I wished he would've called me first.

As if he had telepathic vibes, he called.

"Hey, baby," I answered quickly, hardly letting it ring.

He paused before he said, "Uh . . . hello?"

I realized I never called him baby before, so that made him wonder if I was talking to the right person.

"Yes, I'm talking to you, Sev. Thanks for calling me back. I was about to call you again. Look, I'm sorry about what happened at PJ's thing. I had no idea Makani was going to be there. It was supposed to be exclusive. I wanted to enjoy the party with you. That was why I asked you to be my date. I really need to talk to you."

"You texted all of that already—" He stopped, and I could hear him take a deep breath. "Listen, talk to me in person. I'm on my way."

"Okay."

"I'm coming up Pacific Coast Highway now." He hung up.

I quickly rushed to my closet to get myself together. I threw on some jeans and brushed my hair back into a ponytail with some gel. Right on time, as I was jogging down the stairs, the doorbell rang. I pulled the door open. Before he could say a word, I rushed into his arms and threw my lips to his. His thick lips readily accepted mine. He pulled back and looked at me intensely, staring through me to see if I was for real.

"I love you," I said as I pushed myself back against him.

"Do you?" His arms squeezed my waist as he bit his lower lip.

"I do."

"You mean it, or you just saying that because you feel like you're going to lose me?"

"I mean it."

He smiled and replied, "Let's go."

I closed the door behind me as we got to his car. "Where we going?"

He had the naughtiest grin as he peered at me, but he refused to answer.

We got into the car, and he drove down the road. I felt relieved because he was talking to me, and I finally told him that I loved him, but my heart was still racing. I still had to say to him the most crucial part. I looked out of the window, going over in my head how I was going to tell him. As we rode toward the highway, he reached over and placed his warm hand in my lap.

"Tori, listen to me when I say this. I'm a man, but I have feelings. I don't want you to break my heart, so when you tell me you love me, I believe you, and I will assume that I'm the *only* man you want in your life."

"You're the only one I want. I'm done talking to other guys."

He nodded and replied, "Good because I don't want anyone else but you. I've been in love with you since the first time I saw you. I didn't want to scare you away with telling you that because you were clear from day one about what you wanted."

I reached over the armrest and kissed him. He didn't have anything to worry about. I was his, and he was mine.

"I was seeing Makani, but I wasn't having sex with him. I've only been with you."

"I heard him say that at PJ's event. I only walked away because I wanted to punch him in the face for grabbing you, but he was clearly drunk, and I would've looked like an asshole for punching a drunk guy in the face."

"I should've told you before how I felt, but I was afraid that I was in too deep with both of you. They canceled my show," I said, wiping the tears that seemed to emerge out of nowhere.

He frowned. "Why?"

"I'm not dramatic enough. They were the ones who had Makani show up to cause drama with you. The producers wanted you guys to fight over me."

"Wow. I heard these shows don't care anything about people's real lives."

"I really thought this would be my opportunity to shine."

"If they can't see that you're a star, they don't deserve you. Something else will come your way. Well, I was going to take you to the carnival, but are you feeling up to it, or do you want to go back home?"

I shook my head. "I don't want to go back home. The carnival sounds like fun. You gonna win me a bear?"

He chuckled with that sexy laugh. "Of course."

I held a red ring, and in one fluid motion, tossed it across the booth like a Frisbee. I closed my eyes, hoping it would land on the bottle, but it bounced off the side of a bottle and landed on the ground. That was the last ring of three.

"Shoot," I said, feeling disappointed.

"Nice throw," Sevante teased with a sparkle in his eyes.

"I tried." I shrugged. "I guess you can do better, huh?"

Sevante paid the booth attendant five more dollars and smiled as he took three rings from him. He prepared to throw the first ring by kissing his Jesus piece around his neck. The ring then flew from his fingers, and it clattered to a stop around the neck of the bottle.

"Ah," I squealed. "What? How you do that?"

He bowed deeply, grinning. "I got that magic touch, baby."

The attendant pointed to the wall of prizes and asked, "What would you like?"

"Um . . ." I examined my choices before pointing to an oversized white teddy bear holding a red heart. "That one."

Pulling it down, the man then tossed it to Sevante.

Sevante handed it to me and said, "You asked me if I was going to win you a bear, and I told you I would."

"You did. How'd you do that?"

"I'm lucky."

"Okay, I see you, boo. Hey, let's ride the bumper cars," I said, smiling.

"You think all that bumping around will be safe since you're uh . . ."

"Please, it's way too early for that. Come on."

I tugged his hand, and we made our way through the crowd and stood at the back of the line.

"You ready for me to annihilate you?" I asked.

"That's *if* you'll ever catch me," he replied affectionately, kissing the top of my head.

The line moved up quickly. Sevante gave the attendant the tickets, and we chose the cars we wanted. We put on our seat belts, and I made sure the bear was securely at my side.

I looked back at him and said, "You're going down."

"We'll see about that, shorty," he laughed.

The automated voice announced, "Get ready in three . . . two . . . one!"

Everyone revved their cars at the same time and took off. I was laughing so hard as I spun in a circle and was speeding, ramming other bumper cars out of the way to get to him. We locked eyes, and he took a sharp turn to get away from me. Suddenly, someone rammed into the side of his car and sent his car sputtering out of control. It slowed him down enough for me to catch him. I smashed into his bumper car head-on, and we bounced apart.

"Got ya," I hollered.

We couldn't stop laughing. The cars shut off, and the ride was over. We unbuckled ourselves and hopped out. I held my bear by the neck, and he took my hand in his.

"Let's get some cotton candy," I said with a wide grin.

"I was wondering when you were going to want some."

I giggled. "This is so much fun, Sev. I'm glad you picked me up tonight."

"I'm glad I did too."

We walked past the roller coaster and the funhouse. There wasn't a line at the snack bar, so we walked right up.

"Let me get cotton candy for my gorgeous woman," Sevante said.

The young lady pulled down a pink cotton candy in a bag, and he paid for it, then handed it to me.

"You want some?" I asked.

"Just a little bite. That stuff is like pouring sugar in your mouth."

"I love it." I opened the bag and tore off a piece for him. I put it up to his lips and opened his mouth.

"Thank you," he said while chewing.

"No, thank you." I took a piece myself, and it melted as soon as it touched my tongue.

"You know what this reminds me of?" he asked.

"What?"

"The first day we met, and we went to the Santa Monica Pier. You had that purple cotton candy, and I watched your lips as you ate every bit of it."

I giggled. "You did?"

"Yeah. I couldn't stop staring. You made that shit look sexy."

I laughed, shaking my head. "You wanted to jump on me right then and there, didn't you?"

"I did, but as you can see, I'm a gentleman. I waited."

"Was it worth the wait?" I asked.

His head moved toward mine, and he placed his fingers on my chin. I smiled against his lips before we kissed. His tongue entered my mouth, and I accepted it. His kisses were so sweet and felt so good. I could kiss him all day, every day.

Chapter 47

Alistair

The first night with Autumn was a challenge. She cried when wet and hungry, which was every couple of hours. I needed sleep and was exhausted by the morning. I looked up some YouTube videos on how much to give her in the bottle and how to burp her after feeding. I needed a nanny. I didn't trust Google with this kind of thing. Reviews made me nervous as hell. I called Alohnzo to talk to Tahira.

"Hey, Tahira, I don't want to bother you, but Kinsley abandoned the baby, so I went to get her."

"Oh my goodness. Is the baby okay?"

"Yes, she's fine. It's just I don't know much about babies and need some help with her. Do you know of any nannies?"

"As a matter of fact, Tru mentioned that Ximena is back, and she's looking for another family to look after."

"Really?"

"Yup. Call Tru."

"I don't have her number." I grabbed a piece of mail and a pen from my dresser. "I have a pen and paper. What's her number?"

She recited the number, and I wrote it down. "She's going to be happy that Ximena will get to stay in Sand Cove if you hire her."

"Thank you so much, Tahira."

"You're welcome."

I ended the call and dialed Tru.

"Hello?" she answered.

"Hey, Tru. This is Alistair. Kinsley has decided she doesn't want to be a mother. Long story short, I have the baby, and I need help caring for her. Tahira said that Ximena might be looking for a family to work for . . ."

"Yes, she's looking. Alistair, I'm sorry to hear about Kinsley, but I'll be happy to refer Ximena. She loves babies. What time do you want to interview her?"

"Can she come by now? I know it's short notice, but I would really like to get someone hired so I can get some sleep."

"I hear the exhaustion in your voice. I'll let her know, and she'll be right over."

"Thank you."

"You're welcome."

Since Autumn was sleeping, I made a quick sandwich because I was starving. By the time I was halfway finished with it, Ximena was at the door. I left the sandwich on the plate on the counter to answer the door.

"Hello," I said. "Come in."

"Hi," she replied, walking in. "Beautiful home."

"Thanks. Have a seat."

She sat in the chair across from me. "Tru says that you need someone to care for your baby."

"Yes, she's sleeping right now, but I need someone to start today."

"Today? No problem. She's newborn?"

"Yes. Is that okay?"

"It's fine. Would you prefer live-in?"

"That would be ideal since I need someone throughout the day. How much are you looking to start?"

"Since live-in and my cost of living would be taken care of by you, I only require minimum wage."

I nodded. That was fair, but I had a better offer. "How about you have a room, food, and your own car maintained by me so that you can take the baby to necessary doctor visits and checkups. Also, I'll give you twenty dollars an hour. I'll pay at the end of every week."

"Yes, I accept."

"Good. It may take a few days to get your bedroom together, so for now, you can sleep in the living room or in her nursery. I have a baby monitor, and I'm working on putting her nursery fully back together."

"No worries, Señor Kelly. Thank you for the opportunity. I will take care of the baby. What's her name?"

"Her name is Autumn Rose."

"Beautiful. May I see where she is sleeping?"

We stood up, and she followed me up the stairs to Autumn's nursery. Ximena smiled as she peered into her bassinet.

"Goodness, she's so pretty."

"Thank you."

"You must be such a proud papa."

"I am."

"Tru told me about her mother not wanting her. I'm sorry to hear that. Babies need their mothers, but it's okay. You will be just fine."

"Thank you, Ximena."

"Okay. I'll get my things and let Tru know. I'll be right back."

"All right."

Chapter 48

Tahira

End of summer . . .

The summer months flew by. I was working hard with the event planner to get our wedding together, but there was no rush because Alohnzo and his partner were developing new things at Pinnacle Vineyard. They were working hard on their premium wines. Although I hadn't booked as many acting gigs as I had hoped for, being with Alohnzo made me happy.

I stared out of the window, looking at Sidra and Grant as they stood over the grill. I loved everything about the two of them. They were so much fun to be around. Grant had bonded with Alohnzo, Alistair, and Noble during their weekly golf adventures. Sand Cove felt better than it ever had before.

Alohnzo wrapped his arms around me. I leaned back into his embrace.

"It looks nice, doesn't it?" he asked.

"It sure does. I can't believe it's the end of the summer already."

"I can't either. Another summer down."

"Did you already take the case of wine down?" I asked.

"I did about an hour ago. It's seven o'clock. You ready to get out of here?"

"Yeah, I'm ready."

Alohnzo and I headed out of the house and walked down the stairs to the beach. The sounds of Earth, Wind, and Fire's "September" greeted us as soon as we stepped outside. As we were walking down the stairs, Alistair was walking down with Ximena carrying Autumn in a baby bouncer.

"Aaaaw, can I hold her?" I asked, holding out my arms.

I loved holding Autumn because she was such a good baby. Alohnzo and I spent a few afternoons a week visiting, and I couldn't get enough of her.

Ximena stopped to take Autumn out of the bouncer. As soon as she handed her to me, I melted. I reached for the blanket to drape around her, and Alistair gave it to me.

"How y'all doing tonight?" Alistair asked.

"We're good. You?" Alohnzo questioned.

"I'm good. I can't wait to eat this food."

"Me too. I've saved my appetite all day," Alohnzo said. "Did Sidra say what kind of food?"

"Texas BBQ," I replied.

"What? Oh, hell yes! I thought I smelled the grill early this morning," Alistair said.

Sidra had the cutest long table with pillows for seats on the sand. Above the table were lanterns strung up to form a tent. Jarrell was sitting at the table, playing a game on his phone.

"Heeey," Sidra said as she stepped away from the grill where Grant was taking off some corn wrapped in foil.

"Hi," I said, walking over to hug her with the baby in my arms.

Alohnzo and Alistair replied, "Hello."

"Aaaaw, Alistair, she just keeps getting cuter and cuter," Sidra said.

"Thank you. That food table is looking good. What you got over there?"

"I got some Texas-style smoked brisket and ribs, macaroni and cheese, potato salad, Dr. Pepper baked beans, fried okra, pickled jalapeños, corn bread . . . The list goes on. You'll have to check it out. Oh shoot, I forgot the pies in the house." She pulled out her phone and dialed. "Tori, you and Sev bring out the pies, please. Thank you."

I sat at the table with the baby sleeping gently against my chest. The sound of the music didn't bother her one bit. "Hi, Jarrell. How are you?"

"Good," he replied, looking up from his game briefly.

"Alistair, did Autumn stay up last night? She's knocked out," I said.

"No, but she played all afternoon," he replied.

I looked up to see Tru, Noble, and the twins walking from their end of the beach. It seemed as if the twins grew an inch while they were away.

"Don't go in that water! Stay right on the shore," Tru instructed as they ran toward the water.

"I got the kids for you," Ximena said.

Tru gave Ximena a warm smile as Noelle and Noble Jr. ran to her open arms.

"Good evening, everybody," Noble said.

"Hey, guys," Tru added.

Everyone greeted them.

Tru came to the table and hugged me, careful not to squish Autumn.

"Oh my goodness. I feel like every time I see her, I want to bite her," Tru said, gently touching Autumn's cheek. "Alistair, is baby girl still keeping you up at night?"

"A little bit, but not so much anymore. Ximena has been a tremendous help. Thank you so much, Tru."

"It's no problem," Tru said. "I'm happy you needed her help because now she's back with us in Sand Cove."

Sidra said. "Tori, y'all set those pies right on this table."

Tori and Sevante had two pies in each hand as they placed them on the table. We had gotten to know Sevante the times we were running on the beach, and he was out surfing. I thought they were the cutest couple.

"Now that everyone is here, I want to share our news," Sidra said, as she reached for Grant's hand. Grant held her hand and smiled proudly. "Grant and I got married at the courthouse a few days ago. We're husband and wife now."

We all clapped and cheered for her.

"Congratulations," Noble shouted.

"Mommy, you didn't tell me that," Tori said with wide eyes.

"Well, I wanted to save the announcement. I just want to say thank you to you guys for welcoming us to Sand Cove. You have made us feel like family. We are happy to be here. This is my first hosting, but Lord willing, it won't be my last."

"We love you, Sidra," I said.

Everyone clapped.

"The food is ready, so you can eat when you like."

I wasn't ready to give up the baby yet, so I said, "Alistair, you can eat. I'll hold the baby."

"You gonna spoil her, Tahira. I brought the bouncer so she can sit in it."

"I know, but I can't help it," I said.

Alistair and Alohnzo went over to the table to make a plate.

"You got baby fever," Tru teased. "I know it's not hard to imagine what it would be like. She looks like she could be your baby."

I smiled. "I do have baby fever. How could I not? She's a doll."

"She really is."

"How you doing tonight, Tru? You seem a little down lately."

Tru sighed. "I'm trying my best, but things are hard. Money is tight, but I don't want to talk about it. We're supposed to be having fun tonight. You want some wine?"

"Yeah, can you bring me just a little bit? Alohnzo got a crate over there from the vineyard."

"Ooooh, I love that wine. I still have a few bottles Alohnzo gave us. What happened to the launch party? I was looking forward to it."

"They've been busy over there. Alohnzo had to push it back. The date is still to be determined," I replied.

"I can only imagine. The vineyard was already a busy functioning business before he acquired it. I'm sure a party is the last thing they're thinking about. I'll be right back with the wine." Tru walked away.

I rocked the baby on my chest, and her warmth felt good as I placed a gentle kiss on the top of her head.

"Auntie Tahira," Alohnzo said as he sat next to me with his plate.

"Uncle Alohnzo. Hey, that plate looks yummy."

"These baked beans are too good. You want me to make you a plate?"

"Not right now. I'm enjoying little sunshine here."

Alohnzo smiled as he stared at me. "When do you want to have a baby?"

I smiled back at him. "As soon as possible. You ready for that?"

"I've been ready," he said. "I wouldn't mind."

"Ahem," Tru hummed as she walked up with two glasses of red wine. "I heard y'all. Baby-making plans in full effect, right?"

We laughed at her.

"We have to get this wedding together," I said.

Alohnzo nodded. "Definitely. I want it to be your perfect day, so you let me know what you need from me."

"Y'all still so damn cute," Tru said. "Noelle, Junior, you guys hungry?"

"Yessss," they said in unison.

"Come to the table and get what you want." Tru started getting up.

"Baby, it's okay. I'll fix their plates," Noble said.

"Thank you, boo."

"Come on, y'all," he said to them.

Tori and Sevante joined us at the table.

"Hey," Tori said.

"Hi," I replied.

Alohnzo nodded with food in his mouth.

"Hey, girl," Tru said.

"Isn't the baby cute?" Tori asked Sevante.

He agreed, "She really is. That's your baby?"

"No," I replied. "She's Alistair's baby. She's my niece."

"Oh, okay. I hear you and Alohnzo are getting married soon. Congratulations," Tori said.

"Yeah. I'm getting the plans together. I'll be sure to include you guys on the invite."

"Sidra, you sure can cook," Alistair said as he walked toward us with a plate.

"Thank you," she said as she two-stepped with Grant. "Eat all you want. There's plenty."

As I looked around at everyone, I smiled. There wasn't any negativity, no gossiping. This was how Sand Cove was meant to be.

We were a community, one who would keep one another's secrets, no matter how dark they were.

It would stay that way for years to come, and no one spoke of Luca Moretti ever again.

The End